REVIVE

THE REDEMPTION SERIES BOOK 4

ELLIE KIRSON

REVIVE

By: Ellie Kirson

Cover design: Amy Queue

Editing: Kat Lindquist

Proofreader: Amy O'Brien

ISBN: 978-0-6489706-4-4

To obtain permission to excerpt portions of the text, please contact Ellie at ellie.kirson@gmail.com

To keep up to date with all upcoming releases and information, please subscribe to Ellie's newsletter:

https://landing.mailerlite.com/webforms/landing/a7m2t8

Kindle readers: You can follow Ellie on **Amazon** and you will be informed as new releases become available.

Created with Vellum

I have a very special unicorn friend, that loves Garrett just as much as I do.
It would be cruel and unfriend like to not dedicate this book to her.
So, beautiful Lita, this one is for you.
I thank the universe everyday for bringing you into my life. I know we say this all the time, but I love you, just the way you are.
To me, you are perfection. x

WOULD YOU LIKE TO CONNECT WITH ELLIE?

Facebook: http://www.facebook.com/Ellie.kirson/

Newsletter: https://landing.mailerlite.com/webforms/landing/a7m2t8

Email: ***ellie.kirson@gmail.com***

Ellie also has a Facebook reading group "Ellie's Ghost Team" if you wish to join all the girls in there.

ALSO BY ELLIE KIRSON

The redemption series *(in reading order)*

Renegade

Reclaim

Mortemous- Early years Novella

Reborn

Revive

Rectify

CONTENTS

PROLOGUE

I'VE BEEN on every kind of battlefield. I've seen the worst of the worst and fought some of the hardest battles known to man. But as the bullet's echo reverberates in my brain and I watch the love of my life fall to the ground, I feel like my heart's been ripped out of my chest. Years of training and discipline fly out of the window as I rush to her side.

I don't think about the fighting going on around me, nor am I coming up with a plan of action. All I see is her blood spilling out onto the floor around her, and all I am feeling is terror that I'm losing her again. I rush over and slide to her side on my knees and press my palm to her face.

"No." Her voice is rough, and her eyes scream in pain.

"Shhh," I say, trying to soothe her as I determine the extent of her injury. Blood is seeping through her clothes at her abdomen, so I place my hand over the bullet wound and apply pressure to stave off the bleeding, wincing at the additional pain it must cause her.

Two more bullets zip through the room, but I keep my focus on Mila, protecting her with my body. Teeth gritted, she breathes through the pain until her eyes shutter, nearly stopping my heart.

"Fuck! Ansia, can you hear me?" I shift her slightly, trying to get a response. She moans, and my breath hitches in relief.

Lucas appears beside me, ripping his shirt off his body and passing it to me. "Put pressure on it. You need to get her out of here. Go!"

"No," she moans and tries to move, but I hold her down. When her beautiful eyes open, they struggle to focus. "Rett," she sighs.

"I'm here. I got you. I have to lift you, okay? It'll hurt. I'm so sorry," I whisper, and slide my hands beneath her body. She cries out as I lift, and I hate that I'm hurting her further. "Sorry, baby."

"The bombs, Rett," she pants, her eyes flying wide, and my entire body jolts and locks in place.

"Bombs?"

"Mmmm," she moans, her body growing heavier as she fights unconsciousness. Panic squeezes my heart painfully as her eyes close again.

"Where?" She doesn't answer. "Ana?" I jostle her in my arms, trying to get a response, but her eyes refuse to open, and I get nothing. I yell to the others, "Get the fuck out!"

Carrying Mila in my arms, I race out. She bounces in my arms, and my fear becomes a living thing when she doesn't respond at all. I shove my face next to hers and almost trip when I feel her soft breath fan across my cheek.

We sprint through the front door and turn toward where the cars are parked. It takes me a split-second to locate Mila's mustang.

"Keys!" I bark, not caring who answers.

"In her pocket," Ayda yells back. She clings to Ryder's hand the same way I cling to Mila.

"You take her." Roxy orders. "Logan, Ayda, Ryder, and I will take the bikes. The rest of you go in the SUV."

I don't bother answering. I search the area for Tobias, he races after Austin, blood coating his fur. Knowing he is then care of, I focus on the woman in my arms. I reach the Mustang and pray Mila had the foresight to keep it unlocked. When the door opens, I gently place her in the passenger seat and recline the seat back gently.

Slamming the door closed, I rush around to the driver's side and yank open the door. I turn it on, and the souped-up engine roars to life. I floor the accelerator, and dust and dirt flies around the vehicle as the tires slide and gain traction.

I try to force myself to calm down, but panic and dread claws at my throat as she starts losing color in her face. I look in the rearview mirror, seeing two bikes and an SUV following me, but no one else is on our tail. I reach over and place a hand over the shirt on her wound and put pressure on it again. My other hand grips the wheel as memories assault me from years ago.

I won't lose another soldier, especially not the love of my life. This can't be how our story ends.

"Hold on, Ana. Please. God, please hold on," I pray to whomever the fuck is listening because I can't lose her, not after I just got her back.

I knew something bad was going to happen. I felt it before we even went in tonight. I knew, and I did nothing to stop it. Now, I could lose the person that means everything to me.

The tires hit the main road, and I press my foot down harder on the accelerator. The bikes and SUV behind me slow to a stop, and then the building behind me explodes into a plume of billowing flames and falling debris.

If I wasn't rushing to get Ana medical help, I might appreciate the fact that my girl just destroyed an entire fucking building.

"Rett," she whispers, and her voice is a balm to my panic.

"Hey, I'm here."

"Is everyone out?" Her voice is strained and broken with harsh breaths.

"Yeah, baby. Stay awake for me. I'll get you to the hospital."

"No hospital. Greg."

I nod, because that's what I meant. I've spent the better half of the last year trying to get her to tell me what happened in the years we were separated, but she's like a fucking vault.

One thing I do know is that Ghost Team likes to keep low-key. And that means no hospitals, just Greg. The gay doctor.

Her eyelids fall closed, and I press my foot down harder, the engine snarling in protest. My heart pounds inside my chest and vibrates in the pit of my stomach.

"Ana, baby. Stay awake." She doesn't respond, and I slam my palm against the steering wheel. "Fuck!"

My hands shake as I scroll through the screen on her audio system, searching for Greg's number. Finding it and hoping her phone is connected, I hit it.

It dials and rings.

"Marshmallow?" His voice is chipper as he picks up.

"It's Garrett. Mila's hurt."

Just like that, he switches to a professional tone. "Tell me what happened."

"GSW to the abdomen. She's lost quite a bit of blood."

"Is she alert?"

"In and out," I answer, keeping one eye on the road and another on my girl.

Like she knows we're talking about her, she mumbles, "Greg. Hurts. Slade. He needs to know."

My stomach pitches uneasily. "Who's Slade?"

"No one," Greg answers brusquely. "How far away are you?"

"Ten minutes out."

"I need to make a call. Bring her straight in when you get here. We'll be ready."

The call disconnects, and I curse. It seems to take forever to get back to headquarters, but when the gates come into view, I stop and put in the code. I practically push the gates open with the nose of the Mustang and fly through when they open far enough.

I stop at the front door, rip the keys from the ignition, then race around the nose of the car to the passenger side. Lifting Mila out, I boot the door closed and head to the front door as it opens. I follow Greg through the building until we reach the infirmary.

"I've called a surgeon to help," he informs me as I lay her on the bed.

"Is that safe?" I ask as I watch him cut the clothes from her body.

"He's my brother," he explains, but I'm not convinced. "If I didn't think I could trust him, he wouldn't be coming."

"I'm just making sure she's safe."

"Oh, I know." His eyes come to mine, knowingly. "I've taken care of her all of these years without your help. I'm still fairly capable of doing it, now that you're back."

"Back?" My eyes narrow as I realize this doctor knows more about me than most people around here. "You know?"

He swivels to grab a syringe off the medical table before turning back and inserting a IV into her hand. "I don't just know, I lived it. I knew her back then...I even knew you."

His words shake me. I've been amongst these people for the better part of a year, yet none of them know my history with Mila. Greg knows, yet he's said nothing? He hasn't even hinted at the knowledge he has.

"You know what happened to her?"

His lips thin, and the action spikes my anger. Jealousy rears its ugly head, and I have to force it back.

"If you know something, tell me," I snarl.

"No."

"No? You know our history. If you care about her like you say you do, you'd tell me. I can help her."

"She doesn't need your help."

"Greg," I growl in warning.

He snorts, "Mr. Wolf growls, and everyone obeys, right?" He smiles at first, then glares. "Wrong. They are Mila's secrets, and she doesn't want you to know. I have to respect her wishes."

"You respec—I'm trying to help!"

"No, you're not!" he yells. "You come in here, making demands and being a dick. Let me tell you something, Wolfman. Fuck off."

As my eyes widen in shock over the vehemence in his outburst, the door bursts open, and a man rushes into the room. He moves to my side of the bed, and he starts conversing in medical terminology with Greg. He looks at me, a question in his eyes as they talk, and Greg stops to give me a pointed look.

Message received.

I take one last look at the woman that owns me, body and soul, before I step out of the room and collapse into one of the chairs in the hall.

1

MILA

A YEAR AGO

My heart throbs so hard, I'm sure he can see it through my shirt. My insides are a trembling mess of want and fear, but my hand that grips the gun stays steady, pointing at the only man that could ever truly break me.

His watchful green eyes are different, and yet the same. They've aged some, like he's seen harsh things in the years since we last laid eyes on each other. His habit of assessing me has matured, becoming more honed. He probes, pushing at my mental barriers, trying to see inside me, but I'm different now. I'm not that shy girl that was so easy to read anymore.

I steel myself and remember why I can't have him. I can't give into what I desire most because there is another who owns my heart as well. To keep that one safe, I have to stay away from Rett.

I was prepared to walk into that room and see him, but I wasn't prepared for how my body would react. It yearns for him, craves him on a level that I haven't felt in years. The distance between us cooled and muted my longing over time, and just like a bull being released from the chutes into the fighting arena, it rushes in with renewed force, trampling everything in its path.

Garrett Michaels is my red cape.

The silence stretches on, my threat lingering in the air like a dark cloud. I need to know why he's really here. I don't believe in coincidence—everything happens for a reason. I need to know that his reason has nothing to do with our son.

I've spent the last four years hiding with the women I call family. We have a solid, unbreakable foundation of friendship, but they don't know about my son. Slade is protected from every angle because I can't risk Levi coming after him.

Levi wants me back, but like he changed my name to hide me from Garrett, I've done the same to hide myself from him. Mila Romero disappeared the day she rode out of the complex, and on that day, Mila Santos was born.

"I'm with my team. You knew I'd be here. You got all the fucking details. I'm the one who was blindsided, Mila, not you. And yet, you're the one with the fuckin gun pointed at me," Rett growls but doesn't move away from my threat.

My eyes flick to the chain around his neck. Three military dogs tags sit heavily against his broad chest. Three, not two. "You still see your family?"

"What?" His eyes flicker with confusion.

"Answer the question," I snap at him.

"Mom, mostly." His eyes narrow suspiciously. Clearly, he isn't aware that his father sold me. Years later, and that prick never told Rett. "What does that have to do with anything? And why is your last name Santos?"

"It has to do with everything. And it's none of your business."

"Like hell it's not. Where've you been all this time?"

I tilt my head from side to side and plaster an insincere smile on my face. "Here and there."

"That's it? No explanation, no 'I'm sorry,' just some bullshit deflection and half-answers?"

His response pisses me off. I read his fucking records. His time as a Ranger is heavily documented. He is honorable, a good soldier. He lived his charmed life while I lived in a nightmare, and now he thinks I owe him?

"I don't owe you shit," I sneer viciously, and he has the audacity to look offended.

"The fuck you don't!" He takes a single step forward, and I fire a bullet at his feet.

He halts and stares at the smoking hole inches from his foot. Slowly, he raises his eyes to mine, and I see something in them I never wanted to see. Pity.

"What happened to you?" His words are soft, and I hate the way they make me want to cry.

"Life happened, Garrett. I lived, and I survived. I did it on my own, and that means I don't owe you *anything*. You're here to do a fucking job. That's it. When this is all over, you leave and we never see each other again."

"No." He shakes his head and pins me with a look of pure determination. "It's not the end. *We* don't end. I searched for you. I did everything I could to figure out where you were."

I snort derisively. I was right under his nose this entire time. His father knew exactly how to find me. If Garrett really searched for me, he didn't try that hard.

He continues, his words more intense. "I've fought battles that weren't my own and won. If you think I'm a quitter, you're gravely mistaken. I'm not leaving here without you."

"You have no idea what you're saying," I scoff, exasperated.

"The Mila I knew wasn't stupid. I'd be willing to bet you aren't either."

"I'm not the girl you once knew. She's someone I don't even know anymore. We were over the minute I left, and I don't see a good reason why that should change." A fresh wave of torment washes over me as I speak those words, and it's mirrored in his eyes.

"Tell me what happened."

"No."

"Mila, whatever it is, I can fix it," he growls, and once upon a time, it would have scared me. Now, it just turns me on, and I hate that. I need to get out of this room and away from him.

"I'm done, Garrett. Get the fuck out. Find another hole to fuck because this one isn't taking applications."

His eyes widen at my words, and I watch his Adam's apple bob in his throat as he swallows.

"I wasn't—" he starts, quieter now.

"You were, and I meant what I said. I don't want you. I didn't want you then, and I don't want you now. I had my chance to find you, and I didn't. Now, leave."

He stares at me incredulously, searching for the lies in my words, but because I've had to learn to hide my truth, he won't find any. I lift my chin defiantly, watching his shoulders slump as the hope in his eyes extinguishes. I lock my spine and cement my feet to the ground, fighting against my body's pulsing need to go to him.

When I don't move, when my hand remains steady on the gun and my eyes closed off to him, he nods. Turning on his heel, he heads to the door. I hold my breath, waiting for the door to close behind him before I succumb to the pain inside my chest.

At the last second he turns back and smirks. "Still can't lie for shit, Ana."

As soon as the door closes behind him, I collapse on the ground. I force myself to breathe through the anxious energy trying to force me to follow him. I can't want him.

There was a time I'd have done anything to hear the devoted words he gave me, but everything is different now. I can't be that starry-eyed girl that begged him to love her. It's simple. As Slade's parents, being together would likely mean a death-sentence for our son.

Once my breathing is calmer, I pull myself to my feet and head out of the room and make my way to the infirmary. I should go back to the team, but if he is there...I just don't trust myself.

I push open the door, and Greg looks up from his computer. He reads my face, and his lips thin. He taps the vacant chair beside him. "Marshmallow?"

"It's bad," I sigh, and flop dejectedly onto the seat.

"How bad? Like you wanna play Doctors and Nurses-bad? Or you want to shoot him-bad?"

I wince, "Both, but I can't do either of them. I knew him being here would bring up past crap, but it's like my damn vagina hasn't had dick for eight years."

He grins, flashing his perfect teeth. "We knew this, though. You knew it would be hard."

"Yep." I pop the ‘p’ and relax back into the seat.

"Slade is safe. Maybe it's time?" he hedges, and I narrow my eyes.

"No. Slade’s safe right now because no one knows where he is. Half the people in my life don't even know he exists. Garrett's parents are friends with Levi's family. If he and I were to be together, how would that work? Huh? I can't see his parents. They could never know we were together. I probably can’t even see Slade, fearing that Garrett or his stupid family would find out."

"You won't tell him?"

"It's best I don't."

Greg leans forward in his chair and grabs both of my hands in his manicured ones. "I love you. You’re my girl, and I will support you, no matter what. But you are so fucking wrong for not telling him. I know Garrett, and I know his family. The two are not the same. If you think he wouldn't protect Slade just as much as you do, you’d be incorrect. Not telling him is a cop-out, Marshmallow."

"It's not. How can I be sure he won't say anything?" Then I remember. "Is his father still alive?"

My question surprises him. "I'm not sure. Why?"

"He was wearing three dog tags. Families of deceased soldiers are given one, right? Like a respect thing?"

He nods. "Yes. Though if his father’s dead, why would Garrett wear it? I thought you said he and his father didn't get along."

I snort and stand, patting my friend on the shoulder. "Things can always change. I know that better than most."

I press a kiss to his cheek and head to the door.

"Marshmallow?"

"Hmmmmm?" I turn back to find him looking at me seriously.

"Don't get pissed off because you’re making assumptions. Talk to him. If not for you, do it for Slade. He deserves to know his father."

"Slade knows exactly who his father is. Everything I do is for my son."

He nods, his face saddened by my words. "You deserve happiness.

After everything, maybe this is the universe telling you it's time to move on?"

"But what if being with him, letting him in, hurts Slade?"

Greg smiles kindly, "There was a time you trusted Garrett more than me. Maybe open yourself up to find that again. This is a second chance, baby girl. Don't fuck it up by dismissing it straight away. And don't shoot him!"

Laughing, I flip him off and close the door behind me.

2

GARRETT

ALPHA TEAM HAS BEEN WORKING with the Ghost Team for two and a half weeks. In seventeen days, I've barely heard a peep out of Mila. She struts around this place in skin-tight jeans and tops that make my dick hard.

In fact, I don't think I've had an entirely flaccid dick this whole time. She's in my every thought, day or night, and it's frustrating the fuck out of me that she just ignores me.

Everything we had—the friendship, the love—it's like it never existed.

Every day that we were apart, I had hope because I knew, deep down, that a love like ours doesn't just *end*. It exists, and it fights. But now that she's right in front of me? Day by day, that hope dwindles.

Is everything we went through, this love I've carried inside me all this time, all for nothing?

My Mila, the girl who sat with me in our silence, is so far removed from the woman that I see today. This woman is callous, forthcoming, demanding, and so fucking confident. I miss my Mila. This new version seems so foreign, but she wears my friend's face. My love's face.

Her eyes are the same glossy brown with specks of honey floating in their depths. But they're now guarded and hold secrets she isn't prepared to share.

I'm not completely stupid. Ghost Team is made up of people that have lethal secrets or dangerous histories. I know she's running from something or that her past is potentially dangerous. I can help. I *want* to help. I know people, and I'd trade my life for hers in a heartbeat.

She shuts me out instead.

Her team isn't any help. My commander, Logan, already tried that approach, and it backfired.

I switch the shower off and grab a towel, but I quickly shift and brace myself against the sink as a wave of dizziness washes over me. I sway on my feet and struggle to regain my equilibrium.

Fucking drugs.

Greg said it would take a day or two to feel back to normal, but as I try to swallow the wave of nausea lodged in my throat, it feels like it might never pass. Seventy-five hours ago, our headquarters was infiltrated. Men that we can't identify stormed in, caught us off guard, drugged and kept us bound. We were freed only after Roxy agreed to go with them on the condition that they released us.

I don't remember anything. One minute, I was working out in the gym on the bottom floor. Next thing I knew, I felt a needle pierce my skin and everything went black.

We woke up in the infirmary a day ago and Logan explained that we were all taken and kept hostage. Everyone was fine and didn't suffer any extreme effects from the drugs, thankfully. Greg checked us over and ran a few tests. After being cleared, I waited until Mila had awakened and was okay before I left. I headed to my room to shower and crash out for a few hours.

No one else remembers anything. I didn't even realize they had taken us from the building. If I'm going to be honest, it freaked me the fuck out. I'm a trained soldier, a Ranger, but they got the drop on me. They were able to get close enough to inject me without my knowledge.

We've been working around the clock, trying to figure out where Roxy has been taken. Most of us are still battling the aftereffects of the drugs and have had to return to our rooms to rest periodically.

Ayda, Ryder, and Logan have been holding down the fort while the rest of us drown ourselves in sleep and water, trying to flush the poison from our systems.

Logan held a meeting with Alpha Team to explain the Assistant Commissioner's involvement in the attack. Apparently, he was working closely with Roxy's mother, Katarina, who is the one that kidnapped half the team and blackmailed her daughter.

The dizzy spell passes, and I slowly dry myself off. The minute I step into the bedroom, I collapse on the bed and pass out as the exhaustion becomes too powerful to ignore.

I wake up a few hours later, feeling a little more coordinated than before. I groan as a shrill ringing pierces through the room, and I reach for my phone to shut it up. Squinting, I click the text messages open.

Logan: Meeting asap. Meet me in the boardroom.

Tapping off the screen, I pull myself to my feet and shuffle to the dresser to grab a clean pair of jeans, underwear and plain black shirt, I shrug on my clothes, slide my feet into my boots, and quickly brush the fuzz from my teeth.

Five minutes later, I step into the boardroom. My eyes instantly search the room until I find her. Dressed in black jeans and a tank top, her hair falling in soft waves, she glances at me briefly and averts her eyes.

"We think we've found her," Logan announces. His distress over the last few days has been obvious. I have no idea what's going on with him and our missing team member, Roxy, but she means something to him.

Since being stolen by her mother, we haven't had any leads on her location. While it's been frustrating for most of us, our commander's been going out of his mind. I recognize how he feels, having felt the same when Mila went missing. It leads me to believe Logan broke his own rules and got his heart involved.

"What did you find out?" I ask as I grab a bottle of water before joining them around the round table.

"An anonymous source contacted me, providing a location."

Austin snorts, and Mila questions, "Where is she?"

"Here." Logan points at a location on the map. "The issue with the source is that they could be criminals. We've no idea. All I know is they'll be there, collecting someone that was also taken by Katarina. They've asked for safe passage."

"We could potentially be letting criminals walk free," Lucas concludes, pushing his glasses up further on his nose.

"I won't ask you to bend the law and risk your jobs, but I'm doing it." Logan folds thick, tattooed arms across his chest.

"We have no problem with that either, so we'll assist. We won't hold it against you if you choose not to come. But we're going to get my sister back," Ayda admits.

My eyes flick to Ana, who nods in agreement. Where she goes, I go. "I'm in," I state, my eyes never leaving her.

She tenses slightly, but besides that, she shows no reaction to my statement. The other members of Alpha Team also agree to go. We're more than just a team. These men have become my family. We follow each other into every situation and we make sure we leave together.

Logan is our commander by rank, but he's never done anything for us to doubt him. We trust him completely, and if it comes to it, I'd happily walk away from my position for him.

After Lucas brings up the area we need to focus on, Mila steps forward.

"These are old maps, but they're accurate. If we go in through the back, we should have enough cover to be able to get in unnoticed," she states, piquing my curiosity. I watch her closely as she continues, "It's once we're in that we'll be blind."

Alarm bells go off in my head. It's bad news to walk into anything blind. We need to be strategic. The people we are up against are cunning. They got into our headquarters without raising any alarms and took out our entire team. They shouldn't be underestimated. "I don't like that. We need to check it out first and get a better idea of what's inside," I declare.

"No." Logan's response has my head snapping in his direction. He shifts slightly before pointing at the building in question. "It's one open area. There is a level above, but for the most part there isn't rooms or areas they can hide."

I furrow my brows. "How do you know this?"

Slowly, Logan's eyes come to mine. "Because it's the warehouse where my father was killed."

"What?" I snap, my eyes bouncing between everyone. "How do you know that? Those files were locked and sealed?"

"I unsealed them," Blair states, interrupting. "Well, the real ones anyway"

"And I was there," Logan admits and the entire room freezes.

"Back the fuck up." Austin's palm slaps down on the table, causing the entire room to turn their attention to him. "You've been searching for your father's killer for a long-ass time. But you knew who he was?"

Mila winces and shifts back slightly. Her eyes are drilling into Logan, and I follow her line of sight. My eyes narrow as the pieces fall into place.

"She," he corrects Austin, and just like that, I connect the dots.

His rage when we first arrived. The way he and Roxy clashed at every encounter. Mila's cautiousness in wanting to protect her friend. "It was Roxy," I whisper, but everyone hears. "You were angry when we first arrived. The hatred poured off you. It was her, wasn't it?"

When Logan says nothing, I turn to Ayda. "Wasn't it?" My voice comes out in a growl.

I'm pissed we weren't told. I'm angry that these girls hold secrets and don't share them. What else do they know? Are they all killers, cleared because they just decide to be good for once? Is Mila?

"Yes," Mila states, her eyes turning glacial as she steps up beside Ayda. "But she isn't the same person she was."

I hear the double-meaning in her words. She doesn't mean that Roxy's the only one that's changed. "And that fucking changes everything then, does it?"

"No." Her eyes flash with pain before she drops them and looks away. "But Logan's realized who she is and has seen the changes in her. He cares enough to share her bed, and he knows the truth. Everyone changes, Rett. Life moves on."

Her words have the desired effect as my heart cracks inside my chest. "Not everyone," I murmur and swallow my emotion, unwilling to expose my weakness in front of my friends.

Logan and Ayda continue making plans, oblivious to the tension in the room. Mila pays attention, but her posture is stiff, telling me I wasn't the only one affected by the exchange.

She's right. She *is* different. I'm finding it difficult to reconcile the old Mila to this version, and I don't like it. Everything I once knew is different now, yet I still see glimpses. Perhaps that's what I need to do —try and remind her of who she was.

As Ayda and Ryder start bickering about the plan and his lack of approval for her going in alone, I interrupt before they pull us off-topic.

"I think we need to do this at dusk, right before the sun goes down." I keep my eyes on Mila, but she continues to ignore me. "We need time to prepare and get the supplies in order."

Logan doesn't agree. He doesn't want to wait, but eventually, we convince him that the plan will work better if we are smart about it. His patience is wearing thin, and I know he's concerned about Rox, but everyone's at risk if we go in stupid.

We go over the plans one last time to discuss strategy and roles before he dismisses us to get some rest. Mila hightails it out of the room, and I follow her, determined to close this gap between us. We need to talk. I catch up just as she steps into the elevator, and I squeeze through the gap before the doors fully close.

Leaning against the back corner, her arms folded defensively, she watches me. My lips twitch as I lean back and mimic her position. When I don't say anything, she raises a manicured eyebrow and leans forward to stab a button on the elevator panel. I frown when I realize she isn't going to her apartment.

"You're going out?" I ask, noticing the floor she selected opens to the parking garage.

"Yep."

"Where?" Her eyes narrow at my question. "We have to be ready to leave in twenty-four hours. I don't think now is the time to leave."

"Well, lucky for you, Sergeant—"

"Staff Sergeant," I correct pointedly. Then I realize I sound like my father and wince.

She grins and winks. "I know. I just don't care. Just like I don't care that you think I need to stay here. I'm a big girl who can look after myself, and I know how to tell time."

"Where are you going?" I ask, brushing off her hostility.

She snorts, "None of your business. I don't think you understand how this works. I have my team, and you have yours. Beyond that, find somewhere else to stick your nose."

The doors open and she storms out. I follow her into the garage, and she unlocks a black Mustang with the fob in her hand.

"Is this a booty call?" I call after her, loud enough so that she hears me.

She stops and spins on her heel. "And if it is?"

I slow my steps until I'm in front of her. Her scent invades my nose and causes all the blood to rush to my dick. Even after all these years, she still smells the same. "This isn't the time."

"And this is still not your business," she retorts and goes to turn away, but I grab her arm and stop her.

"I'm making it my business."

She shrugs out of my grasp with almost no effort, but she doesn't scoot away. She surprises me by stepping forward, so close that her heat presses into my chest. I stare into her exotic eyes and search for the tiny flecks of honeyed gold I remember so well.

"That's not how this works," she says with a smile, and I feel my eyes drop to her lips. "You don't make the rules here. I go to the meetings. I know what I need to do, and I'll be here before we leave." Her eyes turn threatening, she shoves me back a step, and goes to her car. "Stay out of my shit."

"Ana."

She opens the door to her Mustang and slides in, closing the door quickly behind her. I shove my hands in my pocket as the engine roars. As her eyes flick to mine in the rearview mirror, I smirk and fold my arms across my chest.

Positioned behind her car, I'm not moving until she gets out and speaks to me like a normal person. She needs to stop running away from this.

My smile drops as the engine revs. The tires squeal as she throws it into reverse, and I dive out of the way to avoid being run over. I grunt as my body hits the ground, and I roll over in time to see her disappear out into the night.

Getting up off the cold concrete, I brush myself off. I shake my head and walk back to the elevators. I don't know how to bridge this space between us. How do I get her to have an open conversation with me when she is so closed-off?

It doesn't matter what I do or how much space I give her, she's still angry and defensive. I have no clue what I did that makes her so angry with me.

3

MILA

I BLOW out a relieved breath when I see he's okay, and I watch him stare after me as I pull out of the underground garage. I didn't want to run him over, just wanted to make a point.

He can't just come back and pick up where shit left off. Things may not have changed for him, but my entire world shifted in the time we were apart. It feels like a long-ass time since I was that quiet, complacent girl.

A lot has happened.

It's not that I think he's had it easy. In fact, I know he hasn't. It's just that his version of Hell is different from mine. In one way, I think I'm more accepting of this new version of him than he is of me. Every time we're in the same room, I can feel his eyes on me, trying to pull back my layers and find answers...to find that young girl that once was.

There are no layers. There's just me, and I'm different. Honestly, it hurts a little. I like this version of myself. I'm better, stronger than I was. But he wants to strip it all back, and it angers me because it took a lot to be who I am now.

His disappointment hurts. He thinks I'm hiding, and I'm not. I have secrets, yes, but I'm not pretending to be someone I'm not to hide them.

Perhaps Greg was right. Slade should know his father. Rett has a right to be the dad I always knew he could be, but I'm not convinced it's safe. I'm not sure I know this Garrett, and every chance I try, I get frustrated because he wants the old Mila.

If he can't accept me growing up, how can he accept his son?

I groan in frustration as I pull onto a quiet suburban street, past the park I've taken Slade to a few times. By the time I pull into the driveway, my grin almost hurts my face. I turn off the car and head in, pushing thoughts of Garrett to the back of my mind.

I close the front door behind me and call out, "It's just me."

"Hija?"

I step into the living room to find Mama and Slade playing with dinosaurs on the floor. "Hey, Mama. Hey, baby boy."

"Mama!" His smile lights up his entire face, and a feeling of contentment washes over me. He stands and rushes in my direction, and I drop to my knees to catch him.

I bury my face into his shaggy, dark hair and inhale his sweet smell. "Hey, baby. Did you have a good day?"

"Abuela has been teaching me Spanish, and we made cake."

I gasp, "Cake? Did you save me some?"

"Yes." He nods so hard, his hair flops into his eyes, and I have to brush it back. He grabs my hand and pulls me towards the kitchen. "Come see."

I follow him and leave Mama to clean up the toys. This house is small and not flashy, but it's enough for the two of them. The house belongs to a friend of Scott's, and none of the utilities are listed in Mama's name. Slade is home-schooled, but under a different name, of course.

I wanted my son to have an education, but safely. This was the only option. There's a tutor that I've had vetted that teaches him. Any money I earn, I give most of it to Scott, who handles the expenses for Mama. Anything else, I handle.

For the most part, my son has a normal life. I visit him as much as I can, and when I can't, I call. He doesn't ask questions about me often, but when he does, I answer them as honestly as I can. I've answered his questions about his dad the same way.

The rules of friendship Garrett and I had, I've made for my son and me. We don't lie to each other, and we don't break promises.

He knows about Rett. He also knows that I never told his father about him. For now, he's okay with it. But I'm prepared for the fact he won't always be so accepting. I'm not sure what I'll do when that happens, but I'll deal with it when the time comes.

"Oohh," I say excitedly as he shows me his cake. "Looks so yummy."

"Abuela and I did it. It's chocolate and has cream in the middle," he says proudly. He rushes to the cabinet and grabs three plastic plates while I cut a piece each for us.

He helps me carry the plates to the table, and Mama joins us. "How was your day, hija?"

"Fine, Mama. Same old stuff."

Mama knows it all. I had to tell her because keeping her in the dark would more than likely get her killed. What if she ran into Eva? Or Levi?

She is also aware of my 'job,' though I generally don't go into details, and I definitely don't explain my friends' backgrounds. She knows enough to be cautious and to call me if anything suspicious happens.

I did, however, mention that Garrett would be working with us. Sensing where she's going to take the conversation, I work to steer her away.

"This cake is delicious, mi hijo." I wink at Slade, and he puffs his chest out in pride.

"And your new friends?" Mama pushes.

"What new friends?" Slade asks, and I shoot mama a narrow-eyed look. He notices, just as observant as his daddy. "What? Don't you want me to know?"

I sigh as Mama pats my hand and offers her advice. Thankfully, she does so in Spanish. "He'll find out eventually, hija. He's asking more questions and deserves answers."

"I know," I reply back in Spanish as well.

"Know what?" Slade sits a little higher and looks between us. My eyes widen when I realize he understood what I said.

Mama chuckles, "He knows some words. Not all." She smiles at Slade affectionately before speaking to me again. "Talk to him, hija. He is smart and will understand."

I nod to Mama, who gathers our dishes as I turn to my son. "Abuela is correct. I do have new friends, people my friends and I will be working with for a little while. You remember how I told you your papa and I used to be friends?" He nods and swallows, his green eyes attentively watching me. "And that we lost touch when he went to the Army?"

"Yes, but you're still friends." He shifts in his seat, figuring out where this is going, and his excitement is barely contained in his little body. His eyes twinkle at me, and I hate that this will probably hurt him.

"Yes, baby. He...well, he's part of the group I'm working with now."

His beautiful eyes light up. "Does that mean he could come here? I could show him my dinosaurs and cars, Mama. Do you think he'll like them? I know! We could play soldiers, and he could teach me all the secret code words!"

"No, baby," I reply, and the way his face falls hurts my heart. I would rather stab my own eye out than hurt him the way I am. "It's not that he doesn't want to, he just doesn't know about you."

His brows pinch. "Just tell him, then."

I blow out a slow breath and think of the best way to explain this. "When your papa and I separated, there were a lot of people that didn't want us to be together. Those people still don't. I want to tell him, baby. And I promise, when the time is right, I will. But if those people find out we're together, they'll find out about you. Right now, I need to keep you safe."

Stormy-green eyes come to mine. "But Papa wouldn't hurt me, would he?"

"No," I say, and I believe that with my whole heart. I'm not worried about Garrett hurting his son, but his ties with his family and their ties to Levi could. That's what's stopping me.

"Then he could keep me a secret," he pleads, and I grab his face to press a kiss to his cheek.

"You are the only thing in the world that matters to me. I promise to tell him as soon as I'm sure it's safe. I won't risk you, hijo." As the realization of what I've promised settles in, my stomach sinks. "It's time for bed, baby. Go brush your teeth."

"We don't break promises, Mama," he chides as he gives me a firm look.

"I know, hijo." I smile to reassure him. "Go on. Get ready for bed."

"Okay." He slides off his seat and presses a kiss to my cheek. "Do you have a picture?"

My eyes widen in surprise. "Of your papa?" I ask, and he nods. "No, baby"

"Can you get me one?"

My eyes flick to Mama as she rejoins us, and she shrugs. I squeeze my eyes shut and turn back to my son and nod, "I'll try."

His smile is bright enough to blind me as he fist-pumps the air and runs toward the bathroom. Laughing, I follow him to make sure he brushes properly. Then I walk him to his room, tuck him in, and read him a story.

By the second book, his eyelids grow droopy, and I know it won't be long until he falls asleep. Standing from his bed, I make sure he's tucked in and kiss him softly. "Sleep, baby. I love you."

Silently, I walk out of the room and close the door behind me. I walk down the hallway until I find Mama sitting in the living room.

"He's right, hija," she says once I take a seat.

"I know. It's just not that easy," I state. "If it was, I would've told him years ago."

"How long will you keep running? You spend all this time with Garrett now. He's a smart boy and will figure it out."

"Maybe," I muse. That's what I am afraid of. It's why I avoid him as much as I can. Garrett has always been highly observant, and even more so now. It won't take him long, and I'm worried he'll find out and not come to me first, that he'll call his mother or take this into his own hands.

"The boy I knew—" Mama begins.

I snort, "The boy you knew...is different. *I'm* different. I can't be sure about anything, and until I am, I won't take that risk."

"Are you scared, hija?" Mama leans forward and takes my hands in hers. Like everyone else, she's different too. Her hands are more wrinkled and rough from years of hard work, but her grasp is still warm and comforting.

"Scared of something happening to my son?"

"No." Her knowing eyes find mine, and she smiles. "Scared to trust yourself."

I blow out a harsh breath. "My track record isn't exactly good, Mama. Every decision I made had bad consequences."

"Not all decisions, hija. Some were the right ones. The important ones were right. You kept your baby, and every choice you made to keep him safe worked. You chose your friends. Those were not bad."

"My gut tells me it's not time," I argue because I feel that in my soul.

"I trust you to do what's best. But sometimes there is no...how do Americans say it?" she ponders before it comes to her. "No reward without this risk."

"I know. I'll work on it. That's the best I can do." I lean forward and press a kiss to her cheek. "Do you need anything?"

"No. Mr. Scott has been very good to us."

"He's a good man."

"He is."

"I'll call tomorrow. We have a job, but I should be back the day after."

"Okay. Be safe, hija. I love you."

I kiss her once more. "I love you too, Mama."

I drive back to HQ with a heaviness in my heart. It's getting harder and harder each day to live separately from my son. I crave him, his joyful personality and beautiful nature, in my life. But living with him is too much of a risk. I keep myself apart while still remaining present in his life, so if Levi finds me, Slade will remain safe.

My baby is so forgiving and understanding. Not many kids would just accept this as their life, but he does. He accepts it and thrives. I am completely blessed and so in love.

I remind myself that one day, we will have a life together permanently. It's just not now. I'm doing it all for him, and I'm just not finished making it safe yet.

I put in the access code, and the barrier raises, allowing me entrance. The Mustang's engine vibrates in here as I swing into my parking spot and switch off the ignition. Stepping out, I engage the lock and alarm and move toward the elevator.

"Why do you hate me?"

I yip a little and spin in surprise as Garrett steps out of the shadows with the saddest green eyes I've ever seen.

4

GARRETT

HANDS IN MY POCKET, heart on my sleeve, I beg for her answers. I need to understand what happened. Her brown eyes switch from fright to something softer, and for a split second, I see the girl that owns me body and soul.

"Hate you? Why would I hate you?" She shifts on her feet but watches me as I approach her.

Tension hums in the air. I could leave her alone. I could walk away and hope she'd come to me freely. But I did that once, and I lost her. I won't be a coward. I'm not leaving here until I know what's going on. "You *do* hate me. You're hostile, evasive. You avoid me all the time, and you close yourself off."

Her head drops, confirming my thoughts. I did something unknowingly, and she hates me for it.

"I don't hate you, Rett." My heart thumps at my old name. "Maybe once I did, but not anymore."

"Then what happened? You're so different." She nods, and I take another step forward, elation singing in my body when she doesn't move away. "You're running from something. Is it this place? Do you not want to be here? I can help—"

"Stop." She gives me a pointed look. "It's not this place. I want to be here, and those girls are my family. I'm finally where I want to be, thanks to them."

"But you aren't who you are." I throw my hands up in frustration. "This isn't who you are. I know you, and the Mila I know doesn't walk around half dressed carrying a Glock in her pants."

"The Mila you knew was a fucking moron," she snaps. "This *is* who I am. I don't ask for shit, I demand it. I lead, and I won't ever follow. I love who I am. It took a lot for me to get here."

"But it's not you."

She steps forward, fire burning in her eyes. "It is. You think just because you stuck your dick in me that one fucking time that you know me? You don't. You think you can tell me what's right for me? You can't."

"That's not what I am saying!"

"That's *exactly* what you're saying. Eight years have passed, and people change. You're standing here, telling me I'm not who I am, but you're wrong." Her fist pounds against her chest. "I know me, and I don't give two fucking pussy flaps what you think, Garrett Michaels. You can shove your pretentious notions up your stupid ass. Don't come in here and try to tell me who to be. I'm fucking proud of who I am, and what I sacrificed to get to this point."

"What happened? Please help me understand." My brain doesn't get it, refusing to connect this vulgar woman with the girl who sat with me in silence under the willow tree.

"No," she snarls, and when her arm snakes around to where I know her Glock is, I step back. "It's my past, and it's done. I don't owe you an explanation or excuse as to why I'm the way I am."

She turns away, and my heart pounds inside my chest. I'm running out of time. "I'm trying to understand because I love you."

Her steps falter as she tenses. "You need to stop saying that."

"I won't ever stop. I've waited eight years to find you, and I won't give up fighting for you."

She snorts and turns her head to look at me. "You'd fight for me, but you won't accept who I am? That's not love, Garrett. You don't get to pick what you want to love and what you don't. You love all or none of it."

"And what if I want it all?"

Her face falls, and she slowly turns to me fully. "You don't. Your parents were right. We don't fit, especially now. Let it go."

"No."

She shrugs. "Suit yourself."

She pushes the button, and the elevator doors open. She steps in and turns to watch me. Her eyes glitter with so much emotion and confidence, I find myself drowning in their depths.

Right before the doors close, anguish darkens her eyes, and it's then that I realize that she still loves me. I feel it with every fiber of my being. She's just scared.

Of what, though? It doesn't make sense. If what she says is true, then she's completely capable of taking care of herself. Scared isn't something I would associate with this Mila.

She also went out tonight. One thing I have learned is that this team is smart. They've spent the better half of the last few days searching for Roxy. They are strategic and resourceful, and they band together when shit hits the fan.

They've been extremely focused on getting Roxy back, so why did Mila leave tonight? What's so important that she had to go?

I don't believe it was a booty call. It's barely eleven P.M. I mean, I'm no expert, but surely it would last longer than a few hours. She barely looked ruffled. Either her guy was a shit lay, or she left here for another reason.

There's only one person I can think of that would be more important. Pulling my phone from my pocket, I scroll through my contacts. Finding the number I need, I hit dial. It rings twice before he answers.

"Garrett."

"Dominic," I answer, my eyes on the elevator in case she comes back.

"I haven't found anything new. I'd contact you if I did."

"I know. I have a new assignment. I need you to find her mother, Mrs. Diez."

"First name?"

I pause. In all the years Mila's mom worked for my family, I never heard her first name. "I'm not sure. I'll find out, but can you do a small search of the last name for now? She would be here on a green card, and I think she's close to my current location."

"Yep, can do. It'll be easier once I have a full name, but I'll see what I can find."

"Thanks. Send me the bill." I hang up.

I hired Dominic to find Mila twelve months ago. He comes with a glowing reputation, and he is cunning. He also has zero ties to my father. He found stuff on Mila from the days after she left, but the records are sealed. He's been working with a colleague to uncover them, but someone keeps throwing up walls to keep them out.

Sighing, I scroll through my phone to find Mom's number. If anyone knows Mila's mom's name, it's her recent employers.

"Garrett?" Her voice is thick with sleep and concern.

I wince. I should've waited until morning. "Hey, Mom. Sorry I woke you."

"It's fine. Is everything okay?"

"Yeah, sort of. Do you remember Mrs. Diez?"

She hesitates slightly before answering, "Yes?"

"Do you know her first name?"

"Ah..." She pauses for a moment before answering, "No. Your father hired her and always called her Mrs. Diez."

"I know. I did too. Any chance you have employment records with her name and everything on it?"

"Maybe. I'm not sure. What's this about?"

I push my fingers through my hair and continue to stare at the elevator. Maybe Mila's right. Perhaps I should stay out of it, but I need to know what happened. For years, I've had no answers, and now, I have the opportunity to ask the one person that knows, and she won't tell me.

"Garrett?" Mom's voice is growing more worried as I continue to ponder in silence.

"It's for a job," I lie. Years of being a Ranger trained me to sound convincing. "We need a translator. One I can trust."

I don't know why I lie, but something inside me tells me to. When she asked me why, a heated surge filled me with the need to protect Mila. I've learned to trust my instincts.

"Is that all?" she asks, hesitant.

"Yes," I swallow.

"Okay. Can it wait until morning?"

"Yeah, that's fine. Let me know."

"I will."

"How's Tobias?"

"He's looking at me like I lost my damn mind talking on the phone this late," she laughs.

"How rude of you," I chuckle.

"It's fine. He sleeps more than I do anyway."

"That's true. I'll let you go back to sleep. Sorry I woke you."

"It's okay. Stay safe. I'll see what I can find."

"Thanks. I love you."

"Love you too."

5

MILA

THE RESCUE WAS A SUCCESS. First, we got Roxy out safely. Second, Garrett didn't try to play the hero. The expression on his face when I set off the bomb still makes me giggle. He was so mad.

I relax on the sofa with my team as Roxy eats in an unladylike fashion and catches up on what happened while she was gone. Her dark, ebony hair is wet from her shower, and her eyes are red from exhaustion. She was kidnapped by her own mother to train an army for her.

Roxy is a highly-trained fighter. If royalty exists in the underground, Lex would be a king. I know from what I learned in Levi's complex that her family is dangerous. Roxy was raised, trained to be his human weapon. But like me, she was smart, and when she saw an opportunity, she went renegade on his plans and got her and her twin out from under her father, Lex's control.

Her older brother, Jacob, and younger sister, Mia, stayed. I met them both when I was with Levi. Turns out, Jacob was Logan's anonymous source, and the person he wanted to rescue was Mia. Go figure. I find it really ironic that he hunted my friend for the very same thing he did today.

In fact, Roxy and Ayda are still being hunted. Their father wants them dead because they broke some stupid code and betrayed him.

They've been careful for years, and now they fear it's all going to come to a head.

I think Roxy's finally understanding that she isn't in this alone this time. We're a family, and though her biological family may be different, this one always stands together. I have their back, and I know they have mine.

Guilt punches at me because I still hide half of me from them. The most important part. *Slade.*

I smile as our poking into Roxy and Logan's relationship results in her screeching about colored assholes and boobs. Her voice rises as her frustration with us grows, just as the man in question steps into the room. Credit goes to Ayda as she tries to shut her sister up and warn her, but Roxy is too far gone to stop.

Logan stands behind his woman, muscular arms crossed and decorated in ink, and a smirk planted firmly on his face. When she finally finishes her speech, she looks at our expressions, a suspicious look sliding across her face. Since she's facing us, she has no idea he's behind her.

"Please...continue," Logan states, laughter in his voice.

Roxy's body stiffens as she glares at all of us, particularly me, before turning in his direction. His eyes twinkle playfully and remind me of childhood moments I'd long forgotten.

"Anything else you wanna add, baby?" His lips twitch in a smile, and I bring a hand up to my mouth to stifle my laugh.

Full of defiance, Roxy squares up to him. "He has really good hands too." She tilts her head to the side, smiling sweetly. Roxy ain't sweet. "Big and masculine, which he'll be well-acquainted with in the foreseeable future because he is acting like a jagoff."

I snort as she storms off, and his face drops. Not sparing any of us a glance, he charges after her and leaves us all giggling like school girls.

Slowly, our laughter dwindles and is replaced by yawning. One by one, we say good night, and I watch as the girls head to their rooms.

When Charlie's head of red hair disappears behind her closed door, I listen to make sure everyone's settling okay. When it seems like everyone's turned in for the night, I slip out the front door and head to the elevator.

Walking into the ground-floor gym, I look around to make sure I'm alone. There are two sections to this gym. The first section is for the public. The memberships of gym junkies help add to our cash pile, but it also adds a layer of camouflage to keep us hidden. The second part of the gym is hidden behind a coded door, and it's specifically designed for Ghost Team.

Entering my code, my son's birthday, into the electronic keypad, I push the doors open and move toward the shooting range. A selection of weapons are hung up in a case on the wall, and I stroke my finger over the intrinsic beauty of each gun.

Every time I'm here, I am reminded of the first night I met Kage. Guilt is a bitch of a feeling. It doesn't matter how much time passes, it can buckle you at any time. I don't think I'll ever forgive myself for what I did to Kage. The last time I saw him plays repeatedly in my head, the pain he felt because I broke his heart.

Just another one of my stupid, selfish mistakes.

I slide down the wall and pull out my phone. I dial the only number I have on speed-dial, and she picks up on the first ring.

"Hija," my mama sighs. I know she worries and waits for my calls, especially when she knows I've been out on a job.

"Mama."

"You okay? Safe?" I smile at her concern, but I hate being the cause of it. For a long time, I was a good child and Eva the rebel. At times, I wish she wouldn't worry about me and focus on Slade instead.

"Yeah, the job was a success, and we're all safe." I hear her sigh, and I smile. "Is he there?"

"Yes. I'll get him," she responds. A minute later, a different voice trickles through the phone.

"Mama!"

"Hey, baby. Did you have a good day?"

"Yes. I made paper mache today. We painted it and made hot air balloons. Mine is blue and green." A smile splits my face, his excitement contagious.

"Wow, that's amazing. You'll have to show me when I come see you."

"Did you know the Civil War had a balloon corps?"

"What?" I chuckle. "Really? Like hot air balloons?"

"Yeah. They were used to spy on the enemy. How cool is that?" he exclaims.

"That's really cool, baby."

"When will you come see us? I wanna show you all this stuff," he questions, and it triggers a longing inside my chest. My son shouldn't have to ask where I am all the time or when I'll be visiting. Moms are supposed to be present all the time, not occasional visitors.

"Tomorrow, sweetie. I promise."

"Okay. Te amo, Mama." Tears prick at my eyes at his declaration.

"Te amo mucho," I respond softly.

The line disconnects, and I drop my phone into my lap. I don't know what's harder: seeing him everyday for a few hours or not seeing him at all. I feel like there's this giant void inside my chest that I can never fill. It's raw and it churns with pent up energy that can't be used.

"There's someone else?"

I gasp when I hear his voice and search the dark room for him. Movement to my left has my head whipping in that direction as he steps out of the shadows and into the light.

"Garrett," I whisper, panic flaring inside my chest. I run the conversation over in my head and try to pin-point anything he may have heard that could lead to my son.

He sits down in front of me, tucking his knees into his chest and resting his arms against them. "That's who was on the phone, right? Why didn't you tell me there was someone else?"

I should lie, save us both the pain, but I see his agony glittering in his green eyes, and I can't bring myself to do it. "There isn't anyone else."

"Then who was on the phone?"

"A friend."

"You tell your friends you love them?"

"Yes," I frown. "Don't you? If you don't, maybe you need to."

He huffs and falls silent. Normally, silences have me edgy, I need to break it and find out why people don't speak, but this silence is different. Silence with Rett always was.

"Explosives, huh?" He relaxes his legs and crosses them, leaning back on his hands.

I try hard not to stare, but his body was made to be ogled. Every ridge and dip looks like it was carved from marble. His skin is clear and golden, likely soft to the touch. My fingers twitch. My eyes flick to his, and he arches a brow in question. It takes me a second to remember what he asked, but when I do, I nod. "Yeah. It comes in handy."

"I don't like it," he mumbles

"Me using explosives?"

"No, explosives in general. They kill people," he clarifies. "Have you killed people?"

I fiddle with the lace on my shoe and contemplate how to answer his question. "Depends, I guess. 'People' is a broad term."

"Well, that's a non-committal response. Care to explain?" He stares at me, his eyes shining with moonlight that spills in through the window.

"Well...you have criminals, right? Pedophiles, rapists, abusers, and all those cocksuckers. Then you have innocent people." I shrug, "If you're talking about the former, then yeah, I have. The latter? No."

"Do you like it?"

"Killing?" He nods, and I shake my head. "No. While they deserve it, I don't find joy in it."

"You were so excited when the bomb exploded."

I nod and smile, "Yeah, I like to blow shit up. I like to know that something I build works. But that doesn't mean I like killing people. There's a difference."

"Is there? My training says they are one and the same."

"Maybe your trainer needs a different perspective."

He snorts, "Maybe."

"Probably," I say pointedly.

He sighs and sits forward, resting his arms on his knees. His eyes probe mine, and I know he's going to ask me something serious.

He's reading me, paying attention, looking for a lie. "Is what we had real?"

I frown, because of all the questions I was expecting, this was not one of them. "Huh?"

"I've held our relationship in my head for so long, making it out to be some Romeo and Juliet shit. But now you're here, right in front of me, and I'm left wondering if it's just something my head and heart conjured. So, I want to know. Was it real?"

I could easily fall into his arms, tell him what's inside my heart is true. That he's tattooed on my soul. A big part of me wants to, but I'm not ready. I am not sure I ever will be.

My eyes flick down to the chain around his neck and I tilt my head, studying them. "The tags. Did your father pass away?"

His face pinches in annoyance, probably because I'm avoiding his question. " No."

"Why three? I know when a soldier dies, one tag is left with their body, and the other is given to his family," I muse, and he nods in confirmation. "So whose is the third?"

He smiles, and I almost pass out as my core throbs. He's so fucking beautiful when he smiles. "I'll tell you my secrets if you tell me yours."

My blood turns icy as memories of Levi flood to the forefront of my brain.

"I need to go," I huff suddenly, snatching my phone from my lap. I leverage myself to my feet, and my tired and sore muscles protest.

"What just happened?" He rushes to follow me.

"Nothing. I'm just really tired, " I try to deflect.

"Don't lie to me," he growls, gripping my arm and spinning me to face him. His intense gaze drills into me, trying to decipher what I'm not telling him.

"I'm not. I'm tired and just realized the time, that's all."

He searches my eyes, looking for anything to discredit my claim, but when he finds nothing, he drops my arm on a grunt.

I turn toward the exit, and just as I push the door open, he calls out.

"Hey, what's your mom's name?"

I pause halfway out the door and look at him over my shoulder. "What? Why?"

He gives a sheepish shrug. "Mom and I were talking about how much she misses her. Did you know my mom can't cook for shit? Mom just realized that she didn't even know her first name. Since dad took all the paperwork with him in the divorce, we can't find out."

"Divorce? Your parents got divorced?"

He nods. "Yeah. Probably about a year after you left."

"Wow."

"That surprises you?"

"Well, yeah. No offense, but your mom wasn't exactly the type to stand up to your dad."

"That's true, but after I refused to come home because I didn't want to see him, she found her courage."

I stare into empty space, unfocused. Did Garrett not go home because he knew what happened to me? Does he know I was sold to his father's motorcycle gang friend?

"Mila?"

"Hmmmmm?" My eyes refocus to find him waiting patiently for an answer. "Lilliana," I state, then frown when my gut clenches.

"I'll let her know." He smiles in thanks before shoving his hands in his pockets and turning away.

The pit in my stomach increases in size with every step he takes away from me. I hate it. Before I second-guess myself, I blurt out, "It was real." He halts and turns back to me with hopeful eyes, so I continue, "All of it. You didn't make it up. It was real."

He opens his mouth to respond, but I push the door back open and step through before he can say anything. Self-preservation kicks in, and I hightail it back to my room.

It will never matter what the distance is between Rett and I. I still crave him, and my heart still cries for him.

6

GARRETT

It's been five days since my talk with Mila. She had walked straight into the gym, not paying attention to her surroundings, as if she didn't need to. That probably wasn't the first time she went there to make a phone call. She's so used to being alone there at that time of night that she didn't even bother to check.

I know that section is for Ghost Team only, so I'm assuming she didn't realize we were given codes to use it too.

Austin hits the button to call the elevator. Alpha Team is silent as we try to process what we've just seen. When I first saw all those women in shipping containers, trapped and malnourished, my blood ran cold.

Their captors are the people Mila referred to the other night. Abusers. The ones she doesn't consider people and deemed fit to kill. I understand what she means now. I couldn't imagine being trapped inside a container with all those women, no food or water, waiting to be auctioned. Waiting for some sleazebag to purchase me, make me into a possession.

The girls reacted in a way that was impressive. They became unified and plotted a plan of action, and I can see why they are a force with whom to be reckoned.

"We need some plan in place," Austin presses, clearly as disturbed as I am.

Logan nods, lost in thought. We can't do anything about the women yet because we need to get José before he realizes we're on to him and vanishes. Our position is tenuous. If José finds out we're even so much as sniffing around, he'll go into hiding, and all of our hard work would be for nothing.

José is just a small piece of Lex's world, but he is the one that coordinates the drug trade. Bringing him down will eliminate a chunk of Lex's reach.

"I'll contact the temporary commissioner and get things started." Lucas taps away on his tablet, and we fall into silence.

I personally don't think it's necessary. I saw the silent exchange between the members of Ghost Team and know they're planning something. They won't wait for us and will get the women out alone if they have to. They're not required to follow political protocol or a chain of command, so they have no reason to wait.

I should tell the guys, but remembering the state in which I saw those poor women, their survival may not last until we have clearance to go in. For their lives' sake, I keep my thoughts to myself and hope I'm right about the girls.

Abusing women is a hard limit for me. I've fought against beastly men, but this lack of humanity almost brings me to my knees. Maybe it's from years of witnessing my father's abuse against my mother or seeing the world at its worst. I don't know, but my stomach threatens to revolt every time those images appear in my mind.

One thing I learned from rescuing Roxy was that these women we work with aren't to be underestimated. They're the definition of badass, and standing in their way would do more harm than good. My heart thumps heavily when I think that Mila's one of them.

I don't know whether I'm proud of her or fucking terrified. She was always the shy girl I needed to protect. In all those years I'd known her when she was my best friend, my loyalty and protection was always hers.

I went about it in the wrong way, but I was a stupid rich kid. After my time in the service and working with Alpha Team, I realized I was simply a coward and took the easy way out. I didn't fight for her when I needed to. I always thought our best communication happened when we were silent, but I was wrong. Things were left unsaid, and I've regretted not saying what was in my heart ever since.

I told her I loved her, and we made plans for our future together. But I never told her how deep my feelings ran, how imprinted she was on my soul. Perhaps that could have changed things, taken us down a different path.

I didn't, and now I'm left trapped inside a storm, and I don't know how to get out.

I chuckle at the irony as I unlock my apartment door. I'm a methodical man; I find solutions and map out plans for wars. I think outside the box because that's my job. But this? Her? It's like my brain malfunctions and can't compute.

I head to my bedroom, strip off my clothes, and jump in the shower. I wash off the sweat from this morning's training session with my team. Roxy and Ayda are training us in preparation for our upcoming operation with José. While I'm skilled and prepared for most types of combat, it doesn't hurt to refresh my training.

Tomorrow, we infiltrate José's world and bring him down. We have a plan and a group of highly skilled and prepared people. Soon, it'll all be over, and Alpha Team will return to life pre-Ghost Team. The dread that sinks into my bones is almost suffocating.

I don't want to return. I've finally found my woman after years of searching, and leaving her behind feels so fucking wrong. I don't know where we stand. I can barely have a conversation with her. Walking away feels like the coward's way out.

Again.

I step out of the shower and dry off. Dressing in black sweatpants, t-shirt, and a black hoodie, I head out of the apartment and into the elevator. I push open the front doors and step out into the night. I breathe in deeply, forcing my lungs to expand, relieving their tightness.

I walk to clear my head and plan. I could quit Alpha Team, hand in my badge and come back here. Even if she doesn't want me, I can't bring myself to completely walk away. I could watch over her like a creep, and when she needs it, I'd swoop in and help.

I know that for sure. Whatever she's running from will come back. They always do, and when they do, I'll be here.

A few hours and about fifty laps around the building later, I decide to head back in. I need to rest, though I'm sure I won't sleep. It's been years since I was a Ranger, yet my sleeping patterns are still screwed.

I take the stairs back to my apartment and shove the fire door open before stepping out into the hall. I almost trip when I see the figure seated against the door to my apartment.

My heart kicks to life when I recognize her. She shifts slightly when I get closer, and when she doesn't move to stand, I sit on the floor beside her. It's almost midnight, and she should be sleeping. The fact she can't and has seeked me out gives my heart a burst of joy.

"I know you figured it out," she whispers.

"That Ghost Team is going to go and get the women being held hostage?"

She blows out a breath, "Yeah." She shifts so she's facing me. "Did you tell the guys?"

"No." I shake my head, and she sags in relief.

"Good," she responds.

I interlock my fingers in my lap to stop myself from reaching out to touch her and stare straight ahead. "Why doesn't Roxy just tell Logan?"

She shrugs. "She doesn't play well with others. She's always been self-reliant, and she tends to lock herself away. In some ways, Logan challenges her and draws her out of her shell. But the job comes first, and those women need our help."

"Logan would help," I push, not being a fan of her going into the unknown without me.

She nods, her hair falling in soft curls over her shoulder. "I'm sure you're right. But he is in law enforcement, and there's too much red tape, just like he said. We don't have to follow that protocol, and she doesn't want to put him in a situation where he has to risk his job."

"She said that?"

"She didn't need to." Her eyes flick away for a second before coming back to mine. "It's how we all feel."

"Right." I purse my lips in disagreement. "If my time with the Rangers taught me anything, it's that you stick together. We're all working this case."

"We are working on José. Those poor women weren't included."

"Yet, here we are."

"Yep."

Silence falls, and desperation creeps in. This might be my last chance to have her alone, to say all those things I never said, before we have to leave.

"Rangers, huh?" Her voice is nothing but a whisper, but it sounds much louder in the quiet hallway. "Bet your dad was proud."

I snort, "If he is, I wouldn't know. I haven't talked with him since you left, and I couldn't find you."

Her smile drops, and her eyes fall to her lap. She knows where I'm about to take this conversation.

"I looked for you, Ana." I swivel to face her. "I swear to God I did, but I couldn't fucking *find* you. I came home from boot camp, and you were just gone. He told me you wrote a letter. He even gave me the fuckin' thing. But that couldn't have been you. I'd bet my life you didn't write it."

Her head comes up, and pain pounds my heart when I witness the glittering of welling tears in her eyes. "I didn't."

I nod and reach out, taking her hand. "I know. Why did you leave? What happened?"

Her eyes darken. "You say that like I wanted to, that I had a choice. I didn't."

"Then why didn't you reach out to me?"

She slides her hand from mine. "You've no idea what I went through." Her hand reaches out and flicks the chain around my neck. "But that's okay because you think you're some hero. Soldier boy went to war. I had my own fucking war, and I didn't have a team of men helping me. I don't have a stupid necklace or badges of honor."

She stands, brushing off her butt as I stand as well. Her eyes stare into mine as she continues, "You act like you're the only one that lost something, that had to make sacrifices. You're not, Garrett. I lost everything I ever knew and was forced to live a life I never fucking wanted."

My shoulders drop. "I'm sorry."

She gives me a sarcastic laugh. "Well, I'm not sorry. I made choices, and I'm not proud of some of them. But I made them, and I have no one to blame for the consequences but myself."

"That's not why I'm sorry. And what choices?"

"Choices that lead me here. Tell me, Mr. Know-it-all, did you ever talk to Romeo after I left?"

My face pinches in confusion. "What's he got to do with this? Did he know where you were?"

She snorts, "Answer the question."

"Yes, I spoke to him."

Her anger breaks, and for a split second, I see a broken girl shattered by my words. "Good night, Garrett."

She turns and heads down the hall.

"I used to think I was a coward," I call after her.

She turns back like I knew she would. Challenge this Mila, and she spits flames from her mouth. Her gaze rakes over my body before finally settling on my face. "You were."

I stare at her, trying to tell her without words that I already know that, that I'm sorry, and I fucking wish I could take it all back. I let her see it all, opening myself up and letting her in. Her lip wobbles, and I move to her subconsciously. In two strides, I'm in front of her, my hands framing her face. "Let me in, Ana, please."

"I can't. It's not safe." Her voice cracks, and my knees buckle under our shared agony.

My eyes drop briefly to her lips as her breath fans my face. I wipe away a tear that slides down her cheek and stare into her eyes so hard, I can see the honey flecks of color in them.

I can feel her pulse spike under my fingers, and her chest bounces with heavy breaths that match mine. The need to kiss her claws at my throat so strongly, I can almost taste her on my tongue. I move in closer, making my intentions clear. When she doesn't pull away, my lips twitch with the need to claim her.

"Tell me to stop." My voice is thick with desire, and when her breath hitches, and she doesn't say anything, I press my lips to hers.

The contact sends an electric current flying straight through my body, stopping at my dick. I groan when she opens for me, and my tongue slides along hers for the first time in eight years.

There is nothing shy about Mila, no hesitation. She is all woman, and she knows exactly what she wants. She demands it. Her arms come up, and her nails slide through my hair. My hands find her delicious ass that's taunted me for weeks, and I squeeze.

I back her up until her body hits the wall. Gripping her butt, I lift until she wraps her legs around my waist. She is positioned perfectly, and when I grind my erection against her heat, she groans and tugs my hair in appreciation.

I rip my lips from hers and press them to her jaw line, creating a path down her neck, while I continue to thrust into the apex of her thighs. She's panting, her nails scratching a path over my body like she can't get enough.

"Garrett," she puffs out. "Stop."

I freeze, not sure I've heard her right. I pull back slightly, keeping her against the wall.

"What?"

She licks her lips, and my eyes follow the movement with greed.

"You said if I ever told you to stop, you would."

Stunned, I lower her feet to the floor and take a step back, adjusting my throbbing cock. "What just happened?"

"We can't do this."

I throw my hands up in frustration. "Why not? I know you felt that, Ana."

She tilts her head up in defiance, and the longer she stays inside her head, the more her expression closes off. "You're leaving tomorrow. I won't repeat history."

"I can stay—"

"No."

"No I can't stay? Or no you don't want me to?"

"Both. I'm not the same, okay? I have nothing to offer you. You've made it clear you don't like this version of me, and I have no desire to regress into the girl I once was. She doesn't exist anymore. This won't ever work."

"How the fuck do you know? You keep shutting me out!"

She nods. "It's better this way, safer, for all of us."

My heart threatens to stop, and my brain locks onto what she said. "Wait, what?"

"Huh?"

I step forward, regaining the little ground she put between us. I watch her carefully, wanting to know if she lies to me. "You said 'all of us.' What does that mean?"

Her face falls, and she stumbles back, almost tripping over her feet. Righting herself, she scoffs. "You don't get your dick wet, and now you're looking for shit that ain't there?"

I raise an eyebrow at her. "When I get too close to the truth, you make crude jokes about dicks and vaginas. Tell me, Ana, how close am I?"

"You wanna fuck? Get it out of your system?" She cocks a hip, and proves my point.

"No. If I have you, I want forever, not one night."

"Well, have fun palming your dick to thoughts of me. Make sure you lube up because chafing fuckin' sucks. Stick a finger in your ass and wiggle it a bit. It works." She winks and spins away.

I watch her power-walk to the elevator and stab the button repeatedly. She waits five seconds impatiently before deciding to take the stairs instead.

I was right. Mila isn't protecting herself. She's protecting someone else.

7

MILA

"YOU OKAY?" I ask Roxy, and she climbs off her bike after Ayda.

"Don't have a choice," she shrugs, but I see the hurt in her eyes and the way she winces as she moves.

Blood and dirt coat her skin from her fight with José and his men earlier, but she's still focused. Even when injured, she won't stop until this is finished. We slowly follow her toward the tree line, using the tree trunks to remain hidden.

There's no doubt our vehicles have alerted them already. They'd be trying to call their boss, but he is currently lying in a pool of his own blood thanks to Rox.

We watch the guards, about twenty of them all together, talk between themselves, protecting the shipping containers holding the women. The guards are clearly in distress. One paces while on the phone, while the others talk with wild and impatient hand gestures.

Blair organized transport for the women, and they're waiting for our signal. Once we get rid of the guards, we'll be able to safely remove the women and get them the help they need.

"Careful with the guns. Double-check your targets because those containers aren't bulletproof," Roxy states.

I roll my eyes. "I don't miss."

She smirks at me. "You ready?"

We nod, and she steps out from behind the trees. Blair, Charlie, and I hold back a few paces to provide cover from the back with our long-range weaponry. In addition to those, Charlie has her automatic bow and arrow, Blair has her sniper rifle, and I have my trusty Glock and a spare pistol.

"Time to play," I grin, snapping a magazine into my Glock, chambering the first round.

I raise my arm at the same time Charlie raises her bow. We fire, and two bodies jerk and fall to the ground as the other guards turn, alerted of our presence.

Roxy races forward with Ayda on her heel as the guards start shouting orders and grabbing weapons. Another body goes down as Blair's next bullet finds its mark.

The guards start firing in our direction, so I dart to my next position. A moving target is harder to hit. Two more bullets leave my weapon in rapid succession, and then I'm tracking and firing. Bullet after bullet jerks from my gun, causing it to vibrate in my hand.

I grit my teeth as each body falls to the ground, finding grim satisfaction in eradicating this bile from the earth.

Not five minutes later, Blair signals for the buses to move in. I step over the bodies of dead guards and resist the urge to put extra bullet holes into their bodies. I take comfort in the fact that they no longer share the same air we do.

They were holding women against their will and preparing them for auction. Gurgling sounds come from my left, and I move in that direction. Crouching down in front of a man clearly fighting for oxygen, I smile when his eyes widen in fear.

I tilt my head as his body fights to survive. I could end his suffering. A bullet between his eyes would make this process smoother, but he made innocent women suffer, and I can't find it in my heart to give a shit about him.

I look up and frown when I see Roxy sway on her feet, her skin ghostly white and her lips devoid of color. Sweat coats her skin, and when her blue eyes lift in my direction, they seem unfocused and slightly confused.

I check first to make sure the others have got the women covered before heading over to Roxy. Sliding an arm around her back, I help support her weight.

"Come on. I'll take you to Greg." I know she doesn't want me to make a big deal about this, and the minute I do, she'll fight me.

Her tongue tries to moisten her dry lips, and she sluggishly shakes her head. "No. It's not done."

"It is. Let's go."

She doesn't protest as I half-carry her to the Mustang. She struggles to walk, and her heavy, uncoordinated steps stumble often. I slide her into the passenger seat and clip the seat belt around her.

"Do you have paper?"

"Maybe. Why?" I frown, confused. Maybe she is worse-off than I thought.

"Can I have it and a pen?" she mumbles, slurring. I'm getting increasingly concerned..

I open the glove box hurriedly, knowing the longer I delay, the more she'll argue. I grab a notebook and pen and hand it to her. She scribbles something down before ripping out the page and handing it to me.

"Tell one of the women to give it to Logan," she asks. "Please."

"A love letter?" I chuckle.

She attempts to glare at me but doesn't have the energy. "Just do it."

I nod before closing the door and running back to the others. I pass a woman that seems less shell-shocked than the others and ask her to give the letter to Commander Carter. She nods but doesn't say anything. It'll have to do. Roxy needs medical attention, and I don't have time to play messenger.

Rushing to find Ayda, I find her at the first bus giving the driver directions. Interrupting them, I let her know I need to get Roxy to Greg. Obviously worried, she agrees and lets me know the others will cover us.

I race back to the Mustang and slide in the driver's side. Starting the ignition, I stomp on the accelerator and head back to HQ, keeping one eye on my friend as her eyes flutter with pain and exhaustion.

By the time I get back, Roxy is passed-out, and Scott has to carry her to the infirmary. Greg does what he does best, and I sit in the waiting area outside his makeshift operating room. Eventually, the rest of the team trickles in as we wait for the news on our friend.

Hours later, Greg finally emerges, exhausted. "Her injuries were severe. She had internal bleeding, and I had to perform surgery to stop it and repair the damage."

"From what?" I ask, confused. "Don't you get internal bleeding from a severe impact?"

Greg nods as Ayda explains, "When she jumped off the roof to save Ry, she had the rope secured around her waist."

"That'd probably do the trick," Greg states with pursed lips.

"She'll be okay, right?" Ayda stands, her hands clasped tightly, her fingers white.

"Yes, Cupcake. She'll be fine. She'll probably sleep for a while, though. She lost a lot of blood, and her body needs time to heal."

Ayda nods several times, as if trying to convince herself that her sister is safe. "Can I see her?"

"Sure. Just be quiet, okay?" Greg smiles and accepts her hug when she wraps her arms around him.

"Thank you." She presses a quick kiss to his cheek and darts off to find Roxy.

"I'm going to grab a shower," Charlie says as she stands, relieved like the rest of us that her friend's okay.

Blair decides she's going to as well and follows her out.

Greg drops down into the vacant seat beside me. "So it's all over? Alpha Team is gone?"

I stare at my hands and hate the way his words make my hands shake and my heart hurt. "Yeah. It's better this way."

"Are you trying to convince me or yourself, Marshmallow?" He nudges my shoulder and tries to make me smile, but I feel heavy.

Now that Rett is gone, it's like I can finally feel the rest of it. I thought I'd be relieved Rett's gone, but I don't. I feel like I'm grieving him all over again.

"Both," I admit and give him a watery smile, cursing when my eyes burn with the need to cry. "I have to keep Slade safe, and this is the only way."

"Is it?"

"What're you saying?"

"I'm saying that you went through hell. You had every opportunity to say it was too hard and just give in, but you didn't. You always find a way. This feels like you're giving up. That isn't who you are; that's the old Mila."

"I love him enough to let him go."

He gives me a defiant snort. "That's bullshit and you know it. True love is when you can't breathe without the other. It's finding a way back to each other, no matter the circumstances. When they start slipping through your fingers, you cling the fuck on or go down with them. You don't just let them go." He pats my leg. "The thing about love is, it comes from the heart. Each beat is for love, and when you're dying, you hold on because of that love. You don't have the love, Marshmallow, your heart gives up."

8

GARRETT

A MONTH after taking José down, I pace the office in frustration as the Assistant Commissioner leaves the room. Roxy Mortemous has been labelled as dangerous. We've been given orders to bring her in, and if she doesn't cooperate, we have permission to shoot on sight. We have permission to fucking kill Mila's best friend.

Fuck no.

My brain is short-circuiting as the situation becomes more daunting, and Logan continues to stay within the confines of the law. He treats this mission like he would any other, as if the person we've been ordered to bring in isn't the girl he loves.

If we try to kill Roxy, or take her against her will, we're going to go up against the entire Ghost Team. It goes against my entire being to be on opposite sides of Mila. There's no way I can do it. I'd rather shoot myself in the head than point a gun at her.

I'd follow Logan into almost any situation, but this is crossing a line, and I won't do it.

I could hand in my badge right now, but if the team goes ahead with the mission, I'm stuck fighting the guys that have become my brothers. I already lost one best friend. I can't lose any more.

Logan snaps at Ryder's accusation that Logan orchestrated the mission. I understand where he's coming from. Roxy lied to him about going after the women. He's been pissed since she shot out his tires and stopped him from following them.

Once the clean up at José's hotel was done, and we took Ryder to the hospital with a gunshot wound to the shoulder, we came back to the station to find busloads of the women Ghost Team rescued being treated.

"No, I didn't fucking know about this. And before you fucking ask, I don't want to kill her. Shit, Ry. I fucking loved her," Logan spits out, drawing my attention back to the conversation.

"Loved," Ryder snarls. Roxy earned his loyalty when she jumped from a fucking building to rescue him after he got shot. She saved his life and could've died in the process. He wears a sling while his shoulder heals from its injury and has been relegated to light duty for another four weeks.

"I...what?" Logan's face contorts.

"You said 'loved,' asshole. Past tense. She fucked up, and just like that, you flipped a switch? That's not love. That's being a fucking coward," Ryder pushes back, determined to get Logan to see past his anger.

Logan groans, clearly frustrated. "Maybe we can talk to her. Convince her to come in."

"Ha!" Austin smirks, and I have to agree with him.

"She won't. You know that," I state.

"The girls will have her back too. You know what that means?" Lucas murmurs.

Ryder stops pacing and looks Logan dead in the eye. "We agree to this, we'll end up having to kill them all."

"No," I growl. "Fuck that. They may work differently than us, but that doesn't make them wrong. It doesn't mean they should die."

Austin watches me and frowns for a moment before nodding in agreement. "They did the right thing. They just don't have the red tape to walk through that we do."

"If we don't do this, then we risk our jobs. Again," Logan throws out.

Ryder shrugs. "So be it. I'm not doing this, Carter. Roxy saved my life, and I'm not repaying her by throwing her to the wolves. She did the right thing, and I won't be the one punishing her for it."

"Me either," I add. "If that means I don't have a shiny badge, then I'm okay with that."

"Do you understand what you're saying?" Logan asks incredulously.

I nod.

Austin shoves a hand in his pocket and nods his agreement. Logan turns to Lucas, who also agrees. Logan gives us one last chance to back out and rescind our vote before walking over to the door and letting the Assistant Commissioner join us again.

Deckker smiles and takes a seat in the chair at his desk. His arrogant gaze bouncing between us before Logan wipes it straight off his face.

"We won't do it," Logan announces, and Deckker's face falls.

"You can't say no. You'll lose your badge," he says sternly. "These orders are from higher up the food chain, Carter."

Logan nods. "We are aware."

Austin pulls his hand from his pocket, and tosses the badge onto the desk.

"You don't want to do this," Deckker sputters. "This is your career. You don't want to just throw this away."

I also pull my badge from my pocket and silently walk to the desk. "What you're asking us to do doesn't line up with our ethics."

"Those women are killers!"

Lucas tosses his badge down, and Ryder follows with his. "They saved my life and a hundred women's lives. I think the good they did outweighs the bad."

Logan is the last to step forward. He chucks his badge down and braces his hands on the table. "Roxy isn't who you think she is. She doesn't deserve this. Just so we're clear, if anyone comes near her, they'll have to go through me. This case is closed, Deckker."

We head to the door, and I follow Lucas out, the others behind me.

"This case is not closed," Deckker growls. "Other officers will come after you, and this job will be handed to them. You can't kill an officer, Logan. It's against the law."

I turn to find Logan smirking, and I feel my own lips twitch. "It's against the law to kill anyone, Deckker. Good thing Ghost Team doesn't work within the law. I mean it. Stay the fuck away from them."

Logan slams the door closed, and we chuckle. I can't speak for the others, but I don't feel so heavy anymore. The badge I've carried for years was heavier than I thought it was. I joined Alpha Team four-and-a-half years ago to find the woman that vanished from my life.

I've found her, and it's time to get her back.

It takes a few hours to fill out all the discharge paperwork, but when it's done, there's a collective sigh of relief amongst the team. We pack up our shit and hand in our guns. Then, together, we head out.

As soon as I step outside, a tingle of awareness creeps across my body. I stop, using my senses to search for whatever has me on edge. I turn back to see Logan talking to Deckker, who wasn't done talking, evidently. Logan shakes his head at him, before heading toward us.

"Where to?" he asks, shoving his hands into his pockets.

"We can go talk to the girls," Austin shrugs.

"No need," I interject. My body feels heightened, alert, but not in warning, and that only means one thing. "They're here."

Logan tenses. "What?"

"Behind you," I state, my eyes locking on to her body. She's in the shadows, but I can make out her shape. I'd know it anywhere.

Logan turns abruptly and looks straight to where Ghost Team stands. He doesn't stop as he makes his way toward them, and we follow. The girls step out of the shadows, and my eyes instantly find Mila's. Her expression is guarded, no doubt because they know about the mission we were given. They are all cautious.

"What are you doing here?" Logan growls, but it's not in anger. He's concerned with Roxy being this close to the station when the cops want her.

"Can we talk?" Roxy whispers, no concern over the danger she's in.

Logan stalks off across the parking lot, into the shadows, and pulls her to where she'd be hidden from anyone inside the station.

"So, how's it going?" Austin chirps.

"Great," Mila deadpans, giving me a look like she's waiting for me to lunge at her. "Especially when there's a hit out on our friend."

I bite back a smirk, and my eyes flick to Lucas, who gives me a swift nod in acknowledgement as a smile spreads across his face. My attention shifts to Blair, who is none the wiser.

Lucas locked her out. They may know about the mission, but they've no idea we turned in our badges or the fact that we were discussing working with Ghost Team full-time.

That was my idea.

"We good?" Mila asks, and I turn to watch Logan and Roxy joining us, their hands intertwined.

Logan looks at Ryder, smiling like he's on top of the world now that he got his girl. "You tell them?"

"Tell us what?" Blair frowns.

"We're no longer Alpha Team. As of an hour ago, we're out of a job," Lucas smiles, hard.

"No," She pulls out her phone and starts frantically tapping away at the device. "That's not true."

"You won't find it on there, princess." Her neon-pink eyes snap to his. "I know you've been in the systems all day. I let you, but I only allowed you to see what I wanted you to." He grins. "Sucks huh? When someone fucks you around?"

"You stupid—"

"Right," Roxy intervenes. "So they are jobless and want to know if we will give them one?"

"You want to work for Ghost Team?" Ayda asks, but she's looking curiously at Ryder.

"Yup. That's the idea," he replies coolly.

"I'm cool with it," Charlie shrugs.

"I'm cool as long as you all stay the hell out of my business." Mila's eyes snap fire in my direction, and the challenge makes my dick twitch.

"Same," Blair shoots in Lucas' direction.

"Yeah. We're good," Ayda mumbles.

"Let's get going then. Even though they've still got to organize a new Alpha Team to target us, standing outside the cop shop is giving me the heebeegeebees," Mila shivers dramatically, strutting towards her car.

I watch her hip sway like a man possessed. The movement has me hypnotized and standing in the parking lot like a fool.

Austin nudges me. "Are you even listening to me? Does everyone ignore me?"

Thank fuck I've never been a blusher, otherwise I'd seriously be embarrassed right now. "Sorry, man. What's up?"

He pouts, and I roll my eyes. "Can you give me a lift? I ran here," he asks.

"You can't run home?" I frown playfully.

He throws his arms out, exasperated. "It's dark!"

I bark out a laugh and head to my car. He follows, jumping in the passenger seat. I make my way to his place, drop him off, then head to Mom's to collect Tobias and a few other things I need.

It's time for Ghost Team to meet the sixth member of Alpha Team. I could leave Tobias with Mom, but he was Monty's. Tobias has been with me since I lost my best friend, and I'm keeping it that way.

Twenty minutes later, I've loaded up my car, and Tobias and I follow Roxy's bike back to the new HQ. We drive through the gates, and I can't keep the smile off my face as I pull my car in next to Mila's mustang.

For the first time in eight-and-a-half years, I feel like I'm finally in the right place again. Now all I need is my girl, and everything in my life will be as it should've been this entire time.

9

MILA

I GROAN as my phone blares from the bedside table. I reach out with my eyes closed and feel around until I hear a heavy *thunk* as it hits the floor. Cursing, I lean over the side of the bed and grab my phone off of the floor. Hitting the accept button, I blindly bring it to my ear and grunt.

"My office." Scott's voice is commanding, but I don't react to it the way I would if it was any other man. His commands are more about urgency than glaring demands. I throw off my blankets and move to the closet for clothes.

"See you soon," I respond and hang up, tossing my phone on the bed.

I shove my legs into black jeans and grab a hoodie and sneakers. I pocket my phone, grab my keys, and lock the door behind me as I leave.

A few minutes later, I enter his office, following behind a sleepy Charlie. Blair is seated next to Lucas as they tap away on their iPads. Austin leans against the back wall and winks when I smile in greeting. Charlie joins him, and I lean against the opposite side wall.

Tingles skate across my skin as Garrett walks in. Glancing around the room, his eyes darken the moment they see me, and the most intense shade of dark green stares at me. His gaze slides over my body, and I can feel every place his eyes touch.

His eyes linger on my red hoodie for a moment before he focuses on my face again. The entire exchange happens in a matter of seconds, but he still manages to summon every single ounce of desire my body possesses.

My skin is tight with awareness, like my body knows he's close without having to see him. My mouth turns dry as he continues to eat me up with his eyes as he moves in my direction. I haven't forgotten the kiss we shared, nor the willpower it took for me to stop it.

"Now that everyone's here," Scott starts, snapping me out of my lust-filled haze. "There's something you all should know."

Garrett settles against the wall beside me, crossing his arms, highlighting his defined muscles. It's serious arm-porn, and I'm pretty sure my panties are combusting.

I have to work hard to keep my eyes from wandering and to look at Scott as he continues, "We have guests that arrived this morning. Two girls, eight years-old." My body tenses, and I can scarcely breathe.

"Who?" Garrett asks, oblivious to my inner turmoil for now.

"They are Roxy and Ayda's nieces."

"Kids?" Garrett's nose scrunches, and my stomach drops. "Why would kids be here?"

Scott's eyes flick to mine, and I feel Garrett stiffen next to me. *Fuck.* I send a pointed look in Scott's direction and hope he gets the message.

"I agree with Garrett," I state and surprise myself when my voice comes out steady and unfazed. "This isn't any place for children."

"Ayda and Roxy disagree. Their sister Mia met with Ayda last night. Mia was beaten pretty badly and asked Ayda to take the girls to keep them safe. Rhian, one of the twins, was also hurt and is being treated by Greg. I understand you don't think it's safe, but this might be the safest place for them right now."

"How so?" Garrett inquires.

I take a step to the side to create some space between us and turn to face him. "You know a little of Roxy's background, but Ayda's is different. Those women we saved? Those things happen all the time, and it isn't just outside the family."

"I don't understand," Austin pushes off the wall, his eyes focused on me.

"Ayda was a whore," Charlie inserts.

Austin blanches, and Garrett asks, "What does her sexuality have to do with this?"

"Ayda wasn't a whore by choice," I explain, and his eyes widen in acknowledgement. "Ayda was used by her father. She doesn't talk about it much, but we know enough to know what damage was done. Her father forced her to perform sexual favors so he could make alliances and friends. That's what Roxy saved her from."

"That's what you meant when you said Roxy isn't the same person that killed Logan's father?" Garrett asks, understanding.

I nod, "Roxy's always done what she's had to do. For the most part, she's completely selfless. She's stubborn as shit, but she'd take a bullet for anyone in this room."

Roxy spent most of her life trying to protect her sister. Ayda's the reason Roxy became the fighter she is today. Her protection extends to everyone in this room and to any innocent life outside of it. Roxy isn't going to walk up to you and give you a hug and tell you she loves you, though she's working on that. But she'll protect you with everything she has, including her own life.

Roxy had to kill Logan's father in order to save Ayda. It was a huge issue for Logan when Alpha Team first arrived, but he eventually understood. So much so that they announced their engagement last night, which I think is crazy. But love is love, and I'm the last person that gets to argue about that.

"What do you need from us?" I ask Scott.

"Logan and Roxy have gone to collect supplies for them, and the girls will stay with Ayda. But I'd like everyone to help and keep an eye out. Lex isn't going to let them walk away freely."

I nod and watch as the others agree.

"That's all, I think. Unless there's something else?" Scott looks at each of us individually, and when none of us say anything, he dismisses us.

One by one, everyone trickles out until there's only Scott, Blair, and me.

"You good?" Scott questions, his concern evident on his features.

"Yeah. Shit my pants for a sec, but I'm sweet. Rett's observant as fuck, so you need to watch your shit around him."

"Ahh..." Blair raises her hand slightly and turns in her seat, looking at me with dread. "I found something."

I look at Scott, and he looks as surprised as I do. "What?"

"Someone's looking for your mother." Blocks of cement drop into my stomach as panic and anxiety zips through my body. "It's a private detective, and I haven't been able to trace who hired him yet. But I've been able to block most of their attempts."

"No one even knows my Mom's name," I say, my face pinching, until I recall my conversation with Rett. My confusion turns to anger in a heartbeat.

That sneaky fucking bastard.

My fists clench as I address my friends. "I know who it was. I'll handle it. Let me know if anything changes or if this asshole finds her."

I storm from the office and punch the button to call the elevator. How dare he? He lied to me, right to my fucking face. I trusted him, and for what? So he could hire a detective and risk my son's life?

I step into the elevator and don't even bother trying to calm myself down. The elevator stops and opens on his floor, and I charge forward. I pound my fist on his door repeatedly until it swings open.

I lunge at him and shove at his chest. He stumbles back before righting himself and looks at me like I've lost my damn mind.

"You hired a fucking detective to find my mother? What the fuck, Rett?" His eyes widen in shock as a deep growl resonates around the room. My eyes flick to Tobias and back to Garrett.

"How do you know that?" he swallows uneasily before commanding Tobias, "Leave it." The dog obeys, dropping to the ground and panting like he didn't just scare the fuck out of me. I like dogs, but that thing looks like a damn wolf.

"It doesn't matter how I know. Do you have any idea how bad this is?"

"Why? What's going on?"

I grit my teeth and try to control the rage burning inside me. "What part of 'it's none of your fucking business' is so hard for your small, rich-boy brain to understand? I told you her name, and you lied to me about why you needed it. I fuckin' trusted you."

"You won't tell me what happened. I know you're protecting someone, and I just want to help you!" he pleads with me in frustration.

"I don't want your help. I didn't ask for it. You want something, you ask me. You don't make up bullshit fucking excuses and go behind my back."

"I *did* ask you."

"And I told you, it's none of your business. None of it is. Stay the fuck out of my shit!" I storm toward his door, making a wide berth around the dog.

"No," he growls, and I halt. "If you're in trouble or your family's in trouble, I can help."

I turn back to him, angry tears threatening at the back of my eyes. "This isn't helping! This might have fucked up everything I have ever worked for! Did you ever stop and ask yourself why she's hidden? You selfish, dumb fuck! Estúpida culo pequeña polla!" I spit in Spanish. *Stupid ass small cock.* "Stay the fuck out of my life!"

"Eres mi vida," he pleads. *You are my life.*

"Pero no eres mia," I respond sharply. *But you are not mine.*

I slam the door closed and work hard to slow my breathing. This could undo everything. Garrett might've been trying to protect or help me, but he may have thrown our son in the line of fire to do it.

I shove off the wall and head to the elevator, getting in as soon as the doors open and punch the button for the parking garage.

Wasting no time, I reverse the Mustang out of its space and almost collide with Logan's car on the way out of the gates.

My hands squeeze the steering wheel so hard that by the time I pull into the driveway of Mama's home, my fingers are cramped.

I grab my spare pistol from the glove box, not having the foresight to grab my Glock before the meeting, and shove it into the waistband of my jeans. Stepping out, I tuck my hoodie over the weapon and subtly check the streets for any unusual activity, but I don't see anything that's out of the ordinary. I use my keys and let myself in, my heart rate slowing when I hear the sound of Slade's laughter.

"Hija?" Mom's worried voice carries through the living room and into the hallway.

I blow out a relieved breath, "Mama."

I step into the room, and she gives me a skeptical look, her eyes flicking behind me before coming to mine, full of concern. "Is everything okay?"

I shake my head discreetly, not wanting to worry my son. "Where's Slade?"

"In the kitchen with Miss Livi."

I nod and head in that direction. Slade looks up from his books, and his whole face lights up when he sees me. "Mama!"

He almost face-plants on the floor in his enthusiasm to get to me, but he catches himself in time and launches himself into my arms. I bury my face into his hair and hold him tight with shaking limbs.

I breathe him in and take a moment to reassure myself that he's okay. Now that the initial anger has passed and my worries have been abated, I realize I was maybe a little harsh with Garrett. His intentions have always been pure, and I know this is my fault.

I'm keeping things from him. His tiny lie isn't anything compared to mine. He didn't know about the danger he'd put his son in because I haven't bothered to even tell him he has a son.

After a bit, Slade pulls back, worried. He holds my cheeks. "What's wrong?"

I shake my head and swallow my emotions. "Nothing, baby. I just missed you."

He smiles, and I can't help but kiss him on the cheek. "I missed you too. Want to come see what I've been doing?"

I nod, and he wiggles to get down. Holding my hand, he leads me to the table where Miss Livi sits with an unfocused expression on her face, which clears when we come into her field of vision. She's his full-time tutor and someone I trust greatly. She's been with us since he was five.

She knows enough to understand he's in protection, and she's paid a lot of money to be discreet. Together, they show me the mathematics they're learning today, and Slade demonstrates his new skills. He reads to the both of us, and pride fills my heart with how good he's getting. After a bit, I leave them to it and go to find Mama.

I locate her in Slade's room, stripping the dirty sheets from his bed. I walk over and grab a clean bottom sheet and begin helping her remake it.

"What is going on, hija?"

"Rett hired a private investigator to look for you."

Her face pinches in confusion. "What is this? Private what?"

"Like a detective."

"Mierda," she huffs out in frustration.

"I don't think they found you, Mama, but you need to be careful. Levi has a lot of resources, and it wouldn't take much for him to locate the same PI."

"How? Are he and Garrett friends?"

"I don't know, but if Levi is looking for us, he may find the connection either way. I just need you to be more alert."

"Okay. I will watch."

"Blair will be watching too, okay? You guys aren't alone out here."

"I know, hija. We will be fine. You'll see."

As the words leave her mouth, I think: *famous last words.*

10

GARRETT

WEEKS PASS, and this thick black cloud of guilt hangs over my head. Life continues around me, and I feel stagnant like a fifth wheel. Like I'm not needed. I crossed a line hiring the investigator, but I had good intentions.

I try to stay focused on the challenges we have in front of us. Katarina, Ayda and Roxy's mother, escaped after we arrested her for kidnapping her daughter. We found footage of the escape, and it looks like she had help inside the police department.

Logan and Ryder have been in contact with the department to get a list of fired officers or even ones that are suspected of being corrupt. But since we left the department ourselves, they aren't too forthcoming with assistance.

I've been working with Blair and Lucas to create a program that runs traffic cam footage and other hackable surveillance systems through facial recognition software in the hopes we can locate her. But for now, she seems to be in hiding, and we have no leads. Our two IT specialists have also been working on getting information from the police databases surreptitiously since they didn't willingly give us anything usable.

Ryder and Ayda seemed to have sorted out their shit. There'd been added tension in the group with their inability to see eye to eye on their relationship, but they left the team bonding barbecue together, so we can only hope it means they're working on it.

They seem to be on the same page, and though I'm happy for them, I'm also envious. Mila and I are still at odds and have not made any progress.

She refuses to talk to me, her anger still very much present. I've taken a step back to let her cool off. Back when we were kids, silence was always the best defense when it came to her anger. But it worries me a little. This Mila is different, unpredictable and defiant. I'm worried she will mistake my silence for defeat, and that's not what I am doing.

The night she confronted me about my PI, I called him after she left and cancelled the search. Not because of her anger, but because what was fueling it. Fear. She's scared of something so much, it drove her into a fit of rage.

If she's that worried, then I have reason to be concerned too. So, I called off the dogs and prayed that I hadn't caused any damage.

I open the back door and let Tobias out. He races off, sniffing around and going to the bathroom. My phone vibrates in my pocket, and I pull it out and swipe the screen to answer. "Mom?"

"Hi, baby." Her cheery voice clears some of the heaviness from my chest. "How's it going?"

"Good. Busy."

"And this new team? Are they friendly? How is my grand-fur-baby settling in?" She inquires, and I cringe.

She doesn't know. She has no idea Mila and I have reconnected, nor that I now live at HQ with the whole team. She knows I'm here, but not the circumstances surrounding it.

"They're good, Mom. Tobias loves it. He has freedom to come and go as he pleases. How's things with you?" I watch Tobias do a sweep of the building. You can take the military away from the dog, but the dog will always do what he does best.

"I'm good, sweetie. Got a lovely Swedish massage from my friend's daughter. She's sweet, about your age, and very pretty. Her mother and I go to the country club together. Gabrielle is her name. She's studying criminal law. Isn't that funny?" I groan at the obvious reason for her call.

"Mom, my life is busy as it is. I don't have time for anyone. It wouldn't be fair to her."

"I understood your father's commitments; the right girl would understand yours," she scolds.

"I know. I'm just..." My words taper off as Mila steps outside, searching the yard until she finds me. "I'm not available."

"What does that mean? Have you met someone?" She's excited, but I can barely focus on her as Mila makes her way toward me. "Garrett?"

"Hey, team's waiting for you," Mila states, stopping a few feet away from me.

"Is that—" Mom starts to ask, snapping me out of my silence.

"I have to go, Mom," I rush out, and Mila's face blanches.

"Garrett, who was that? Is that—" Her words are cut off as Mila snatches the phone and ends the call.

"What the fuck?" I growl.

"Does she know you're here? With me?" The words are muttered softly but well-controlled, like she's being careful with what she says.

"No. I didn't tell her anyone's name beside those of Alpha Team. She doesn't know the details."

Her whole body deflates, and she slowly holds out my phone for me to take. "Please don't ever tell her, Rett. She can't know."

I take the phone and shove it into my pocket. "Is that who you're running from? My father?"

She groans in frustration, "Why can't you just drop it?"

"Because I love you," I say simply. The words might be simple, but the emotional kaleidoscope they represent is anything but.

Her face softens, but she doesn't say it back, and that stings more than I'm willing to admit. She simply stares at me, and I hope she sees I'm being sincere because I never, not once, stopped loving her. I thought about her every second we were apart, which is why I can't let her go now.

There's no way. This is a fight I will not lose.

She gives me a slow nod and a smile, bringing up a million of my childhood memories, before turning and heading back inside. Hope blooms in my heart because that felt like a small victory. We didn't fight, and for a tiny moment, she let me in.

I whistle for Tobias, and he races in my direction. After I give him a quick pat, he follows me inside.

I meet Charlie, Austin, Lucas, Blair, and Mila on my way to the gym. We walk in only to find Roxy and Ayda trying to soothe a frustrated Layla.

"I suck," she mumbles, clearly disappointed in herself.

"So, did I," Ayda says soothingly. "But a person who falls and gets back up is much stronger than the person who never fell."

"It doesn't matter how many times you fail," Roxy chimes in.

"What matters is that you try again, every time." Charlie says as she enters the room, and I follow her lead.

"We don't quit," I add pointedly because the anguish on Layla's face echoes my own. Tobias whimpers at my thigh in agreement, and Mila snorts, throwing a look over her shoulder I can't figure out.

"What are you guys doing here?" Ryder asks, his curious gaze bouncing between Mila and me.

"Roxy and Ayda want to train the girls, so we're here to help." Charlie holds out her arms wide.

"You guys don't need to do that," Roxy mumbles.

"We're family, girl. That means where you go, we go," Mila smiles, and my stupid heart yearns for her and wishes those words were meant for me.

"Plus," Austin notes as he raises his hand, "I want skills. It's not fair you have them all."

"I'll tell you what," Ryder speaks to Layla, who is being held in his arms. "How about I learn with you? I don't know how to use a stick either."

She snickers, "It's not a stick. It's a bo staff."

"Okay, a bo staff then. How about we learn together as a team? Would you like that?"

"Okay."

"I wanna!" Austin raises his other hand, wiggling his fingers.

Charlie chuckles, "We know."

"Same," Lucas nods, tossing in with them.

I step forward and shrug at the same time Logan says, "May as well."

"I'm on her team." Mila thrusts a thumb at Rox. "You think I don't already know how to use that thing? Me and the stick do not agree."

Austin snorts, and I work hard to control my reaction. I swear to God, if he makes one more dirty comment about Mila and a cock, I'll punch him so hard, it'll knock out his soul.

Her eyes narrow to slits as she turns to glare at him, but he only bursts out laughing. But when she advances on him, the smile drops off his face. "Fuck off, asshole. You and your 'stick' *do* agree, yet you got blue balls for days."

He snaps his mouth shut, and I have to smother my smile.

"Will you both shut up?" Ryder says urgently, pointing to the two kids in the room. "They don't need to hear this shit!"

"He started it," Mila retorts.

"Shut up," Roxy snaps. "Everyone that wants to learn, get a bo staff and line up on the mats. Shoes off."

I call Tobias to the edge of the mats and command him to stay. He obeys, and I remove my shoes and socks. Tossing my phone and keys inside my shoes, I make my way to a vacant spot. Roxy hands me a stick and makes her way back to the front of the group.

Layla, who normally sticks to Ryder like glue, chews her nails nervously. She looks around at the men and women surrounding her with worried eyes. Eventually, her eyes land on me, and I smile, trying to let her know it's okay. She's safe and has nothing to worry about.

She surprises me by leaving Ryder at the front of the room and coming to stand beside me.

"Hello," she smiles and I return her grin.

"Hey. You okay?" I squat slightly, my glutes burning from my earlier workout.

"Yes. I just suck. It's embarrassing."

I chuckle, "You know, we all suck at something, right?"

"Yeah?" Two tiny lines form between her brows. "What do you suck at?"

"Spanish," I chuckle and throw a quick glance to where Mila stands watching us. "I was really bad. My mom got me a tutor, and I had to practice a lot. I'm much better at it now."

"That's cool. Was it a lady? Or a boy?"

"A lady tutor." Although she grew up to be, respectfully, rather unladylike.

"Pretty lady?"

I nod, "Very pretty. Like you, Monkey."

"Ryder calls me Monkey. You can't call me that," she intones imperiously.

"How about I call you something different, so I can have a special name for you too?" Her face lights up, and she nods her head vigorously. "How about 'Bella'?"

She frowns, "That seems boring."

"You know how I told you Spanish was hard for me?"

She nods, "Yeah."

"Bella means 'beautiful' in Spanish, so your name can be a reminder that you are beautiful *and* to never give up."

She thinks about it for a moment before a slow smile spreads across her face. "I like that."

I chuckle and rise to my feet. "Okay Bella, let's see what you got."

I face the front of the room, and only then do I realize how quiet the entire room is. Everyone stopped what they were doing to listen to the exchange between Bella and me.

I look at each one in turn, and their eyes reflect awe, gratitude, and respect. When I look at Mila, her head is lowered, and her hair falls like a curtain as she shields herself from the eyes of the rest of the room.

Disappointment crashes into me. I don't know or understand why we're so disconnected. What happened to change things so drastically?

"I'm Bella. What's your cool name?" Layla cocks a hip and pops off sassily.

11

MILA

EVEN THOUGH EACH DAY, I put one foot in front of the other, I feel like I'm not moving forward.

The other night, Ayda broke down and finally told us the nightmare she lived in. She told us of the things her father made her do, and the things he didn't. She's a virgin, or was. But just because they didn't penetrate her, doesn't mean she wasn't violated.

A father should protect their children. My life wasn't all that pretty, but at least I had the love of my parents. What her father made her do shattered my whole perception of the world. It could have been worse for me, but it wasn't. I was lucky.

She is so unbelievably strong, and I am incredibly blessed to have her as a friend.

But hearing her story made me question mine. I thought I was strong too, but I'm not. Deep down, I'm scared. I am scared to love Garrett, scared to spend too much time with my son. As a result, I take the easy way, the cautious way.

I settle against the window frame and watch Layla and Rhian run around the front yard, laughing and giggling. I imagine the smile on Slade's face and what it would be like for him to live here. Maybe I'm doing the wrong thing. Perhaps he would be safer here with us.

My chest squeezes from the pressure I'm under. They never tell you this, never explain the overwhelming demand to always make the right choice. How do I know that what I'm doing and all that I've done has been the right thing?

Giving up on pretending he's not there, my eyes find Garrett seated in the tree line beside the building. Although we allow the girls to run around freely outside, whenever they are alone, he seems to be there. He's protecting them, staying hidden and out of sight as he watches for any danger. Tobias lounges next to him in the sun.

It makes me wonder if he watched me like this when we were growing up. He seemed to always be there at the right times, always knowing where I was. It doesn't surprise me; he's always been a silent observer. I just didn't realize the lengths to which he went.

Like he can sense me watching him, his gaze lifts, and I can almost distinguish the green more prominently today. We stare at each other for a long time before I feel tears threatening at the back of my eyes, and I turn away.

I need to check in with Roxy and Ayds. Our prisoner, Dean Luzzo, refuses to speak and give us any information. Turns out, he's the police officer that helped Katarina escape. He also happens to be Ryder's absentee father.

The real icing on the cake, the part that sends liquid rage raging through my veins, is that he's also the person that Lex sold Ayda's virginity to. The piece of shit traded his assistance with the police for pussy that should've never been given to him in the first place.

The elevator doors open on the gym's floor, and I step out into the hall. Turning toward the gym, I ram into a solid wall of muscle. I inhale, and his deep masculine scent hurls my mind back to a simpler time when all I had to worry about was grades, my sister's stupid rumors, and him.

Garrett. *Mike.*

"Ana," he whispers, but I'm frozen, unable to force my body to take a step back and move away to where I'm not tempted to climb him like a tree and hump his face.

His hands slide around my waist, and I almost moan at the

contact. He leans down, burying his nose into my neck, and my eyes flutter closed. My body moves of its own volition as my hands slide around his waist to hold his body against mine.

That one simple move encloses me in his warmth. His crisp, ocean scent surrounds me and reminds me of winter days on the beach in Cali, just the two of us. For the first time in years, my body relaxes as if it's finally home. He sighs against me, feeling this moment as much as I do, his warm breath tickling the hairs on my neck.

His hand glides up my back and presses against the back of my head, his fingers threading through my hair, and he secures me in his embrace. We don't kiss or say a damn word. He just holds me, and it means more to me than anything else he has to offer.

It's been years since I've been held like this. I didn't even realize I needed it until this moment. It feels so normal, and I feel cherished and loved.

Eventually, he pulls back, tucks a stray hair behind my ear, and trails a finger across my cheek. "Everything I've said to you since we reunited, and I forgot to say the most important thing."

"What's that?"

"That you're beautiful. You were beautiful back then, but you're even more stunning now." He chuckles and shakes his head. "For some reason, I feel a lot of pride. I don't know why, but I'm proud of you, Ana."

His words are a timely reminder of everything that stands between us. All the secrets and lies. Everything I'm trying to protect.

His face falls as his hand tightens around my waist. "What just happened? You just shut down on me again. What did I say?"

"Nothing." I swallow hard, the need to ask him to hold me nearly too powerful to resist. Instead, I push out of his arms and force myself to stand apart.

"How can we move forward when you won't even tell me what I've said or done wrong?"

I'm doing it all over again. First with Kage, now with Garrett. I should've stepped away sooner. Instead, I selfishly held on because I needed the comfort of the contact.

"There is no moving forward, Rett," I whisper and hope he sees how sorry I am. "What we had is over. There's too much between us, too much in the way."

His eyes darken, showing more hazel than green. I've seen this look before on the night Levi was drunk and tried to maul me on the dance floor. "You won't tell me what the fuck it is! How can I help if I don't know what the fuck's going on? I thought by calling off the PI that you would understand I don't want to hurt you, that you'd finally let me in on whatever this is. You hate when other people make decisions for you, so why do you make mine for me?"

"This is not about you or me!" I snarl.

"Then what the fuck is it?" he roars, and my eyes widen. Garrett doesn't yell, especially not at me.

Snapping out of my shock, I slide past him and head to the gym. I'm not going to have a yelling match with him. I made the decision, and he just needs to deal with it.

"Don't fuckin' walk away from me! Tell me what the fuck happened!" he yells after me, not giving up.

I storm into the gym. "Fuck off, Garrett!" I put every ounce of venom I can into my words, hoping it drives my message home.

"You owe me a fucking explanation," he growls back, and I see red.

I spin on my heel and ram my finger into his chest. "I owe you nothing. Nada. Zilch. You lost that fucking opportunity nine years ago."

His angry eyes pin me in place, and my heart pounds at the sheer determination I see in his gaze. "The fuck I did!"

Garrett's body jolts back as Logan and Ryder grab him and force him back a few steps. The whole time, his eyes never leave mine, not when Roxy steps between us demanding to know what's going on, and not when Logan holds him back when he goes to lunge at me again.

"No!" I snap at Roxy's demand. I don't want them to know. They can't fucking know.

My phone pings in my pocket, distracting me, but I ignore it. Roxy stiffens as she watches her sister across the room, but Garrett's eyes are still on me.

"Get the fucking twins!" Ayda cries out, and my stomach drops at the same time Garrett's face drains of color.

He was watching them, and I distracted him.

Fuck!

12

GARRETT

My inability to stay focused created a situation in which someone died needlessly. Mia Mortemous died by her father's sword in order to save her daughters. Lex came for the girls, and I should have been on watch. I was, but then I saw her. I left my post like a poor excuse of a soldier, and a mother paid the price with her life.

We almost lost the twins. Bella and Rhian could have died if it wasn't for the alarm system on our phones. Some of us are taking it as a win because the girls are alive and safe, but I don't.

The team is respectfully cleaning up the mess and getting rid of Mia's body. The twins are with Lucas. Ayda and Roxy are with Logan and Ryder mourning their sister and the fact they couldn't save her.

Trying to breathe past the guilt, I lean back against the trunk of the tree. I should be inside, but I'm sitting right where I should've been when Lex swarmed our gates.

Rox and Ayds blame themselves in the same way I blame myself. We all had a role to play, but I was the one watching them. I shouldn't have allowed myself to be distracted, to abandon my mission.

It's not like any good came out of it. I shake my head, disappointed with my loss of control. I shouldn't have yelled at Mila like that. Months of frustration and rejection built up on top of years of absence, and I lost control.

I thread my hand through Tobias's fur and think of the other friend I let down. Monty shouldn't have died on that battlefield. It was my job to watch his back, and I failed. I failed again today.

The snapping of a branch has my head jerking up, and Tobias turns in the direction of the sudden sound. His nose lifts, sniffing the air. My body is alert as my fingers wrap around the butt of the gun strapped to my thigh.

"You going to shoot me, Rett?" Mila's voice reaches me moments before she steps into the moonlight that breaks through the branches of the tree.

My body relaxes against the tree, and I watch as she nervously watches Tobias. "He won't hurt you. He looks scary, but I promise he'd protect you with his life." I try to reassure her.

"I never thought of you as a dog person," she muses and takes a seat on the grass beside me.

"I'm not. He's a military dog, not mine. A friend's."

"Where's your friend?"

I swallow. Talking about Monty was really hard when he first passed away. I dealt with the grief silently on my own, much like everything else. But this is Ana, and we used to tell each other everything. No lies. "He died."

She gasps and tentatively places her hand on my knee. "I'm sorry."

I nod, and let my head hang heavily against my chest. After a long moment of silence, I decide to speak. "I took Tobias home to his family. My team and I stayed for the service. Gloria, Monty's wife, asked me to take him. She had two daughters, and they planned to move back to her parents. He has been with me since then."

"How did he die?" she asks softly, caring and with reverence.

"He was shot." I swallow because this always hurts. The pain of it is always present, much like the pain of losing the woman beside me. "Tobias stayed with him, protecting him on the battlefield."

She smiles, and it reminds me so much of the girl that stole my heart. "Tobias sounds like a good friend."

I nod and purse my lips before admitting, "I'm not."

She frowns, "What do you mean?"

"I was supposed to be watching his back, but a small convoy we weren't expecting snuck up on us. The other guys were under fire, and I turned my back on my friend to help them. He was shot because he wasn't looking, thinking I had him covered."

"That wasn't your fault," she says soothingly, but it's a lie.

"Wasn't it? I knew my job and knew what I needed to do. Every mission, each member knows their role. He trusted me, and I failed. Just like I failed today."

"I knew you'd blame yourself," she sighs and scoots around so she's sitting in front of me. "You put so much pressure on yourself, but you're only human. You wouldn't be angry at anyone else for making the same mistakes."

"It wasn't anyone else," I snap and instantly regret it when her eyes turn icy.

She squeezes her eyes closed, and I watch her throat bob as she swallows. "No, it's you. The guy that has a protective default setting. The guy that learned to speak Spanish for his friend's secret name. The one that fought social protocol to protect a girl no one cared about."

"Not no one," I mutter.

"No. Someone did," she smirks. Her eyes flick to the building behind me before coming back to mine. "Roxy and Ayda will be in there soon, deciding our next move." When I frown in confusion, she takes a deep breath. "Lex now knows they're here. More than that, he knows the twins are. He won't sit pretty and accept that."

"I understand that."

"Roxy *will* decide to act first. It is not a matter of if, but when. Ghost Team won't let her go alone."

"I know." One thing I have learned is that Mila is loyal, and where her girls go, she goes. A vague uneasiness blooms in my gut. "I've got a bad feeling about this."

"Mike," she whispers, and my heart stalls. "Please don't fight me on this. You wouldn't leave your men to do this alone. I can't leave mine on their own either."

"This is really dangerous," I warn.

"Yes. I won't lie, but it needs to be done. Mia deserves vengeance, and those four girls inside deserve their freedom."

"Is that what they did for you? Gave you your freedom?"

She smiles and leans forward, pressing a quick kiss to my cheek, sending the blood rushing to my cock. "Thank you for understanding."

She ignores my question as she stands, brushing the dirt and leaves off of her butt before leaving to make her way inside. I watch her hips sway from side to side, the uneasy feeling inside me building and battling with the love I feel for her.

When she's halfway back to the building, I call out to her, "Are you a betting woman these days?"

She turns and puts her hands on her hips. "What?"

"In the Rangers, the guys and I would always make a deal before a mission."

"Okay, soldier. What's the proposition?"

"We make it out without serious injury, you give me a chance to get to know this Mila. To be *her* friend."

Her smile drops slightly. "And what do I get out of this?"

"What do you want?" I hold my hands out to my sides before dropping them.

The smile that spreads playfully across her face has my heart pounding erratically. "I want your cock." I cough, choking on my own saliva. "I want it whenever I feel like it, wherever I want it. I want to come, and then I want you to leave. No attachments, no labels."

I nod, too afraid to speak. The painfully hard log between my legs *really* wants her to win.

13

GARRETT

I FUCKING KNEW I should've trusted my gut. I had a feeling something bad would happen, and now the love of my life lies in a hospital bed surrounded by machines and wires.

It's been forty-eight hours since I broke every law known to man to get her to Greg so he could save her life. She was lucky, and now we just have to wait for her beautiful brown eyes to open.

Greg and his brother Noah, the other guy that operated on Mila, have been coming in intermittently to check on her. The girls have come in to talk to her and tell her that they love her. Tobias is staying with Scott for the time being. He brings Tobias when he comes to visit. He sits with me for a while, then leaves taking a sad looking Tobias with him. The time he is here, we don't exchange words, just wait in silence.

I won't leave. I refuse. My heart won't allow me to leave her alone. It needs the reassurance the machines give to keep beating. Austin sits with me too, joking and trying to bring me out of my funk, but there is only one person that has the power to do that.

"Ana, baby, please open your eyes. I need to see you. Te amo," I beg and press my lips to the back of her hand before laying my cheek against it.

There isn't any response, just the soothing sound of the *beep, beep, beep* of machines.

I wake with a start when someone places their arm on my shoulder. For a split second, I am wild with hope, then my heart skips when she lays silent, still asleep.

"Didn't mean to scare you, pretty boy," Greg chuckles. "I just need to get past to check her."

I kiss her hand before moving my chair back out of the way.

"When will she wake?" I asked the same thing a hundred times already, and he always gives me the same damn response.

"When she's ready." Greg replies simply.

Stretching out my stiff muscles, I yawn before readjusting my position on the chair. My eyes fall on a piece of folded paper that must've fallen out of my pocket while I was sleeping.

Scooping it up, I unfold it carefully. It's worn and fragile from years of looking at it. I don't even know why I kept it. She didn't write it, but she did sign it. In my mind, it was always the last thing I had that she'd touched.

It's sacred.

My eyes read the words I've read a million times.

"She didn't write that," Greg whispers, and when I look up, I find him watching me.

"I know." I clear my throat and refold the paper before tucking it away in my pocket. "You knew her back then?"

He nods. "Yes. I was her dance teacher."

My eyebrows shoot into my hairline in surprise. "I didn't know that."

"Why do you keep it?" He nods in the direction of my pocket.

"Seems stupid. I know she didn't write those words, but it was the only evidence I had that she existed. When I got home from boot camp, everything that was hers was gone. There wasn't anything, not even that stupid hoodie she liked to wear all the time."

"That thing was ugly," he cringes and laughs softly.

"It was." I watch the way his eyes shine with a different kind of love as he watches her. One born from years of friendship and loyalty...the kind I have for my brothers. "Were you there?"

His shoulders drop, and I know the answer. He was there, knows what her secrets are. I also know what he's going to say about that. "I can't tell you. I want to. I believe with my whole heart that she deserves happiness." His eyes come to mine. "I believe you can make her happy, but I can't betray her trust. I can't betray—I just can't."

I bob my head. "I get it. She's like a coded vault, and she insists on changing the code every time I think I have it figured out."

He sighs, "I can give you some advice, pretty boy with the green eyes. *Accept* her."

I rear back, slightly offended. "I do."

"No, you don't. She is wild and beautifully complicated. Instead of trying to tame her and making her conform; support her. Let her be who she is now, and don't try to chain her to the girl she was. They are two separate people for a good reason, but deep in her core, she is the Mila we love and adore. She just had to thicken her skin a little to survive."

I stare at the woman in question. I can do that; I can love her exactly how she is. Deep down, she is still the woman I love. She just looks a little different now, speaks a little more...*loudly*. But I just need to know. "Is she in danger?"

His silence becomes a living thing in the room, and when I turn to make sure he's still here, his eyes are almost volcanic with anger. "She's been in danger since she left your house as a sixteen year-old girl. But twenty-four year-old Mila knows how to handle it. She'll ask for help when the time is right, and when it is, don't question her or her motives."

"I can help now," I insist.

He shakes his head, sadness enveloping his features. "She isn't ready for that, and she will fight you on it if you keep pushing. The more she has to fight you, the more she'll push you away."

"The further away she'll be when she needs help. She won't ask," I conclude.

He walks over to me and squeezes my shoulder before pressing a kiss to my cheek that shocks the shit out of me. I don't comment, but as soon as he clears the room, I scrub that shit off.

I appreciate everything he has done, but no.

I pull out my phone and check it. There are messages from Mom checking in and seeing how Tobias and I are doing. I reply, letting her know I'm fine and that I'll call when I can. There's another message from my dad, urgently asking me to contact him. I delete it. I read an email from my real estate lawyer letting me know the closing on my house went through with no issues.

I look up when someone knocks at the door. Ayda smiles softly before stepping into the room. Her long blonde hair hangs in waves down her back. Dressed in jean cut-offs and a tank top, she leans over the side of the bed and kisses Mila's cheek.

"Hey, badass, you really like sleeping, huh?" She takes a seat and looks at me. "How're you holding up?"

I scoff, "Fine. Wish she would wake up, though."

"After Roxy was injured rescuing Ry, she was unconscious for a week. Scared me half to death," she chuckles. "So you and Mila, huh? Kinda didn't see that one coming."

"It's always been me and her." She looks at me with a confused expression, and I realize Mila must not have mentioned our history. "We went to school together. Her mom was our live-in help. She and her sister came as a package-deal."

"Eva's a fucking dog," Ayda snarls, surprising me. Wide-eyed I stare, at the viciousness of it. Then her face lightens, and she turns to me. "You're the guy from the willow tree?"

"Wh-huh?" I sputter.

"The jock dude that fucked her sister or some shit. You're that guy?"

"She told you I fucked her sister?" I wheeze.

"Didn't you?"

"No. She thinks that?"

Ayda nods. "Said she heard you two or something."

"Fuck. I never fucked Eva. I got her off because she wouldn't shut the fuck up. But she never touched me, and I never fucked her. I never fucked anyone but Mila, and I haven't fucked anyone since."

"What?" a new voice whispers.

My head snaps to the side to find Mila blinking her eyes open and staring at me with apprehension.

"Ana!" I almost kick the chair over in my haste to get to her as Ayda rushes from the room to get Greg.

"You didn't?" Mila croaks and winces.

For a second her question doesn't make sense, but then I realize what she means. "No. I lost my virginity the same night you did, baby. Don't tell the guys, but that's the only time I've had sex, and it was with you. Only you."

"Well, fuck."

Before I can respond, Greg comes into the room, closely followed by Ayda.

"Well, hello there, Marshmallow. You look like poop. Let's see how you're doing," he chirps. "How are you feeling? Any pain?"

Mila ignores him, keeping her eyes pinned on me. "I accused you back then of sleeping with her. Why didn't you tell me then?"

I throw my hands up. "You said you heard us. I thought you meant you knew I...you know. I didn't think you meant *that*."

"Oh. My. Fuck." She averts her gaze, and my stomach drops.

"Are you in pain, Marshmallow?" Greg intervenes.

"A little," she murmurs, lost in thought.

"I can give you something to make you more comfortable."

Her eyes pop wide. "Where's Scott? I need to see him."

"Uh, he's doing that thing you asked him to do. With that person," he winces before clearing his throat. "Gotta check your boo-boo out."

"What thing?" I step forward, watching Greg and Mila carefully. I see the way she tenses slightly and the way his hand jumps as he pulls the blankets down.

"He's checking on Mama," Mila says, and I can tell she isn't lying. So either she believes her subterfuge, or she's finally being honest with me.

14

MILA

INCESSANT PAIN PULLS me from my sleep, but as my sluggish thoughts come into focus, the annoying sound of tapping has my teeth grinding. Squinting my eyes open, I'm greeted by snake-eye slits and bright blue hair.

"Blair?" I rasp, my mouth dry like I swallowed a bag of cotton balls.

She smiles, tucking the tablet away in her bag. Grabbing the bottle of water beside me, she holds it up for me to drink. I suck the cool liquid greedily through the straw, and it's a balm for my sore throat.

"How do you feel?" she asks when I've finished.

"Like I got shot," I wince as I try to shift on the bed.

"Want me to get Greg?"

"No, I'm okay. It's not too bad at the moment." I glance around the room, ensuring we're alone. Garrett's barely left my side, and it's made it difficult to ask about Slade.

"He went to his apartment to shower," Blair reassures me, knowing me too well.

"Have you heard from Mama? Is Slade okay?"

She nods. "They're both fine. Though be aware, they think you have a nasty cold, not a gunshot wound."

"Thank you," I say, relieved.

"Scott's been checking in with them daily, but they won't buy the sick story if you don't call soon."

"I'll call them a bit later," I agree.

"Can I ask a question?"

"Go for it."

"Is Slade Garrett's son?" My eyes widen, and she smirks. "Thought so."

"How'd you guess?"

"I don't guess. I gather information. Slade's almost eight-and-a-half. You said he isn't your husband's, and Garrett told Ayda you grew up together. Timelines match, so it makes sense." She shrugs. "It wasn't hard."

"Who else knows?"

"No one. Though, why doesn't Garrett?"

I sigh, "You remember how I said I was married off to Levi when I was almost seventeen?" She nods. "Garrett's father organized it *because* I was pregnant."

"So Garrett's parents know? They wouldn't have told him?"

"When he first got here, I had my suspicions, but he doesn't seem to have a relationship with his father, and his mother spent most of those years drinking. As far as I can tell, they haven't told him."

"Why haven't you? I mean, you said yourself that he doesn't talk to his dad," she points out.

"Because how can I be sure? What's going to happen? We become this big happy family, and he'll want to take his son home to meet his mom. Maybe even his dad? Levi will find us if he does, and then what?"

"Have you seen Garrett's records? He was a Ranger, Mila. Secrets were his job. I think if you explained the circumstances, he'd understand he can't share his son with his family. He won't want to hurt Slade."

I give a humorless laugh, "I know."

"Then what? What reason do you have for keeping this from him?"

"I'm scared," I admit. Because that's what this is. Deep down, I'm fucking terrified. "I hated walking away from him years ago, knowing he wouldn't know his son. Now, I have every opportunity to tell him, and I'm terrified he'll take him from me. My life isn't safe, and we go to extreme measures to protect Slade and Mama. What if Garrett thinks he can do it better? That I'm unfit? I'd lose the one thing I live for, and I can't do that."

She stares at me for a beat, and I know whatever she's about to say will have some hard truths. "You're being selfish. You're taking away Slade's opportunity to know his father and vise-versa. You're doing to Garrett what you're so scared he's going to do to you."

"I know that, I do. But I spent years without my son. Fuckin' years, Blair. I can't do that again."

"We'd never let that happen, and you know it. Besides, I don't think Garrett's going anywhere. It took a lot of convincing to get him to leave this damn room."

"I lied to him. I've had every opportunity to tell him the truth."

She frowns and asks, "He's the one that hired the private investigator, isn't he?" I nod, and she finishes her thought. "He seems pretty committed to figuring this out."

"Appears so."

She combs dainty fingers through her hair before expelling an annoyed breath. "You've made a mess."

I roll my eyes. "Tell me something I don't know."

"I found a paper trail going back eight years. He's been looking for you for a long fucking time."

"What?"

She nods confidently. "Yep. He searched for you. He was so fuckin' close too. This is a mess, Mila, and one you need to clean up. This could all blow-up in your face, and if it does, you risk your son's life. Garrett won't stop because he never did. Most people would give up after a couple of years, but not him. He's determined."

"What if telling him causes it to blow-up anyway?"

"You create and defuse bombs for a living. You have a family that would do anything for you. You preach girl-power like it's a religious belief. Do you think any one of us will let Slade get hurt?"

"No," I answer honestly. I know they wouldn't. I may have joined them in the beginning because I believed they'd be able to help me. But now I know, with everything inside me, that they've got my back.

"Then you have nothing to worry about."

I scoff, but when she stares at me pointedly, I add, "I'll think about it."

"Think about what?" Garrett asks, stepping into the room with wet hair and fresh clothes. His gaze bounces between Blair and me, and I worry that he may have heard our conversation.

"What she wants for dinner, seeing as Greg said she can go back to her apartment," Blair inserts the save, giving me a look that says I'd better think about it. Hard.

I incline my head subtly at her in understanding as Garrett takes a seat beside my bed.

"You don't need to worry about feeding her. Tobias and I will be staying with her until she's recovered," Garrett states with conviction.

My head whips in his direction. "Excuse me?"

"I'll sleep on the couch or the floor, but I'm not leaving you in your apartment alone. You just got shot."

"Blair can stay with me," I state.

"No can do," she sing-songs. "I've seen enough naked Mila to last me a lifetime."

"Naked Mila?" Garret questions, and I have to bite my lip to stop my smile.

"Yeah, she has an aversion to clothes. You'd be lucky if you get sexy lingerie. We mostly got to see her buck-ass naked."

His eyebrows furrow. "Like, in your room?"

Blair barks out a laugh, "No. If you don't believe me, feel free to ask Logan."

He sits forward abruptly in his seat. "What the fuck does that mean?" When she grabs her bag and heads for the door without a response, he turns to me. "What does she mean?"

I shrug, fighting my laughter.

"Mila Diez—" he growls a warning.

"Santos."

"Whatever. Did my brother, my fucking commander, see you naked?"

"No," I chuckle, and he just starts to relax when I add, "I was wearing lingerie."

"Motherfuck—what the actual fuck?"

"What? You think you're the only man that's seen the goods?" I roll my eyes and instantly feel like the biggest asshole when his face drops, and he averts his eyes.

Just like that, I'm reminded that he waited for me. Sexy-as-fuck Garrett Michaels waited for the poor girl. Maybe Blair was right. Perhaps I *am* being selfish.

Shit.

"I'm sorry. I didn't—" I start, but he cuts me off.

"Were there others?"

"Rett, maybe we shouldn't go there."

"We should. It's not like I know anything else about your life in the last eight years. And it was probably stupid of me to think you were waiting for me."

My eyes drop to my lap, and I begin playing with the dressing Greg put on my hand when he removed the IV. I'm not ready to tell him the whole truth, but maybe I can give him a small piece. Hopefully, a tiny bit of the truth will satisfy his curiosity for a while.

"A week before you were due back from boot camp, I got into some trouble." I almost smile when his body tenses, like he's afraid to move in case I change my mind. His eyes plead with me to continue, so I do. "I was forced to make a choice. At the time, I thought I made the smart choice, the choice you would've made. But I was wrong. Sort of."

Over the years, I've thought about if I could've done things differently. Could I have called friends? Ran away? Hidden somewhere until Garrett came home? But at the time, I was petrified beyond comprehension. My mind was a mess, and I really thought I only had the options Anthony, Garrett's father, laid out for me.

"Then what happened?" he whispers, and I give him a small smile to reassure him that I'm not shutting down on him.

"I made the choice, and I had to live with it. There wasn't any way for me to contact anyone. I didn't get to speak to Mama for years."

"What was it? Like a commune with no technology?"

I chuckle. That's a pretty good, if relatively benign, comparison to what my life was like. "Pretty much. I met someone there." I pause to swallow the lump in my throat. Talking about Kage hurts more than I want it to. "He taught me how to shoot, how to make explosives. He was a good friend, and he helped me a lot."

"He was your lover?"

"Not really." I shake my head adamantly. "What we had was a really great friendship with some physical benefits on the side." Garrett's face twists in pain, and I really hate myself for doing this to him. "I'm so sorry if that hurts you. Truly, I am. I hurt him too, and I hate that."

"Did he save you?" I give him a confused look, and he clarifies, "Sounds like you were trapped in that place. But you're not anymore, obviously, so does that mean he saved you?"

"No. I did it with the help of Ghost Team after they found me. Although, he helped me gain the skills I needed to get myself out. He empowered me."

"When I couldn't." His body slumps in dejection.

I reach out and run my fingers through his hair, trying my best to give him some comfort. "I was angry at you for a while," I whisper, and he lifts his head, his eyes shining with unshed tears, the same tears I know are in mine. "I wanted you to find me. I thought you would, but it was stupid."

"I couldn't find you. I tried. Every day for years, I tried to find where you were."

I nod once, allowing the tears to slide down my face. "I know. But it wasn't your job. I spent my whole life up to that point being some sort of distressed damsel. I needed to learn to rely on myself. To fight for me. I lost you, and it tore my heart out. But I found myself along the way. I learned to give voice to my opinion, to question things, to say what I mean. I learned to be my own damn hero instead of running to others to save me."

"But now, you shut people out too. You shut *me* out."

I bite my lip, accepting this truth. "Yeah, I do, but having you back here in my world scares me."

"Why?"

"Giving you my heart again gives you the power to hurt me. You could destroy everything I've built, everything that I've worked so hard to protect. With you, I lose the power I need to do those things."

"I never want to make you feel powerless, Ana." He takes my hand and presses his lips to my palm, sending fiery sparks over my skin. "I love you with every fiber of my being. Every part of you."

I squeeze my eyes closed as I'm assaulted by built-up emotions. I never stopped loving him. Opening up about my past, giving him that tiny piece, feels like I've reopened old wounds that never fully healed. I allow myself to finally feel the grief I'd smothered since I left his house that day.

I missed him so much, his smile, the one he only ever gave to me. I missed his silence and the words that he didn't need to speak because I could feel them. I really missed his comfort and the safety I felt whenever he was around.

Soft lips press against mine, and I tense for a fraction of a second before I give in to him. I kiss him for the years we missed and for the time we may never get again. I kiss him to express how sorry I am, how I wish it was all different.

I part my lips, allowing him to take what's always been his, and I don't regret it for a single second. His tongue licks into my mouth, tasting and seeking. I feel his sorrow, taste his tears. The connection that's always been between us flares to life, reignited by this kiss, and in this moment, everything feels as it should.

He slows the kiss and whispers over my lips, "Look at me, Ana."

I open my eyes and gasp. His eyes are bright, the green eclipsing the hazel, and shining with his unbreakable love for me. I know I shouldn't. I need to protect our son, the little boy that looks so much like his daddy. But Garrett has always been my greatest strength and my greatest weakness.

I drop my shields and let him in. I let him see the love I still have for him, the pain of losing him, and the agony of years apart. That's the truth. Kage may have had a piece of me, but it's nothing compared to the chunk Garrett owns.

A slow smile spreads across his features. My fucking smile. I own that. He reads my every thought right before slamming his mouth down on mine, groaning when I kiss him back with equal intensity. Glide for glide, lick for lick, we remind each other that our hearts and souls were each other's years ago.

We may not have known what it meant then, but we do now. We've fought, wounded and battered, to get to where we are. I just hope we survive when this is all over.

"I know you don't trust me," he whispers, his lips brushing against mine. "Just give me a chance. I can love you so completely, you won't question what we have ever again."

"There's still so much you don't know"

"When you're ready, when you trust me, tell me. I'd wait forever for you if that's what you need from me. Just don't ask me to live without you because that isn't possible. Please, Ana."

I hesitate. There's so much at stake, but I don't think I can keep doing this alone. I don't know if I want to anymore. Garrett's my weakness, but he's also the thing that kept me going. Him and his son.

Mi familia.

15

GARRETT

I PUSH the wheelchair out of the elevator and into the hall. This will be the first time I've been to Mila's apartment, and I'm nervous to see inside her life. Even though we've agreed to take it slow and give things a chance, she hasn't really been forthcoming with any more information on what happened. She gave all she was willing to give for the time being.

That's okay. I'm a patient man and have waited this long to get her back. I don't mind waiting more. I'm determined to prove to her that I deserve her. I'm going to show her every day how much she means to me, and I won't make the same mistakes I did last time.

She hands me the keys, and I unlock the door and prop it open. Tobias takes it as an invitation and walks in. His nails clicking on the tiles as he moves through the room. Wheeling the chair in, I'm surprised that the apartment lacks a personal touch. There are no photos or knick knacks. Don't get me wrong, it looks lived-in. There are scraps of lingerie hanging haphazardly over the couch, and a few dirty dishes are stacked in the sink. There's a pile of laundry on the table. There just isn't any liveliness and personality in her space.

"Where do you want to go?" I ask, stopping in the room that functions as both a dining area and living room.

"I want a shower. I feel gross," she replies, scrunching up her face in an adorable way. Yeah, I've got it bad alright.

"Okay. You need help?"

She raises her brow. "Is that your sneaky way to see me naked?"

I chuckle at her teasing. "No. Though, I'm not opposed to it. But perhaps we should wait until you're a little less injured."

"My vagina ain't broken," she scolds, and I shake my head.

"I have no doubt. But I don't want to hurt you. Besides, you said slow, and that means no sex."

"I did say that." She smiles at me playfully. "Friends first."

"Yep. So, you need help? You know? With the bandage and stuff?"

"No, I'll manage," she says, wincing as she stands. My body twitches with the need to help her, but if she says she can do it, I know better than to force my help on her.

"I'll start cooking dinner. Any preferences?"

"Anything is fine." She waves me off as she shuffles toward her bathroom. I move the wheelchair out of the way and begin straightening up the apartment.

I fold the laundry that's on the table and use the emptied basket to gather up the dirty clothes and place it beside the front door. Then I grab my bag off the back of the wheelchair and put it beside the couch for later. I grab the bag with Tobias' food, bowls and bed. Then I lay the bed out beside the front door where he likes it and fill his water bowl before placing it beside his bed.

Heading back to the kitchen, I rummage through the fridge and find that it's been stocked recently. Deciding to make chicken stir-fry and rice, I grab the ingredients I need and get the vegetables chopped up. I fire up the wok and grease it with some oil before throwing in the chicken. Leaving it to sizzle, I fill the sink with water to wash the dishes.

I'm just finishing up the rice when she slowly makes her way into the room. My hands grip the counter, holding me in place as my eyes take in what she's wearing. I thought Blair was joking when she said Mila doesn't like clothes. My forever-hard dick turns to steel. I'm so hard, I could smash holes into the marble countertop and not feel a damn thing. Her open silk robe floats behind her and leaves absolutely nothing to the imagination.

She gives me a pain-filled smile before groaning as she takes a seat at the table. I bite my lip, trying not to smile. She wants to be sexy, and she fucking is, but her pain is frustrating her.

"Smells amazing in here," she half-moans and half-groans, doing nothing to help the issue in my pants. I discreetly adjust myself, trying not to be obvious.

"It's just stir-fry. Nothing to call home about." I grin and grab the bottle of pain pills Greg gave her. Tapping two out into my hand and getting a glass of water, I hand them to her. "Take these. Dinner will be ready in a sec."

"Thank you."

I lean forward, brushing my lips against her cheek. "Pink suits you, baby. Matches that sweet pussy of yours. Don't tempt me, Mila. I'm a man, not a saint."

She stiffens for a split-second before her lips twitch playfully. "Maybe I want the man," she teases, and I smile against her skin.

Sliding my lips down her neck, I inhale her sweet smell. "Not yet. You're not ready for that."

"Says who?"

I pull back, giving her a peck on the corner of her mouth as I retreat. "When I'm inside you next, I'll have your trust. I don't want just half of you. I want it all." She opens her mouth to respond, but I press a finger against her soft lips. "I won't push. I promised. But I also promised to love you completely, and I can't do that unless you give me all of you."

Standing up taller, I walk to the kitchen and get our dinner onto plates. Sliding one plate in front of her, I take a seat and begin eating. We don't talk while we eat, and when we finish, I take the plates and wash them while she moves to the sofa and selects a movie to watch.

Once the kitchen is cleaned up, I grab a couple of drinks and a bag of Jolly Ranchers before joining her.

We settle in to watch "The Fast And The Furious." Half-way through the movie, she snuggles against me, and I can't help the smile that spreads across my face. Instead of watching the movie, I watch her.

I have an overwhelming need to pinch myself. I've thought about our reunion in a hundred different ways. Never once did it include having a gun pointed at me and eyes laced with suspicion. I've been treading water ever since, trying to stay afloat. I feel like this moment can't be real, but it is. She's real and so fucking beautiful, more beautiful than I could've ever imagined.

Her eyelids droop as she loses the fight against exhaustion. Greg said the painkillers would make her tired, and when she's asleep, I switch off the television. I slide out from under her and then scoop her into my arms.

She mumbles, wrapping her arms around me and resting her head in the crook of my neck. It feels terrific to have her in my arms, and I thank years of gym memberships and brutal training that I'm strong enough to carry her.

Placing her onto her bed, I remove her robe. Forcing my eyes to focus solely on her face, I tuck her in, softly brushing the hair from her face and pressing a kiss to her cheek.

I switch off the light as I leave and head out in search of a spare blanket. I open the door beside hers and poke in my head, smiling when I smell her shampoo. Bathroom.

I try the next door and freeze when the smell of C4 fills my nose. Flicking on the light switch, I inhale sharply. Everything you could possibly need to build a bomb is in this room. Racks of fuses, timers, batteries and detonators line the walls. Work benches are littered with unused parts and wires. Plans and diagrams—pages and pages of stuff written and drawn by my girl are on display.

If anyone outside of my team found this, they'd think a terrorist lived here. A psychotic terrorist. My psycho. I flick through the pages, years of mechanical and ordinance training enabling me to understand the designs and intricate maps.

It's original stuff, designs she created and built, no doubt.

I was worried when I first found out about her skill, but these are genius. She's worked out every single thing, down to the tiniest of details. It's like art, and a strange sense of pride washes over me.

This is the Mila I know, the overachiever. She hasn't just found something she liked and half-assed it. She isn't being reckless like I thought. She's studied this, calculated it and perfected her form.

Placing the pages back how I found them, I take one last look around the room before switching the light off and closing the door. I stand there for a moment, and for the first time, I see how this Mila is still the same. She's just grown-up and, perhaps, even better.

Greg was right. She's still the person I knew at her core. She's just a little more shielded than before. She's no longer just book smart, but street smart as well.

Turning in the hall, I try the last door and finally find the linen closet. Grabbing a blanket and a pillow, I head back to the living room and set up my bed for the night. I grab a quick shower and check on Mila one last time before settling into my makeshift bed.

I set an alarm to awaken me when she's due for her next round of medication before falling into a restless sleep.

My alarm goes off a few hours later, and I groan. Scrubbing the sleep from my eyes, I stumble into the kitchen on auto-pilot to grab the pills and a glass of water before heading to Mila's room.

I knock lightly before opening the door.

She smiles from her position on the bed. "Booty-call?"

I snicker, "Pain pills."

She groans, "Even better."

I help her sit up a bit and support her weight as she swallows the pills. When she's done, I take the glass, setting it down on the bedside table and help her settle back under the covers.

"Thank you," she says appreciatively.

"You're welcome."

I move to leave so she can go back to sleep when her voice stops me. "Will you stay with me? I can't sleep. We could talk if you're not tired."

I am. I'm exhausted, but I'm not passing up an opportunity to be near her. "Nope. Not tired."

"'kay." She pats the bed beside her.

Laying down on top of the covers, I rest my head on the pillow and face her. The only light in the room is from the lamp beside her bed, and it bathes her in a warm, golden glow. Her hair is still wet from her shower hours ago, and it'll probably still be wet tomorrow. She used to complain when we were kids that it took forever to dry. It's longer now, but still the same color.

She hasn't dyed it like most women might. She's left it natural, and I love it. Her face is bare. There isn't an inch of make-up, yet she is stunning. She never needed make-up or baubles. Mila has a special kind of beauty that draws people to her. That hasn't changed.

"Tell me about the Army?" she asks, readjusting her head on the pillow.

"What do you want to know?"

"Well, start from the beginning. What was boot camp like?"

"Brutal," I laugh. "I was expecting it to be hard, but when I got there, it was a really bad reality check. Then I signed up for more."

She looks confused, "What do you mean?"

"When I came home, and you were gone, I was angry at the world and everyone in it. My drill sergeant spoke to me before I left boot camp and suggested I volunteer for the Army Rangers. I went looking for something that filled the void that you left. I took his advice, and that meant more boot camp, but even more strenuous than the last."

"Wow. Was it hard?"

"The boot camp or Rangers?"

"Being a Ranger," she murmurs.

I nod, my cheek brushing against the pillow. "It's not for everyone. But for someone like me, it was good."

"What do you mean?"

I blow out a breath and watch as her hair tickles her cheek. "I didn't go home. I stayed on base and rarely left, even between deployments. I didn't have a partner or kids, so I didn't mind the risk. It kept my mind busy when missing you became too much. Or when I would hit another dead end when a lead on your whereabouts didn't pan out."

"You really never gave up, huh?"

"I did. There was a time when I thought holding on was unrealistic. But some part of me just wouldn't let go."

"I hate that."

"Because you were able to move on?" I ask even though my heart pounds with nervousness.

"No. I hate it because it held you back. I never wanted that for you. You deserve to be happy."

"Were you happy?"

"I wasn't, not for a long time. But then I was. I still am."

"Because of that guy?"

She frowns, "No. I told you, he and I were friends. Yes, we slept together, and he enabled me to be stronger. But I was never his."

"You weren't mine either," I point out. She bites her lip and averts her eyes. I guess she agreed with me there. "What changed that made you happy?"

"The girls." She smiles, remembering events I'm not privy to yet. "We're all so different from how we were back then. We're stronger together, and I love them."

I nod, getting it. I understand the bond that's created when you fight beside someone. They know your secrets you've never shared with anyone else. They live them with you.

"Tell me about Greg?" I ask, hoping this isn't pushing too far.

"I met him in high school."

"You never mentioned him," I muse.

"That wasn't intentional. There was a lot happening at the time. At first, you and I weren't anything, and then we were. He was a med student at the time. So when summer break was over, he went back to college."

"Did you know he's bi-sexual?"

She screws up her face. "Non-selective? Yeah. Why?"

I chuckle, "Roxy and Ayda didn't." Her eyes widen and I nod. "Yep. They figured it out just after he finished operating on you. He came to tell us how you were doing, and his brother let it slip. Their faces were priceless, and Logan and Ry were kinda jerks about it at first."

She covers her mouth in shock. "Oh my God."

"Austin had a fit, saying it's unfair. He's been hounding Greg ever since, demanding he choose just one sex because he can't just have both."

She laughs and grunts, gripping her midsection. "Don't make me laugh."

I tuck a stray hair away from her eyes. "Sorry."

"It's fine. Just hurts."

Concerned, I pay close attention to her for any sign she's in more pain than she is letting on. "Are the pain pills not working?"

She waves her hand dismissively. "They're fine. Just laughing is painful."

"Roger that. So tell me...how did the bi-sexual dance teacher end up here?"

"That's easy. I asked him to help, and he did because he can't resist my charm."

I snort, "Help with what?"

"Nosey, huh?"

I shrug, "You're finally talking, and I have a ton of questions. If we didn't need to sleep, I reckon I'd keep us talking for at least a month."

"Thank God for sleep," she says cheekily. I chuckle, and she continues, "Scott's sister was abused by some men linked to Lex. She was sexually abused and in rough shape when Roxy found her. I arrived a day after her, and they were doing the best they could to help her, but she needed medical attention. Going to a hospital was out of the question because the men they stole her from were still out there. I called Greg, and he agreed to help. He never left."

"What happened to the men?"

"Dead. That was my first job when I arrived. They'd captured one of the men, but the leader was still at large. The guy they had pretended to only speak Spanish."

"Which is pointless if your captors also speak it."

She gives a firm nod. "I seduced the information out of him. Roxy killed the leader that night, and Greg made Scott's sister healthy again."

"Where's his sister now?"

She hesitates before responding, "You need to ask Scott that."

"I thought there were no secrets?"

"No secrets that pose a threat," she corrects on a yawn, "but she isn't a threat."

"Right. So Greg's just part of the team now?"

"Yeah. He can't shoot to save his life, but he has other skills that are just as important. He believed then, and still does, that he does more good here than in some public health system." She yawns again, blinking the tired tears from her eyes.

"Sleep. We can talk later," I murmur quietly.

"'kay." Her eyes droop as she mumbles her agreement.

I kiss her forehead softly, unable to resist, and rise from the bed.

"Stay. Sleep," she mumbles again, and I turn to make sure I heard her correctly. She taps her own pillow as if too exhausted to pat the other one. "Sleep."

"You sure? I can sleep on the couch." She growls in response, and I bark out a laugh. "Okay."

Lifting the blankets, I slide under the covers beside her, keeping my hands and body parts to myself. I lay quietly for a while, convinced there's no way I'm going to be able to sleep. I'm awake now, my body ready for battle if necessary. So when my eyelids grow heavy and my breathing slows to match hers, I smile before falling into the deepest sleep I've had in years.

16

MILA

I WAKE to the sound of soft snoring beside me and smile. Trying not to wake him, I slowly try to roll to my side and hiss when pain flares through my stomach, intense enough that I almost barf.

Fuck.

Garrett bolts upright so fast that I jump and groan when the sudden movement tweaks the pain to new levels. He turns, assessing me, clearly seeing I'm in pain before his eyes flick to my bedside table.

"Shit. We missed your next dosage by an hour." He tosses back the covers and gets up.

I could barely see anything in the light from my lamp last night, but this morning, as bright sunshine breaks through the curtains, I almost drool. His body is a work of art. Deep ridges define four sets of abs. His military tags hang against pectoral muscles that twitch and flex as he moves. I bet he could make them dance. His broad shoulders and thick muscles are enough to make any pussy quiver. But the part that has me most entranced is the deep V at his waist, barely concealed by his sleep pants. They sit so low, I can see a tiny patch of trimmed hair peeking out.

He snorts, and I feel the heat rise in my cheeks. "You jack off with those arms?" I blurt reflexively.

He watches me in shock for a bit before he bends over, bracing his arms on the bed in a way that makes them flex. My breath hitches, trapped inside my lungs, as he crawls forward. "To you? Yeah. I imagined all the ways we could fuck. How I'd worship your body like a goddess, and if I was really lucky, you'd worship me back."

I swallow hard. "Like a god?"

"Like a joker." He smacks a kiss on my cheek and winks before standing.

"Fuck you," I snap, a little pissed he turned my teasing around on me.

"Uh huh. Just like that," he laughs as he walks out the door. I can't help the smile that curls my lips. Playful Garrett can hang out with me any time.

I try to make myself more comfortable, but the pain is practically immobilizing me right now. He returns with my pills and helps me sit up. Swallowing them, I relax against the headboard.

"Will you be okay if I jump in the shower real quick?" he asks after I'm settled.

"I'm not on my death-bed," I state sarcastically.

"You were," he says simply. I swallow at the fear that flashes in his eyes. Greg told me Garrett had brought me in, holding my wound to staunch the bleeding. Realization dawns that he probably saved my life, and I never even thanked him.

"You okay?" He steps toward me, concerned. "You look a little green."

"I'm sorry," I blurt out.

"For what?"

"For being selfish."

"Hey." He kneels beside the bed and takes my hand, pressing a kiss to my palm. Shivers climb up my body as it reacts to his touch. "Where's this coming from?"

"You probably saved my life, and I didn't even thank you."

He shakes his head. "You're alive, and that's all that matters. I'm not going to lie, Mila. I was dying inside when I thought I wouldn't get you to Greg in time, but it's over now. You're okay."

He cups my cheek, and I lean into his touch as if our skin is magnetized. "Thank you."

He rewards me with a smile, and my stomach flutters at the sight. "Anytime. But don't make a habit of it."

"Okay."

"Okay." He kisses my cheek as he stands. "I'll have a shower, then make us something for breakfast."

I smile at him and watch his retreat out of the room. As soon as he's outside, I mentally scold myself. I can't keep giving into him. I know I promised I would try, and I am, but is there even a future for us?

When he finds out all my secrets, he'll hate me. I know it. I've kept his son from him when I've had every opportunity to tell him. Fear keeps my mouth closed. I don't want to lose my son, and if I'm truly honest with myself, I don't want to lose Garrett either.

I lived through that once. I don't think I could do it again. I don't think I'd survive.

If I tell him, would he take the same precautions I do to keep Slade a secret? Once my son's out of the shadows, his life will be at risk. Levi won't give up looking for me. I embarrassed and shamed him, jeopardizing his position in the MC.

The Chaplains thrive on power, and what would people think of the man that couldn't even control his own woman? I escaped from right under his nose and blew up his house. No. There's no doubt in my mind that he's still looking for both Slade and me.

Anthony is still Garrett's dad, whether Garrett's in contact with him or not. Can I, in good conscience, ask Garrett to choose us over his family? Would he even consider choosing us?

I groan in frustration.

I know the answer. I have to have faith, to jump in and hope. But I did that once, and it didn't turn out so well for me.

The shower switches off, and a couple of minutes later, I hear his footsteps pad toward the bedroom.

He pokes in his head. "Need help to the living room?"

I shake my head. "No, I wanna do it. I'll holler if I need to."

"Okay."

Leaving, he heads towards the kitchen, and I hear stuff being moved around as he begins making breakfast as promised.

He's been so patient with me, taken care of me, and stayed with me while I've been healing the last few days.

Every time I push him away, he comes back and fights a little bit harder. He's done nothing to make me believe he'd take my baby or put Slade in any kind of danger.

Blair is right. They *all* are.

What I'm doing isn't fair to him or to Slade.

I slowly swivel my legs over the edge of the bed until my feet hit the carpet. I grab my robe from the back of the door and wrap it around myself. Bracing myself on the door frame and then on the wall, I make my way out to the living room.

By the time I sit in a chair at the table, a thin coat of sweat shines on my skin.

"You don't look so hot." Garrett stares at me with concern, noticing my discomfort.

I brush him off, saying, "I'm fine. I'm just healing."

"I'm calling Greg." Before I can protest, he has his phone out, calling. "Hey, it's me." He snorts at whatever Greg says. "Can you come check on Mila? She doesn't look good." I roll my eyes and earn myself a smirk. "Thanks," he says into the receiver before hanging up.

I raise a brow in question, and he gives me a one-shouldered shrug. "I'm not taking any risks. He fucking lives here, so it's not like he's got to go far." He turns away, like the conversation is over, and begins stirring whatever's in the pan.

"I'm not a damn—" I start, irate.

"Damsel," he finishes. "I know, but you're stubborn as hell, and you honestly look like crap, so I want to make sure there isn't an infection or anything."

"Gee, way to make a girl feel like shit," I sneer.

"You're beautiful, even when you look like crap and are a little snarky."

"I'm snarky because I've survived without you for a while now. I don't need you coming in here and taking over."

He turns off the burner and gives me his full attention. "I'm not taking over. I'm trying to help."

"I know, " I huff. "Just tone it down a little."

"No."

"Excuse me?"

"I won't. Not where you're concerned. Not ever."

I let out a frustrated groan just as there's a knock at the door.

Garrett grins and winks. "Looks like he thought it was urgent."

He walks across the room to answer the door as I mutter under my breath, "I wonder why?"

He chuckles, "Heard that."

"Good," I grumble.

He swings open the door, and Greg waltzes in, carrying his medical bag and making a beeline for me. Seems like everyone had been invited—Roxy, Logan, Ayda, Ryder, and Tobias follow him in.

I glare at Rett before turning to Greg. "I'm fine. The whole team didn't need to come."

"We were down there talking to Greg anyway, so don't blame him," Ayda chides me.

"About the bi-sexual thing?" Just like that, five tiny words render the entire room silent. "What? Too soon?" I flutter my eyes in mock-innocence.

"Never is too soon," Ryder growls.

"Wait! You knew?" Ayda blanches.

"Yes." I shrug. "It's not a big deal."

"The fuck it isn't." Logan snaps. "He did fuckin' pap smears."

I giggle at his stupidity. "There are male gynecologists, you know?"

"Nope." Ryder shakes his head. "Just no."

"Yes," I nod my head solemnly.

"Fuck no. Not my girl."

"Green doesn't suit you, hot stuff," Greg murmurs playfully.

"Purple doesn't fuckin' suit you, so when I bruise up your pretty face, you won't look too good."

I hitch a brow, instantly defensive. "Not if I blow off your face first, Azai."

"Alright, everyone needs calm the fuck down," Roxy intervenes.

Jabbing a finger into Logan's chest, she pins him with angry eyes. "I decide who looks at my vagina, not you. If I want Greg to examine me, it's because I trust him. Don't think just because we're engaged that you get the last say, because you don't."

"Baby—"

"She's right. You two need to get over this shit. Out of everyone, I'm the person that should have the biggest problem with it. While I can't say I wasn't shocked, it doesn't mean I don't trust him," Ayda scolds both Ryder and Logan.

"Thank you, Cupcake." Greg winks at her before shoving a thermometer under my tongue.

"Are you two done now?" Roxy folds her arms, bouncing a glare between Ryder and her fiancé.

The guys look at each other, then back at their women, knowing they aren't going to back down. Logan grunts, and Ryder reels a giggling Ayda into his arms, kissing the shit out of her until she's a puddle of goo at his feet.

"I need to check your wounds," Greg says, and I nod, grabbing the cord that secures my robe.

"Nope! No," Garrett snaps, glaring at me. "I know what you fuckin' have on under that, and you all," he points at the two couples in the room, "need to get the fuck out."

Logan nods without argument, understanding exactly what Rett means. Ryder looks confused as Ayda drags him to the door as Roxy and Logan follow. The minute the door closes, Garrett retreats into the hall, and I can't help but smile.

Some things never change.

"I see you smiling, Marshmallow," Greg says, smiling himself as he snaps on his surgical gloves. "Looks good on you."

"I smile."

"Yes, but not like that."

"Whatever," I hiss when he lifts the bandage.

Tobias lets out a deep growl-grunt as he stands and moves towards me. He sniffs at my arms before watching Greg with yellow eyes. Greg eyes flick from the dog to me, before he raises a question brow. I shrug, and he turns back to look at Tobias who hasn't broken eye contact once. The dog simply licks his lips and parks his ass down.

“Looks like you have an extra protection detail. Does he know I am trying to help?” Greg asks.

I shrug, “I guess. They can smell this shit right?”

Greg’s lips thin in response, before slowly lifting the bandage a little higher. He inspects my wound, touching the area around it. "Looks fine. No sign of infection, and you have no temperature."

"Garrett was being overly cautious. I told him not to worry."

He scoffs, "That boy has it bad. He’s going to worry, and you need to let him."

"I can take care of myself."

He peels the old dressing off completely and disposes of it before opening a new one. Each time he moves, he watches Tobias with nerves, but the dog doesn’t move. He just watches Greg, making sure there is no foul play. Greg covers my wound, ensuring it's taped up before removing his gloves and sitting back on his heels. "I know you can. *He* knows you can. But you don't need to do it all on your own. Relationships are partnerships. You’re supposed to take care of each other."

"We’re just friends."

"Friends that love each other, like you two do, don't stay ‘just’ friends. Baby girl, let your heart go. It's been locked in chains for long enough. Let him in."

"I want to," I admit, swallowing nervously as my eyes flick to the hallway. "But I'm scared."

Greg nods in understanding. "I get it. Just don't let fear stop you from missing out on one of the greatest things in the world."

Standing, he slowly leans forward and presses a kiss to my cheek. "Call me if you need me."

I smile fondly at him. "Thank you."

"Anything for you."

Gathering his things, he closes his bag and heads to the front door and opens it, letting the others come in before giving me a wave and closing it behind him. The door barely closes behind him, before Tobias’ claws scrape against the tile as he returns to his bed.

Weird creepy dog.

Garrett walks out of the hallway and stops at the awkward silence in the room.

"Someone shit the bed or something?" I ask after a moment, trying to break the tension. When no one responds, I press further, "You guys fuck up and fuck the wrong sister?"

"Jesus, no!" Logan balks in horror.

"We wanted to talk to you," Roxy states, and if her pointed look is any indication, she means alone.

I groan, "Garrett, get out and take the boys with you. Girl talk. No dick allowed."

"I would've said it nicer than that," Ayda mumbles.

"Should've just said it then instead of trying to tell me telepathically."

Garrett chuckles, and looks at Logan and Ryder. "Gym?"

They give a quick nod before giving their women a kiss and making their way to the door.

"Behave," Rett basically talks straight into my ear, and I almost jump clear out of my chair. Laughing, he pecks my cheek and follows the guys out.

Roxy and Ayda collapse into the vacant chairs, exhausted. They watched their sister die in front of them, then they killed their father in a bid to protect their nieces. Lex wanted to use Rhian and Layla in the same way he tried to use Roxy and Ayda, and none of us could let that happen.

They've spent most of their time at my bedside or with their nieces, who are mourning their mother. I know they're also trying to deal with their own grief and plan a funeral for their sister.

The battle wasn't over when their father was finished.

"How's everything going? Are you two okay?" I ask, placing my hand over Ayda's on the table.

"We will be." She gives me a half-smile and tries her best to hide her hurt. I see it anyway, being well-acquainted with hurt myself.

It's been a hard few days, and I don't have any words that can help. I hope they know I'm here, injured or not, and they have my support and love.

"We found Rhian and Layla's dad," Roxy utters suddenly, and my eyes widen in surprise. "We went to his house."

"Not to talk I'm guessing?"

Roxy shakes her head, but Ayda answers, "We tried, for the sake of the girls, but he wouldn't concede and sign over custody of them. According to him, they're his property."

"You killed him?" I ask, but from the looks on their faces, I already know the answer.

"Yes," Roxy replies, her eyes hard with pent-up rage. "We saw their rooms, Mila. There were chains. New ones. Like he was waiting for them to return." She shakes her head, trying to dispel the images from her mind. "We couldn't leave him alive. They'd never be free."

"You did the right thing," I soothe, and I believe that. Those men are like Levi, taking ownership over women. Even using their own daughters to gain power and status.

"We also found legal documents in his safe, ones he must have taken from Mia. They appointed us as her children's guardians in the event of her death. Legally, those girls belong to Roxy and me now," Ayda states, and that alone begins to calm the anger brewing in my body.

"Today, they start their new lives as Ghosts. They're finally free," Roxy summarizes.

"When did this all happen?" I say, frowning at not knowing what's been going on lately.

"Last night," Roxy says, pursing her lips.

"We went alone," Ayda clarifies, sensing my disappointment that I wasn't there. "Logan and Ryder stayed with the girls."

I rear back, shocked that the guys would even be okay with that. "They just let you go?"

"They didn't know," Roxy snorts. "We're engaged, and he isn't my daddy."

"You don't call him 'Daddy' in the bedroom?" My lips twitch as I try to keep the smile off my face.

"Do you call Garrett 'Daddy'?" She pins me with a knowing look, and it wipes the smile clean off my face. "That's what I thought. Why didn't you tell us?"

"There was nothing to tell," I say dismissively.

"So the fact that he was the love of your life when you were younger is nothing then? His dad is the one that sold you, right?" Roxy questions, and I nod. "That's a pretty important piece of information, Mila."

"He doesn't know."

They both frown, and I almost giggle when even that is identical.

"What do you mean? He doesn't know?" Ayda pushes.

Sighing, knowing it would've been asked eventually, I explain, "Garrett doesn't know I was sold. He thinks I ran."

"Ran where?"

"To a commune," I wince, and both of them bark out in laughter.

"What?" Roxy chastises, still laughing hard. "He thinks you, Mila Santos, were in a commune?"

"What kind of commune? One for sex-addicts?" Ayda giggles, and I roll my eyes.

They're under the same assumption as everyone else. Every night when I leave to see Slade, they assume I'm hooking up with a man for a booty-call. I let them believe that, same as Garrett, because they can't know the real reason why I leave.

Maybe I should tell them the truth. I mean, the rumors don't bother me. They can believe whatever they want, but I owe them the truth. They've always had my back. They'd support me, and I know they'd protect my son with their lives. But if I'm going to tell anyone, I need to tell Garrett first. It's his son, and it would be a dick move to tell everyone else and not him.

Plus, I don't want to risk him finding out from anyone but me. It's already not fair that Scott and Blair know, and he has no clue. I know I need to tell him, and I will. He'll hate me, but I have to deal with that because I made the decisions that led us here. They were mine, and the consequences are mine as a result.

I just have to find the right time.

Changing the subject, I ask, "How's the funeral coming along?"

Their laughter instantly dies out, and I mentally slap myself. For a couple of minutes, they were probably forgetting the heavy shit.

Maybe it was at my expense, but if anyone deserves to laugh, it's them.

"It'll happen in a couple of days. It has to be low-key and simple. Nothing fancy. But it'll allow us all to grieve the way we are supposed to," Roxy supplies on a wince.

"Well, as close as we can to normal, anyway," Ayda inserts, and I offer a comforting smile.

Having been raised to consider death more like a trip to the park than a huge deal, they're trying to do it the right way for the girls. They're grieving. They cried, but on that same night, they went to war with their father and killed him. That's how they grieved. I'm sure they miss their sister in their own way, but it's not the same as most other people would.

For security's sake, they can't have a traditional funeral. Officials would want to autopsy the body, and that would bring unwanted attention to us. So, they have to do it in secret with no official documents or traditional rites for a burial.

"Where are you going to bury her?"

Ayda nods to the kitchen window that overlooks the back meadow. "Out there. It's beautiful and peaceful. After the life Mia had, she deserves that. The hard stuff is over, and her girls are safe. She can rest peacefully knowing she didn't die in vain."

I nod, swallowing my emotions. Speaking of all this brings up memories of my own sister. Eva isn't perfect. In fact, she's the worst kind of sister, much like we thought Mia was. "Do you think that hating Mia for so long was wrong? Like maybe you made the wrong call?" I ask, my thoughts on my own sibling.

"No." Roxy's reply is instant. "I understand the reasons why she did what she did, but they don't make what she did right. There's always a choice. I made the choice to get Ayda out. I decided to fight against my father. She chose an easier path, perhaps because she was young and couldn't see past the fear of losing her babies. I don't know."

"In the end," Ayda interjects, "she made the right decision. She fought the right battle, and we'll always be thankful for that. But it doesn't just wipe away all the bad things she did. Do we ultimately forgive her? Yes. She deserves that much. But can we forget everything she did before that? No. She knew what she was doing was wrong and did it anyway."

I nod, knowing the same could be said for Eva. I used to find excuses for her behavior, but at what point do those excuses become me enabling her? She never showed remorse, nor did she ever apologize for all the shit she pulled.

I'm in this mess because she wanted revenge. I live with the results of the choices I made, but none of this would've happened if she hadn't been trying to destroy my happiness.

Even when that wasn't good enough, she kept pushing until the love I had for her was completely snuffed out and turned sour. I hoped she was in the house the night I escaped, that she died in that explosion. I don't know for sure. One day, I suppose I will, but I'm not sorry.

You reap what you sow, little sister.

17

GARRETT

IT'S BEEN weeks since Mila was shot. Weeks I've spent lying beside her at night and not touching her. I haven't kissed her since that day in the hospital, and it's getting harder and harder to resist her lure.

She's almost fully healed. She moves around freely and rarely needs her pain medication. She doesn't need me here anymore, but I'm not leaving until she tells me to.

It's almost like old times, before our relationship as best friends transformed to something more. Except this time, I'm not holding back. I spent my teenage years keeping her at arm's length, thinking I was protecting her from my parents and from the nasty bitches at school. I took it so far as to date her sister so that I could keep Mila under the radar.

I stupidly thought she'd always be there, that there would be a *later* for us. But I wasted time and hurt the only girl I ever loved because I was a coward. I was scared my parents wouldn't allow me near her and would do something to tear us apart. I didn't want them to take away my best friend.

I lost her anyway.

Whatever happened created a chasm between us. At times, it feels like we'll never repair it and meet in the middle. Then there are the quiet moments, ones where she speaks without words, and I can hear them so clearly, they render me speechless. I know she still loves me, but that rift is still there, and it stops her from being honest with me. There are times I think she's about to tell me, but then she switches and says something completely outrageous. More often than not, it's about sex.

That's another thing I've figured out. Mila deflects with sex. If a conversation gets too serious or too close to exposing her truth, she blurts out something about vaginas or cocks and completely derails the conversation.

Sometimes I think that's why she walks around in lingerie; it causes a distraction from anything emotional or honest. I'm not saying I'm oblivious to her outfit choice...I've spent the last few weeks in a permanent state of arousal. But I do wish she would just let me in.

I'm not sure what else I can do to prove myself worthy.

I took Tobias and left the apartment to head for the gym as Mila was getting in the shower. He sleeps beside me as I count the reps I bench press and listen to Ayda and Roxy spar. The sound of steel clanging and their grunts of effort becomes soothing after a while. Mila plans on coming down here after Greg gives her clearance to train again. I know she's itching to get back into it. Being stuck in the apartment and only allowed to do light work frustrates the shit out of her.

Even though I knew the day would eventually come when she could rejoin the team in combat, it's still something I dread. I push out a couple of extra reps as the anxious energy tries to grip me. I've spoken to Logan about my worries. Austin too. They both said what I already knew to be true.

I wouldn't stop any other team member from coming back after injury, so why would I stop her? The simple answer is that I'm scared of losing her. The more complex answer is that I'm afraid we won't get the chance to reconnect if the next bullet kills her.

We are starting to reconnect, and I've learned so much about her in these short weeks. Mainly, I can't tell her what to do. She will do what she decides to do, whether I want her to or not. My best chance is to be there when she does. If I argue, if I push her away by being stubborn, she won't allow me to be there.

So, this morning when she spoke about coming back, I encouraged her. I smiled when I wanted to hurl and beg her not to. I helped find her boots after weeks of living in her slippers. I gave my support, so that the next time she gets shot, I'm right there with her where I can try and save her life. Again.

I rack the bar and sit up. I'm toweling the sweat from my face when I feel the bench beneath me shift slightly. Lowering the towel, I smile as Bella screws her face up in disgust.

"You're all sweaty," she states.

I bop her nose with my finger before throwing the towel to the floor beside me. "Sweating is good. Gets out all the shit from your body."

"Don't say 'shit'," she scolds. "Rhian started to say 'shit', and Ryder got cranky at her. Like a bear." She completes her description by trying to growl like a bear.

I stare at her, keeping my face as neutral as I can. "You just said 'shit' twice."

Her eyes widen as she whips around, obviously searching for Ryder. "You made me," she whispers. "It's your fault."

"No, Miss Bella. No one makes you do anything." She rolls her eyes, and I chuckle.

"Can I try that?" she asks, nodding toward the bar of weights behind me.

"You bench?" I ask, and she thinks about it before nodding. "Oh yeah? How much?"

"Like five hundred." She blows her statement off with a shrug.

"More than me," I laugh and stand up. "Lay down. Let's see what you got."

She grins and shuffles up the bench until she is lying under the bar. Gripping the bar and holding most of the weight myself, I lower it so she can reach it. Tobias wakes from his slumber and sits up to watch.

"Okay, hold it on either side." She does as I instruct, and I nod. "Good. You ready? How many do you want to do?"

"Like ten. I'm ready."

"Okay, go."

I have to bite my lip when she makes a screwed-up face like she's lifting a truck, the hilariousness of it almost impossible to ignore, but I manage not to laugh. I count her lifts and hold the weight the entire time.

Once we reach ten, I rack the weight and hold up my hand for a high five. "Good job! I'm proud of you." Tobias barks his approval and jumps up with his tail wagging happily. I chuckle and scratch his ear.

Bella grins, "And I'm not even sweating. It wasn't even that hard!"

Grabbing my water bottle, I take a seat beside her and offer her some. She takes the bottle, guzzling it down. Handing it back to me, she gives me a smile that doesn't reach her eyes. While they're still a stunning shade of green, I see the deep well of grief just below the surface. Sensing her grief, Tobias whines and lays his meaty head on her lap to comfort her.

I notice the way she holds the necklace around her neck, clasping it so hard at times when she thinks no one's watching. I know grief. I've felt it. I've seen it when I told family members their kids weren't coming home and when partners died in battle.

Layla's trying to find her way, her new normal without her mom. Even though she's surrounded by people that love her, I can see the loneliness in her eyes.

"You want to go for a walk?" I ask, hoping I'm about to do the right thing.

"Okay," she mutters.

Gathering all my things, I shove them into my bag and hold my hand out for hers. Standing, she slides her palm into mine, and I lead us out of the gym. We take the elevator up one floor to the communal area, and she follows me out the back door.

The sun is warm today and beats down on my skin as we walk across the grass in silence, past the trees, and into the back meadow. I don't have children, and I'm an only child, so I hope by bringing her here, I'm not making it worse. She misses her mom. That much is clear.

I know her and Rhian haven't been back here since we buried

Mia a few weeks back. But if it was me, this is what I would want. She slows her steps the closer we get to the headstone sitting prominently in the field of flowers.

"It's okay," I say and smile when she looks up at me with worried eyes. I stop and crouch down in front of her with my back to the grave. "If you don't want to be here, we can go. I won't get mad. But you can stay and talk to her. I know she's listening. I can stay with you if you want if you're scared."

She looks behind me for a long moment before her eyes come back to mine. "What if I cry?"

"That's okay. It's okay to cry because you miss your mom. I would cry too," I assure her the best I can.

"Will you stay even if I cry?"

"Yes," I nod confidently so she doesn't have any doubts. "I will stay until you are ready to see her on your own."

She worries at her lip as she thinks, her gaze going between the headstone behind me and my face a few times.

When she finally makes her decision, she nods. "Okay."

Standing with her hand in mine, I walk the small distance to the grave. Her hand tightens on mine the closer we get, and when we finally stop, her fingers are white.

I take a seat, keeping my hand in hers. I watch as she stares at the inscription on the stone. Silently, I wait, knowing she needs to do this in her own time and in her own way.

The sun glints off the sword embedded in the ground on the other side of the meadow. It was left exactly where Mia's brother Jacob put it. Roxy told us to leave it, that no one can touch it. That it was a sign of respect for Mia.

Gradually, Bella's grip loosens, until she is just holding onto my hand. I sit while she stands, working through whatever's in her mind. I sit there, sun beating down on my back, until my ass is numb and my back trickles with sweat. Tobias lays next to me, I'm sure the heat is bothering him too, but he won't move from his post. He is a soldier too.

After what feels like an hour, she slowly lowers herself to the ground. My gaze flicks to my watch, and I watch another thirty minutes roll over. I occasionally shift to relieve one butt cheek, then the other. I can sit here for days if I need to.

A breeze rolls over my skin another fifteen minutes later, and she turns to me.

"What do I say?"

"Whatever you want to say, Bella. Tell her everything in your mind, in your heart. We can stay as long as you want." I offer her a comforting smile.

She leans into my body and whispers, "I miss her."

Wrapping my arms around her tiny body, I press a kiss to her hair. "I know baby. Tell her that, Bella. I bet she misses you too."

"I think I'm okay now," she says softly.

"You want me to go?"

She nods against my chest. "But not far. Will you stay where I can see you?"

Giving her a quick squeeze, I lift her chin with a finger. "See that tree over there?" I nod toward the oak tree in her line of sight. "I'll sit right there. Don't hurry. I've got nowhere to be. If you want to stay all day, I'll wait. Okay?"

She sniffles, swiping at her eye. "Okay. Thank you."

I nod, kiss her forehead, and make my way over to the tree. Sighing when I take a seat in the shade, I lean back against the trunk and watch in case she needs me.

I can see her mouth moving as she speaks, her hands run strokes through Tobias' fur. She gets more confident and shuffles closer, and I can't help but feel proud. I snort when Tobias slowly crawls forward as Bella does, chasing the little girls affection.

I remember the same feeling of pride the day Mila snapped at Eva for slapping her friend. I was so shocked at first, I didn't know how to react, but a warm burst of admiration for the steel in Mila's spine burst through me.

After years of abuse and the lies her sister told, she finally stood up to her. Now, she's a woman that doesn't accept anything less than respect. She demands it. I admire that too, yet I can't meld the two Milas together.

Why is that?

Is it because I missed the growth? Am I jealous because I missed a huge chuck of what made her into who she is today? Because she figured out she doesn't need me, and I'm afraid she doesn't want me?

As the questions build in my mind, I know the answer.

Yes.

Just like I know the answer, I also know it isn't fair. Do I really have any right? I want to, but I don't. She told me she was in a commune, and it just doesn't make sense. I thought my father sent her away, that he got rid of her. But he wouldn't have sent her there. If she really was in some commune, then she did leave like he said she did.

Scrubbing a hand over my face, I try to erase the thoughts from my mind. The past needs to stay in the past. We're making progress, and the longer I linger on memory lane, the longer I hold us back.

I need to focus on the future and forget the past. Perhaps she'll tell me one day, but for now, I'm happy building what we have now.

I groan when I shift my position, my muscles stiff from sitting so long. Tobias raise his head at the noise, his eyes watching me for any sign I might be hurt. Smiling, I readjust my position. Satisfied with his assessment, he goes back to guarding his friend.

"Hey." I look up to find Roxy heading toward me.

"Hey back."

"You've been out here for a while. Want me to take over?"

I shake my head, "No, it's cool. I'm used to it, and I promised I wouldn't go anywhere."

She nods and takes a seat beside me. She watches her niece for a moment before speaking, "Thank you for bringing her here. She probably needed this, and I didn't even realize."

I shrug, "It's cool."

"Seriously. We have no idea how to handle this," she says matter-of-factly.

"It's no biggie. It's not like I have any experience with kids. I just did what I thought I would need."

She tugs at blades of grass, a rare softness in her expression. "I have no experience with this or grief, so I win."

I chuckle, "Okay, but you still grieve, right?"

She nods, "Just not like a normal person. We weren't allowed."

I clench my teeth, angry on her behalf. When we first got here, I'll admit that I didn't trust Roxy or Ayda. But they've proven themselves time and time again. They're good people, their hearts in the right place, and they didn't deserve the upbringing they got.

They're trying to give Layla and Rhian the normal childhood they themselves never got. They're doing their best to break the cycle with them, and that's a testament to their strength.

"Do you think she'll be okay?" Rox asks, dispelling my train of thought.

I nod. "They're tough, but I think they're grieving the right way," I add with a smile. "It'll take time, and it's supposed to. They just need our support while they deal with everything they're feeling."

"And to feel connected to their mom."

"Yeah."

"How do we do that? We don't want to make this worse."

"Talk about her with them. Bring them here. Do you have photos of Mia?"

"No," she winces. "Photos were evidence. The only photos there were of any of us were locked in my father's safe. Any others were destroyed."

Of course. "Maybe the police have a photo?"

"A wanted poster? Somehow, I don't think that will encourage many happy memories," she chuckles.

"Right. Sorry."

"Ryder thinks we should have an arts and crafts day or something. Where we draw pictures of Mia and things that remind us of her."

"I'd be happy to do that. I mean, if I'm invited. It might help."

She turns to me, blue eyes glittering. "You're a good man, Garrett Michaels. I can see why Mila loves you."

18

MILA

FOUR. Fucking. Months. I'd been relegated to no training, light duties, and being monitored by Rett. Today is four months and one day since I was shot, which means no more stupid paper-pushing. No more walking instead of running. I can pick up my weapon again, and I plan to, once I've showered and eaten.

Garrett is still here, living in my apartment and sleeping beside me most nights. He's barely touched me, except for the occasional quick peck on the cheek or kiss to my forehead. Not that I've been in any state for much more, it's just strange. I see his desire, and some nights, I even feel it when he rolls over and pulls me close in his sleep.

But he never takes advantage. He never makes a move, and it's refreshing. It's how I know a man should behave. In the weeks after I gave birth, Levi tried, and I had to constantly remind him of what Greg said. He complained and whined, demanded blow jobs and even tried to take me up the ass. All he cared about was his desire and his needs.

I had to be constantly on alert, deflective, and it got really tiring. I caved in to most of his demands just to shut him up. But I don't feel that anxious fear with Garrett. He wants to help, and he does. But he also lets me heal at my own pace. If I want to do it myself, he lets me.

He stands back and watches in case I need him, but he doesn't try to argue with me. For that, I am grateful.

He's given me the time and space to heal at my own pace. He helps keep me distracted. He even talked me through a training regimen that would allow me to stick with Greg's terms and still allow me to feel like I am doing something.

I step out of the shower and dry off. Once I'm dressed, I head back to the bathroom. Blow-drying my hair, I style it in soft waves before applying my make-up. When I deem myself done, I pack my shit away and head to the living room.

The smell of coffee fills my nose, and I groan in appreciation. "There better be coffee for me," I state, leaning my hip against the counter.

He turns away from the stove and jerks to a stop. His eyes darken as they trail a path of fire over my body. I'm not wearing anything I haven't worn before—black skinny jeans, black tank top and boots, but he looks like this is the first time seeing me like this. A shiver rakes up my spine when his eyes finally make their way back to mine. Pure, raw desire emanates from them, and it's like a solid punch to my solar plexus.

He stares at me, his eyes drilling into me as if trying to make completely clear his intentions. I try to break the connection as my desire becomes too much to hide as his eyes probe mine, seeking and trying to draw out whatever truth they can. I'm struggling to draw in air as all my senses become heightened, and the pulse between my thighs becomes unbearable. I want him. All of him.

But I can't, not until he knows the truth.

That thought extinguishes my desire as the truth tries to knock me on my ass. I drop my eyes to the floor.

"Yes," he croaks, before clearing his throat. "Coffee's in the pot."

I take a moment to regain control of my wayward emotions before looking up. His back is to me, stirring whatever concoction he's making this morning. He's wearing a tight, black t-shirt that seems to mold to every dip and bulge of his torso. It's drool-worthy, and my fingers ache to run my hand down his back and feel every corded muscle beneath my fingertips.

Instead, I walk to the pot and force my mind to PG territory. His cell phone pings, and mine does as well a second later. Turning off the burner on the stove, he brushes his hands on his pants before picking up the cell.

After reading it, he relocks the phone and places it down on the counter before addressing me. "Scott called a meeting."

I nod in acknowledgement. "When?"

"Thirty minutes," he states, and I can't help but feel like his words are slightly detached. Mechanical.

Pushing off the counter as he carries a plate to the stove and begins loading it with eggs and toast, I settle against the counter directly behind him. He isn't surprised when he turns around and finds me blocking his path. He throws me a weak smile, but I'm not buying it.

"What's wrong?"

"That's a loaded question," he states, leaning past me to put the plate down and grab the other one. I work hard to not react with his body this close me, his crisp ocean scent surrounding me and trying to send me stupid. I can almost taste him on my tongue from the smell alone.

Clearing my throat, I stand a little straighter. "Talk to me."

"Like you talk to me?" His words are barbed, and I'm instantly defensive because it's true.

"Right. Good chat. Go fuck yourself then." I shove away from the counter and head toward the hall. Suddenly I'm just not hungry anymore.

His hand grips my bicep, and he spins me back to face him. He moves until my ass presses against the counter again, but this time, he invades my space for a whole different reason.

His finger lifts my chin until I'm forced to meet his gaze. "That wasn't fair of me. I'm sorry. I promised I wouldn't push. It's just that sometimes, it's hard to keep my promise. I'm only human, and I like to work with all the information. Not having it throws me a little."

I relax, my anger losing its momentum. "I know. I know it's not fair that I haven't spoken to you. You've been patient, and I love that. It's just hard."

He cups my cheek, and I lean into his warm palm. "I can be patient, Mila, but you have nothing to be afraid of. I love you. I've loved you for a very long time. After everything, it's still there and stronger than ever. Nothing you do, nothing you say, would ever change that."

I swallow, his words meaning everything to me. It's on the tip of my tongue to tell him I love him, that he's owned me this whole time, and I want him the way he wants me. But something holds me back.

It's not fair for me to say that, to let him believe there's a chance without knowing the whole truth. Everything.

He presses a kiss to my forehead. "Eat, baby."

He steps back, and I miss the heat from his body. I want to grab him and force him to come back to me, to kiss me and reassure me his words are solid and unbreakable. Even if I rip his heart out and try to give it back to him in pieces.

That's what my secret will do to him. I've watched him for weeks with Layla, his Bella. He takes her to her mother's grave and sits for hours while she talks to the headstone. He draws with the girls and watches while she and her sister play in the yard. He loves them. Just like I know he'd have loved and protected his son, and I took that away from him. I stole years of memories because of my own irrational fear. Now, it feels like I'm too deep into my deception that I can't get out of it, no matter what I say.

"You eating?" he asks, snapping me out of my thoughts.

Nodding, I make my way to the table. I take a seat, and we eat in silence. It isn't any different to other days, but this silence feels heavy with everything left unsaid.

Once we're finished, he takes our plates and washes the dishes. He's a clean-freak like his father, and my house has become so organized, it's almost scary.

"Military sure makes people organized, huh?" I joke, trying to lighten the tension.

"If you're about to say 'like father, like son,' I'm going to be pissed." He gives me a pointed look, and I grin innocently.

"Nope, but there are similarities, I suppose. I remember Mama bitching about your dad and his OCD tendencies."

He nods. "Except he ordered and demanded things be done a certain way. He was arrogant and rude about it," he explains, shrugging. "If I want things a certain way, I do it myself or keep my mouth shut."

I stand and tuck my seat in before making my way to the front door. "That's a good thing because I'm not a house bitch. And I won't bow to demands." Giggling, I turn my head to look at him. "I bow to no man."

I swing the front door open and squeak when warm hands wrap around my waist and pull me back into his hard chest. He groans as my ass presses against his semi-hard cock and whispers in my ear, "Oh, you will bow, baby. Not because I asked you to, but because you want to. You'll slide my cock deep into your throat, and I will fucking worship you for the goddess you are."

My body nearly betrays me as my knees almost buckle. I can't control the speed of my breathing as my chest rises and falls with heavy pants. I sway back into his chest as his lips press against my bare neck, sending delicious shivers through my touch-starved body.

Then, as quickly as he's there, he's gone. "We're going to be late," he says, and I can tell he's trying to bite back a laugh.

Smiling to myself, I turn to him, and in one step, I reach out to cup his cock and balls. I rub my palm over his solid length and bite my lip when he thrusts into my hand. "You wanna play, Michaels? You wanna lay down challenges and not follow through? Game on, baby."

I remove my hand and smile up at him before spinning and walking away. I press the button to call the elevator when he catches up to me, Tobias following behind him. Once it opens, we settle on separate sides of the compartment. We ride in silence, watching each other, and when the elevator doors ping open, I smile sweetly as I make my way out into the hall.

I yelp when his palm comes down with a *crack* on my ass cheek. He chuckles, "Game on, little mouse."

19

GARRETT

THE STING from my palm gives me a satisfying smile as I step into the boardroom. Logan and Roxy are standing near the front of the room, and I nod toward them before taking a seat beside Austin. Tobias trots around the room like he owns the place and happily says hi to everyone present. Mila follows us in, taking the seat opposite me. She winces slightly when she sits, and my lips twitch in response.

"Still sore, Santos?" Austin asks in a concerned tone.

"Nope." She lifts her chin before a smile splits her face. "Garrett spanked my ass before I walked in here. Cheek's a bit tender to the touch."

I blanch at her blunt delivery, but know I should know better by now.

Austin barks out a laugh, "I didn't think he looked like a spanker, to be honest. Maybe a love-tapper, but not that." He chuckles harder when I glare at him. "What's next, Ranger? Choking? Like to play a little ball-gag?"

"Nah, but she'd choke on his dick," Roxy answers drolly.

"Roxy!" Logan admonishes her like he's got no idea who the fuck she is right now, and I can't help but laugh.

"If you're all done, we have work to do," Scott reminds us scathingly.

"I'm done." I state, rocking back on my seat.

"You will be," Mila mutters, and my head whips in her direction. "What you got?"

"Fuckin' bad shit," Blair states.

She nods to Lucas, who taps away at his tablet. A couple of seconds later, four images fill the screen.

"These kids, three girls and one guy, went missing within twenty-four hours of each other. Melanie Ferguson, Rachael Thomas, Andria Silvers and Jensen Heaton," Blair lists.

"Each one went missing, then a few hours later, their families were murdered in their sleep. All overdoses," Lucas continues.

"We have video footage of Melanie leaving this gas station about an hour from here. She's accompanied by this man and woman," Blair explains, pulling up a copy of video from security cam footage.

I study the images. All the figures are wearing hoods, but you can tell two are female and one is a male.

"How do you know one was Melanie?" I ask, the angle of the camera making it difficult to make out facial features.

"Because the store clerk identified her. She went in, bought a few items, and left. You can see her as she exits the store, where she joins these two," Lucas answers.

I nod, and Logan asks my next question. "Did the footage catch any plate numbers?"

Blair shakes her head sadly. "They left on foot, and I can follow them until they reach this intersection. Then they disappear out of camera range."

"Of course." Mila rolls her eyes. "That would be too easy."

"And there would be no use for us," Scott finishes.

I watch the video closely, focusing in on the surroundings, trying to pinpoint a reflective surface or anything that may have been missed.

"They were careful and never showed their faces on camera. No other footage has surfaced since this," Blair continues as I watch.

I study the feed as they play it on repeat. I follow the steps they take, taking note if they look at anyone, drop anything, or do anything that might seem insignificant on the surface and missed.

Then I see it. "Stop the video. Rewind about five seconds." Lucas does as the room silences, everyone waiting to see what I see. "There. Zoom in."

"What do you see?" Roxy narrows her eyes in concentration.

"See that box? It's there for a reason. After the terrorist attacks, the government installed a series of cameras so they could monitor for any unsuspected attacks."

"How come I don't know about these?" Blair says sheepishly.

"Only a select few do for safety reasons and to minimize information leaks." I watch as she taps out on her tablet. "The minute you try to bypass their systems, an alarm will go off."

"I can get in undetected," she sighs, assuming I underestimate her skills.

I don't. "You could, but it'll take a couple of days to find the back door through the firewall, right? So you don't trigger anything?" She nods, so I continue, "I might have an easier way."

"What way?" Scott asks.

"I can go to the Ranger base. I still have contacts with the superiors there. I could explain the situation and see if I can get a copy of the footage."

"Will they allow that?"

"Maybe. I won't know until I ask, but we'd get the footage quicker this way. In the meantime, we can use Blair and Lucas as back-up in case I fail." I shrug.

Roxy nods, "Do that and take Mila with you. She has a way of being persuasive, and you might need it. The rest of us will go out and search the area for anything else that might help us."

Logan nods, sliding his arm around Roxy's waist. "Especially that alley. We need to figure out where they disappeared to."

"Who will stay with the girls?" Ayda asks.

"Blair and Lucas will stay behind and work on the cameras. Plus, Greg will be here," Scott answers.

"Let's go," Logan dismisses us.

Everyone stands, making their way out of the room. I wait for Mila while she quickly talks to Scott. Satisfied with whatever he says, she makes her way toward me.

"Are you ready to go straight there, or do you need to go to the apartment first?" I ask as we head to the elevator.

"I'm good. We can take the Mustang. It's been ages since I got to drive." She skips, grinning, and I can't help but smile.

She's so fucking beautiful.

I hit the button for the communal living space level and lean back against the elevator wall.

"So," she starts, and I can sense she's choosing her words carefully. "You still in contact with the military?"

"Yes. Mostly with the guys who were there with me in combat. Being on the ground, fighting side by side, you bond. They saw the same shit I did and got it in a way no one else can."

She nods, averting her eyes. "Why did you leave?"

Now that's a loaded question, and I'm not sure if I want to answer. "You want the truth?"

"Always."

"You. You're the reason. I was tired of waiting for you to come to me. Alpha Team had the resources I needed to find you. As it turns out, not even Lucas has that ability."

"Wouldn't the military have more resources than the police?" she asks, confused.

"Yes. But they frown on using them for personal reasons."

"So why would they help us now?" she questions.

"This is to assist a criminal investigation, not a favor for the guy that lost his girl and couldn't find her."

"Right."

I chew my lip, contemplating my next question, and I decide to go for it. "Where were you? I mean, I know where you were generally. But what town? How far away from home did you go?"

She studies me for a long moment, long enough for me to think I maybe asked too much too soon.

"I was in the next town over."

I shove away from the wall. "What?"

She gives me a wary nod. "Well, for the first four years anyway. Then I met Roxy and Scott. Oh, and Blair. The bitch tried to shoot me," she chuckles. "Then I came here. But yeah, I was close."

I rake my hands through my hair in frustration. Not with her, but with myself. "You were right there, under my fucking nose that whole time? How was I that stupid?"

"You didn't know." She steps forward to soothe me, but I back out of reach, not feeling terribly deserving of her comfort. "Rett, there was no way for you to know. My name was changed. Mila Diez didn't legally exist after I left your house. You couldn't have found me, and even if you had, you wouldn't have been let in. They would've killed you if you tried."

"Killed me?" My eyes pin her in place as the elevator doors slide open.

Gasping at her slip, she spins on her heel and makes a beeline across the living room. She shoves the front door open and practically sprints down the porch stairs, but I reach her just as she gets to the Mustang.

"Where the fuck were you? Did they keep you against your will? Is that what you're telling me?"

"I can't talk about this right now."

"Answer me! I was under the assumption you went there willingly, and if that isn't the case, I want to know."

"Garrett..."

"Answer me," I grind out.

"Yes!" she snaps, and it silences me. Adrenaline pumps through my system, and I feel like I could run for days without tiring. "Yes, okay? Is that what you want to hear?"

"They took you? Kept you against your will?"

"Yes."

I clenched my teeth, anger fueled by her words spiking inside me. I grip my hair and tug, trying to get a handle on the storm brewing inside me. I start to pace, needing to burn off the energy inside that threatens to suffocate me. I try to bring myself under control, but images of her being hurt and chained fill my mind. They make it so I can barely breathe.

"Stop it!" She grabs my arm and forces me to look at her. She reaches up, framing my face in her palms and holding my gaze so I can see her honesty. "I'm okay. I got out. Anything that happened then isn't hurting me now."

She opens herself up and lets me see through her walls so I can see what she's feeling. I find confidence and assurance there, and that begins to slow my heart.

I drop my head back and stare at the sky. How can she be so forgiving? "You should hate me."

"For what?" Her voice is soft, gentle.

"For not being there to save you. I should've told my dad to jam his military career up his ass. I should've told him no and chose you. Instead, I asked for you to wait for me, to bank on an unknown future and be second best in my life."

She blows out a rough breath as if my words are too much for her to process. She drops her hands from my face and takes a big step backwards. I spoke the truth, and she knows what I said is right. I fucked this up almost nine years ago, and now we may never get back what we had.

"Like I said before, I did hate you." Her words are whispered and spoken to the ground. My muscles tense, ready for the heartache she's about to deliver, knowing that's what I deserve. Slowly, her eyes come to mine. "I did. But I was wrong. We were kids given adult choices that we had no business making. We both chose poorly, and we had to live through those decisions. You can't keep beating yourself up for this, and I can't keep pushing you away."

"What're you saying?"

"I'm saying that I'm scared, okay? I'm scared to be happy. The last time I felt like this was with you, and then I walked straight into a fucking nightmare of my own choosing. I'm fuckin' petrified to go there again and ruin everything I've worked so fucking hard to build."

"I don't want to hurt you," I whisper.

She nods decisively. "I know that, Rett. I do."

"So where does that leave us?"

"I don't know. There's stuff we *really* need to talk about, but not right now. Right now, we need to go see your friends."

"When then?" I push, even though I shouldn't. I'm done waiting.

We need to put all our cards on the table and then move on with the rest of our lives.

"Soon. I promise."

I nod and make my way around the car. "I'm holding you to that, Mila Santos. We're best friends. They don't break promises, and they don't lie." I drop my ass into the passenger seat, and she starts the car.

She purses her lips as she reverses out the parking spot, and my eyes zero in on her shaking hands. She's nervous, and that makes me anxious as fuck.

20

GARRETT

THREE HOURS LATER, we pull up in front of the base. After showing our IDs at the gate and stating the purpose of our visit, we wait until we're granted access. An escort takes us to the central building where I'm greeted by my old team.

I make introductions to Mila. "Guys, this is Ana. Ana, this is Anderson, Forrest, Fergo, Hexon, and Parkinson." We agreed on the way here that I wouldn't use her name. Ghost Team works in secret, so her identity must remain confidential.

Anderson is a sniper, and his skills were unmatched...at least until I met Blair. His head is completely shaved, which makes his thick eyebrows and brown eyes stand out.

Forrest is the youngest, and I only worked with him for six months before I left. His red hair is styled similar to mine, short on the sides and longish on top. His muscle mass is a little less than mine, but he's beefed up since I left.

Fergo is the oldest. He has five years on me and is the longest-standing Ranger in the group. He joined our team when his team was wiped out in Iraq on a mission. His hair is peppered with gray, but his blue eyes are as lively as ever. He has a wife and three kids at home.

Hexon is my age and is the geekiest of the group. He doesn't do well in social situations, but he makes an effort to welcome Mila that I appreciate.

Lastly is Parkinson. He has black hair, a short beard, and a scar that runs down his neck courtesy of a knife fight. He won and got his guy, but he got a scar for his trouble. He's also married but doesn't have any kids.

"Not that we aren't happy to see you, but why are you here?" Fergo asks.

"Working on a case. Ana and I need to speak to Commander Paves. There's a government camera that could help us identify a suspect."

Fergo's eyes flick to Mila in question, and I nod, "She's good."

He nods, accepting my word at face-value. I trust her, so by default, they do too. "Commander Paves is in his office. You remember the way?" I nod. "Good. If you need a hand, let us know. We got some shit happening here, but if you need us, just sing out."

"Everything good? Anything I can help with?" I ask, though I don't know how much help I could be now that I'm no longer a Ranger.

"Nah, bro. We're good."

"Come say bye before you leave." Forrest winks at Mila, who smiles sweetly before flipping him off and walking past him and me.

When he looks at me with a popped eyebrow, I chuckle and shrug before following her. Grabbing her arm, I steer her in the right direction. "He was playing."

"Oh, I know. So was I," she grins.

We arrive at Commander Paves's door, and I knock. The door swings open after a moment, and I'm greeted with surprise from my old superior.

"Michaels? What in hell are you doing here?" he asks, but there isn't any venom in his tone.

"I need some help, sir."

He steps aside. "Come in. I'll see what I can do."

Mila walks in, and I follow, thanking him on the way in. He closes the door and walks around his desk before taking a seat.

His office has three glass walls overlooking different combat squad areas and one solid one where framed service awards that belong to the man in front of me are hung. Mila makes her way to the windows off to the side, while I take a seat in the vacant chair on this side of the desk.

"What can I do?"

I pull out stills of the camera footage I brought with me and hand them to him. "These are photos of two suspects and one victim. We haven't been able to identify the suspects because the footage we have access to doesn't show their faces clearly." I point to the photo that has the government security camera. "Except in this one, there's a military surveillance camera hidden in it. I believe we may be able to get a clear image of them off that."

"You need access to it?" His eyes slide to Mila and back to mine.

"She's good. Much like Rangers, her team works in secret too." I say that to settle his suspicions, but I don't miss the way Mila tenses against the window. "And yes, I need access to it."

He nods, "I can do that. I'll call the IT people and let them know you're on the way."

"Thank you, sir." I stand, and gather all the images back into the file.

"What are they doing in there?" Mila asks, motioning toward a group of soldiers through one of the windows, and I wince. Maybe I should've told her not to ask questions.

"That's classified," Commander Paves states.

Mila snorts, "Well, I'm not stupid. Everything here is classified, but it looks like they're trying to mutilate a bomb." Her face screws up in disgust. "And unless it's a suicide mission, that plan is going to fuck up severely."

He frowns, eyeing me. I shrug. "Don't ask me. She knows what she's talking about if that's what you want to know."

"Our men are highly trained when it comes to explosives, Miss...?"

"Ana," she inserts.

"Ana who?"

"Ana none of your fucking business," she smiles and my lips twitch. "Honestly, I don't care how smart they are, *that* bomb is going to explode the minute they try to assemble it. Anyone in a two-hundred-foot radius will die. But hey, you want to be up-your-ass-arrogant, I hope you're one of them."

I freeze, staring at Commander Paves. Years of military training means I've learned to respect authority and rank. Her insults and I-don't-give-a-shit attitude would not be welcomed here. He stares at her as if waiting for an apology. I feel sorry for him because he'll be waiting forever.

"You will have to excuse me, Ana. I am not used to this kind of blatant disrespect."

"You're excused. Reality checks suck, and I don't hand out respect like candy. It's earned. I was trying to help, and you dismissed me as if anyone that doesn't wear a uniform is dumb as shit. Frankly, I find that disrespectful."

"Okay, for argument's sake, how would you build that explosive?"

"What do you need it to do?" she asks.

I take my seat again and watch them volley, and I can't help but feel an overwhelming sense of admiration. This was my life for a very long time, and here she is, slotting in, and I love it. My heart could burst right now, but that would be okay. As long as I get to have that girl, I don't care what else happens. But then the admiration is overruled by worry.

"I have civilians trapped. It's a concrete wall, and we need an explosive that can get us through the wall to get them out."

"You want them dead?" She raises a brow.

"Why would I rescue them if I wanted them dead?" he deadpans.

She points towards the room. "Uh, 'cause that bomb would kill them. You want a black smoke explosive or a chemical one. Probably gas. One they use in mining. It should crack the wall. You'd need to break through the foundation after that, but that particular explosive won't make much noise and should break down the structure enough. Means you'd have time to do that if you need to do so discreetly."

"How do you know this?" Suspicion laces his words and has my spine stiffening.

"Aww, now that's confidential," she winks and turns to me. "You ready?"

Flabbergasted, I stand from my seat again and nod my thanks to the commander. I open the office door, allowing Mila to exit first, then close it behind me.

"You shouldn't have done that," I scold as I lead us to the IT department.

"Ana, is it?" Commander Paves's voice stops us in our tracks. Mila turns and nods at him. "You got ten minutes to spend with my guys? I have a feeling I won't word it quite as well as you do."

She looks at me, and I worry my lip. I trust him, but Mila just made it clear she could be dangerous. She just admitted to the Army Rangers commander that she has extensive knowledge of explosives. To them, that could mean a possible threat.

I shouldn't have brought her here.

"Yeah. I have ten," she answers, and I groan.

"Mila, I don't think this is a good idea," I whisper.

"It's fine. You know where to find me, right? If shit goes bad, I'll just blow something up. That's my bat-signal, okay?" She raises a brow as she walks backwards toward the commander.

Resigned to my fate, I nod. I'll be able to see her from where I'll be, so I'll have eyes on her the whole time. If I suspect anything, we'll leave, and I won't take no for an answer.

I glance around the room and find Hexon with his eyes on me. I give him a pointed look, trying to silently send a message. He nods his head subtly in acknowledgement, and I relax a little more.

He has eyes on her too.

I enter the IT room, and one guy steps forward, pushing glasses up on his nose and addressing me. "Commander Paves advised me to assist you, Staff Sergeant."

"Thank you." I open the file and pull out the image with the camera I need on it. "Are you able to pull up the feed for this camera for the time and date stamped on this image?"

"Yes, sir." He moves toward a cluster of screens and begins typing away.

I position myself behind him, keeping a clear line of sight to Mila. She moves around the room, nodding and looking at diagrams or information. She talks to the men as Commander Paves watches her.

She takes a pen and begins writing something. I'm transfixed by her. The way her nose scrunches as she concentrates is just like she did in high school. She gets so focused and has no idea the attention she draws. I bet half the men in that room have a hard-on for my girl.

"Sir?"

I turn my attention back to the guy helping me. The screens now show the intersection where our missing girl, Melanie, was last seen. I watch the screen as three individuals walk into camera view.

"Can you pause that?" I ask, and he nods, hitting a key on his keyboard. "Zoom in." He does, but I think I already know what I'm looking at. "Fuck! Can you print that?"

"Sure can. How many copies, sir?"

"Ten."

"Yes, sir."

I stand up straighter and look toward the explosives department, but Mila's gone. My chest tightens as I search the area. I hold my breath, narrowing my eyes, searching through the moving bodies until finally my gaze lands on her talking to Hexton.

Fuck.

The air whooshes out of my lungs as I sag in relief. I need to get the fuck out of here.

"Here you go, Staff Sergeant."

I turn around and grab the photos, thanking him before heading straight for my girl. I know one thing for sure. My fear of losing her is becoming almost irrational. I need to know where I stand. Being in limbo is killing me.

I thank Hexon, and we say goodbye to the rest of my team before making our way out of the building.

"That was a little exciting," Mila gushes.

"Gave me a fuckin' heart attack." I growl.

"Oh, chill. I was fine."

"Mila, you just walked into a government building filled with the most elite soldiers you can find and claimed you were practically an explosives expert."

"I am," she frowns.

"That makes you a risk, dangerous and someone they'd consider a potential target."

Her eyes widen as she realizes her error. "I was just trying to help."

I stop as we reach the car. "I know, baby. But next time, don't be so smart, okay?"

"You want me to be dumb?" she asks, offended.

I shake my head. "I want them to *think* you are so I don't lose you. I'm one man, and though I'd be willing to fight every last man in there, I'd lose."

She slides into the seat and starts the car.

Gripping her hand in mine, I wait for her gaze to meet mine. "Necesitamos que arreglar esto, Mila. No te puedo perder."

We need to fix this, Mila. I can't lose you.

21

MILA

EVERYONE'S WAITING in the meeting room when we get back to HQ. Garrett explained our findings on the way back, and to be honest, it made me feel sick.

Although he spoke to me most of the trip home, I could sense his worry as he constantly looked in the rearview mirror. He treated every car as suspicious and every pedestrian that looked our way as an enemy. I understand and know he's just being his normal, observant self. But the commander wouldn't have let me leave the building if he honestly thought I was that much of a threat.

I take a seat on my side of the table and look at Roxy. "You're not going to like what we found."

"What did you find?" she asks hesitantly.

Garrett slides the images across the table toward her. "Katarina was the other woman."

"Dickhead One was the guy." She looks at Logan. "Fuck."

He nods, "That explains what we found."

"What did you guys find?" I question.

"The alleyway was a dead-end. It only has one way in and out of it on the surface, but there's an access point to the underground drains. We thought she was underground this whole time, so I guess it makes sense."

"But why kidnap these kids? They've no criminal background or affiliation to criminal organizations. They're just normal," Ayda says as she frowns.

Austin rocks forward in his seat. "You guys don't see the connection?" The twins look at him and shake their heads in confusion. "They're stand-in kids. Melanie, the youngest of the kids that were taken, is Mia."

"Rachael is me." Roxy blanches, staring at the image. "Andria is you," she says to Ayda, who visibly pales.

"Jensen is Jacob," Charlie concludes. "Wow, that's really fucked up."

"What's she trying to do? Rebuild her family with someone else's children?" Ryder asks.

"Looks like it," Blair answers through disapproving lips.

"That's really sick," I snap. "What kind of mother replaces her living children with kids she kidnaps? That's some royally fucked-up shit."

"She *is* fucked-up," Roxy sighs. "I'm not saying this to excuse her behavior, but she wasn't always like that. Lex broke her, and my guess is, her children turning against her was the last straw."

"Especially when we did it in such a spectacular way. We don't agree, we literally fight on separate sides, yet we all went up against her. Together." Ayda continues.

"That has to put a severe dent in her pride. She would've realized then that she lost us," Roxy concludes as Logan wraps his arms around her waist.

"So instead of accepting it, she stole kids from the streets and is building herself a replacement family," Austin growls.

"Seems like it," Roxy murmurs, and I feel for her. I watch how much it affects her every time she has to make these decisions. The pressure to make the right call. It's her family, and this is her mother. I understand this can't be easy.

"Should we contact Jake?" I ask.

She blows out a breath, "That's another thing. There's movement in the underground, talk of territories and war. Lex's death triggered it, and as his heir, Jake will have his hands full."

"Do we need to worry about that?" Garrett inquires.

She turns to him, nods and explains, "Yes. At the moment, we're dealing with people and groups that we know. We can pinpoint people, we know how they work, where they are, etcetera. When you introduce new criminal organizations and players, then add in a war for territories, it's definitely something we need to keep an eye on."

"Could Katarina have something to do with that too?" I ask, thinking it would make sense.

"Maybe," Roxy muses.

"It's highly possible," Ayda adds. "Our grandfather ruled Lex's organization before him. He was appointed heir because Katarina was an only child, and women aren't allowed to rule."

"She could be trying to take back her birthright," Garrett surmises.

"It might pay to reach out to your brother," Lucas says decisively. "He might have information we could use."

Roxy shakes her head. "He won't give it to me. Not without something in return."

"So, we find Katarina's location. Give him that in exchange for information," I offer.

"No." Ayda's face contorts in anger, and Ryder grabs her hand, sliding his fingers between hers. "She has four kids down there. Victims." She gives me a pointed look, and I wince when I realize where this is going. "Do you think my brother will care about them?"

"That's a hard no," Austin answers, though he doesn't need to. Everyone in this room knows what Jake is like.

"So we find the location, get the victims out, and leave the rest to Jake? Give him the location in exchange for information on this war," Charlie suggests.

"That could work." Logan looks down at Roxy nestled in his arms.

"Then what?" she frowns. "We decide whether or not to help him fight his war? No fucking way. If he wants that life, it's on him."

"So we stay out of it?" I ask. I understand why she doesn't want to get involved, but ignoring it isn't going to help the situation.

"Innocents could get hurt," Ryder interjects.

"We can monitor it, but I'm not helping my brother," Roxy says harshly, glaring at Ryder.

Ayda bristles at Roxy's outburst. After all, her twin is kind of attacking her fiancé. Ryder squeezes Ayda's hip like he's warning her or reassuring her.

"I understand that. I'm the last person that wants to help him after everything he did to Blue. I was thinking objectively. There are others in the line of fire too," Ryder replies.

Roxy sighs, "I know that. Sorry."

"How do we find Katarina?" I blurt out to get us back on track. Roxy has a lot on her mind to process right now. She doesn't mean to be heartless.

She is so used to sorting things out on her own that she sometimes struggles to take everyone's opinions into account. She's trying, though, and I'm so proud of her for doing it. There was a time when she'd take off, process, strategize, then come home and talk to us when she had it worked out. She's trying to involve us, but that means she gets a little edgy because she's overwhelmed.

"Feel like going back to see Garrett's friends?" Blair grins.

"No," Garrett growls. "I'll take Aus or Lucas. Mila's staying here."

Curious, Logan asks, "Why? What happened?"

I snort and earn myself a Garrett-glare. "She announced to the base commander that she's an explosives specialist. She even helped build them a bomb."

I grin as Charlie holds her palm up for a high-five. "Go, girl."

"Don't encourage her," Garrett scolds. "She painted a target on her back."

Roxy steps forward, narrowing her eyes. "What kind of target? Should we be worried?"

"No," I roll my eyes. "They don't know who I am. I used a fake name, and the license plate on the Mustang is fake."

"Should you go back there?" Ayds asks, directing her question to Garrett.

"I'll be fine. I'm one of them, so they trust me. But Mila will need to stay here."

"Fine," I shrug. I have somewhere else I need to be anyway.

"So it's settled?"

We nod, and Lucas stands up. "I'll go with him. I might be able to see what they do, get an idea of what Blair and I are dealing with."

Logan nods his approval and dismisses us. I catch up to Garrett on our way out of the room and hand him the Mustang's keys. "The plates are still on there. It's probably best they can't track us."

He nods and murmurs, "Will you be okay?"

"Without you, you mean?" I raise a brow teasingly before I submit to his seriousness. "Yes, I'll be fine. I'm all better."

"Okay. I'll see you when we get back." Then he looks pointedly at the panting dog sitting beside me. "Tobias, stay." The dogs ears prick up as if he is offended. Or perhaps he is silently saying "duh".

I snort at the thought and nod my agreement to Rett. Smiling, he steps into the elevator with Lucas. I wait for the doors to close before spinning back to where I know Blair is watching.

She tosses me a set of keys, and gives me a no-nonsense look. "You scratch her, I scratch you. You dent her, I dent your face."

"Yeah, yeah. I'll bring the Barbie car back in one piece," I call out over my shoulder as I open the stairwell door. "Mind Tobias for me, will you?"

"Hey! No." When I don't respond and hear the door to the stairwell close behind me, she rips it open again. "Santos! I said, no!"

I laugh and turn back to her at the bottom of the first flight of stairs. Offering an enthusiastic smile, I respond, "Thank you. You're the best."

She groans in response, "You're a bitch."

"Yep." I pop the "P".

"You owe me! Give Slade a kiss from Aunty Blair," she yells just before the door closes again.

I race down the stairs, my excitement fueling me with adrenaline. My visits to Slade have been few and far between, and I miss him so much. But sneaking away has been difficult with my injury. I still speak to him everyday, but I'm looking forward to seeing my baby.

I wait inside the communal living area until the Mustang is out of sight. Then I waste no time, jumping in Blair's pink VW and racing out of the gate.

By the time I pull into Mama's driveway, my heart is racing, and my cheeks hurt from my smile. Knocking, because Garrett has my keys, I wait. I can hear the whispering behind the door, and moments later, it opens.

"Where is your key, hija?" Mama scolds, clutching her chest. "I didn't know who it was. Scared me."

Smiling, I press a kiss to her cheek. "Sorry, Mama. I didn't bring my keys."

She huffs out a breath and closes the door behind me, locks it, and calls out to Slade, "It's your mama, nieto!"

"Mama?" He pokes his head out of his room, and the minute his green eyes spot me, a smile breaks out across his face.

He runs toward me and I catch him as he jumps into my arms. My healing abdomen protests slightly, but I hold him to me and squeeze a little harder than I should.

"I missed you, Mama." His words are mumbled into my neck as his tiny arms almost choke me.

"I missed you too, baby. So, so much." I close my eyes and inhale him.

When I open my eyes, I see as Mama wipes her eyes, and I frown. "Are you okay? What's wrong? Has something happened?"

"No, hija." She shakes her head and moves toward the living room. I follow her in, and she collapses into her chair.

"Talk to me, Mama," I whisper, stroking my son's hair as he lies against my chest.

"I don't want to make you mad," she says, worried, and I instantly know what's wrong.

Eva.

She brought her up a couple of times over the years, and, regretfully, I got mad at her for it. She has every right to worry about her other daughter. I don't think there's anything Slade could do that would make me love him less.

"Talk to me. I promise not to get mad," I say sincerely. "What's got you so worried?"

"She's my daughter, hija. My blood. I know you don't like her, but I can't help but worry."

I swallow, and calmly respond, "I know. It's okay. I understand that."

"Why did she do it? Why would she hurt her familia in such a way?"

"She's angry, Mama. She blames me for her rape."

"She should blame me."

"No." I shake my head aggressively. "She should blame the men that took advantage of her. I hate that it happened to her, I truly do. But everything she did after that, everything that happened because of her, was her choice. She knew what she was doing."

"I know," she sighs sadly. "I'm disappointed. It angers me that she could do such a thing to her sobrino. To her hermana. I'm angry."

I nod and agree, "Me, too."

"And now she's your husband's puta," she spits out. "She gives herself to any man. Sells herself. It makes me sick."

Mama doesn't know about the explosion. She doesn't know that the daughter that sits beside her may have killed her baby girl.

Eva broke enough hearts, and I don't even know if she survived. Either way, I wasn't going to let her death break Mama's heart. She's already hurting because of what Eva's done. She hates what Eva became, the choices she made, but she still loves her and hopes for her redemption. I feel nothing but hatred for her.

Whether she survived the explosion or not, my sister is dead to me.

22

GARRETT

I'M EXHAUSTED by the time we make it back to HQ. It's almost three A.M., and I'm dragging ass. We spent hours combing through the cameras and came up with nothing. Katarina is either extremely careful or fucking lucky.

I push open Mila's front door and silently close it behind me. Frowning when I don't see Tobias' bed beside the door, I turn in search of it. I smirk when I find he has pulled it closer to the sofa and is curled up, quietly wagging his tail to greet me. Pulling off my shirt, I place it in a pile before doing the same with my pants. I make my way towards him, dropping down to give him a pat. Standing I decide to sleep out here, on my makeshift bed on the sofa, because I don't want to wake her this late at night.

A smile spreads across my face when I see her sleeping form tucked under my blanket. I look back at Tobias and grin. My heart skips and warmth fills my blood with happiness at the thought that he loves her as much as I do. In my absence, he took it upon himself to become her protector. She doesn't realize it yet, but he will protect her with his life.

She looks so peaceful. I hate to wake her, but I know how uncomfortable that sofa is. She'll wake up regretting this tomorrow and more than likely be in a bad mood. I don't want that.

Kneeling on the floor beside her, I brush her hair off her face before pressing my lips against her warm cheek. "Ana."

She mumbles grumpily and swats at me. Chuckling, I stand and slide my hands beneath her body and lift. She groans, tucking herself into my chest, burying her nose into my neck, and I almost send us both to the floor when her tongue licks my bare skin. My blood roars to life and surges toward my cock.

Thankfully, I make it into the room without injuring either one of us. I decide I'll sleep on the sofa. My dick is so fucking hard, I won't be able to sleep unless I do something about it.

"I need to pee," she whispers, and I tense.

"You're awake?"

She lifts her head, giving me a sleepy smile that makes my heart skip. "Uh huh."

I lower her feet to the floor, and she heads to the bathroom. I leave her to it and head back to the living room. I'm straightening the blankets when her voice breaks the silence.

"I thought you were coming to bed?"

I rake nervous fingers through my hair and thank the universe the back of the sofa shields my raging hard-on. "Uh, I can sleep here tonight."

"So you can jack off?" she blurts out sassily, and my whole body locks as her tease causes precum to leak from my cock.

"What?" I stammer.

"I hear you," she says and shrugs. "Do you hear me? Because that would be kind of hot."

"You...what?"

"I hear you when you masturbate out here."

"Oh, God," I blanch.

"And it turns me on, so I join in on the fun."

I move around the sofa, my eyes searching for any sign she's fucking with me. When she stares right back, challenging me to do something about the sexual tension firing between us, my steps are more determined, making it clear what I want. I want her, and I'm tired of waiting.

The only thing that's ever made sense in my life was her. I know with every inch of my soul that she's the only girl for me. Distance taught me that. No matter what I did, I couldn't move on. My heart only wanted her. It beat for her. She is my life-force and everything good in my world.

"If you don't want this, say so," I growl.

"I want this," she answers confidently.

"We do this, and you're mine. We don't wake up tomorrow and change our minds. This is it."

"I didn't ever regret you," she whispers as I palm her cheek and lift her eyes to mine. "I regret a lot of my life and the choices I made, but I never regretted you."

"Say it," I demand. "Say the words, Ana."

"I love you." Her eyes shine with honesty, leaving no room for misinterpretation, and my heart threatens to explode inside my chest.

I press my forehead against hers and try to swallow the storm of emotions within me. I want to take everything she's offering immediately. Another part of me wants to savor every second of this because it feels like I've waited a lifetime for it.

"I'm scared," I whisper, laying myself bare for her. "I can't lose you. Not again."

"The only way you lose me is if you decide you don't want me," she says, her nervousness causing the slightest tremble in her voice. I pull back and search her eyes. There is hesitance there that I don't understand. She takes a deep breath and continues, "Maybe we should talk—"

I press a finger to her lips to silence her. "Talking has always been overrated. I know what I want. I want you, and nothing you say could ever change that."

"Kiss me," she challenges. "Make me feel good. Remind me what it feels like to be loved by you."

Reaching around her body, I grip her ass in my palms and lift. She wraps her legs around my waist, pressing her heated core against the solid steel in my briefs. I make my way to the bedroom using only muscle memory as I lose myself in our kisses. We pause a moment, and I look down at the radiantly sexy woman in my arms. She's wearing nothing but panties and a threadbare tank top, her pebbled nipples clearly defined, making my mouth water.

She chuckles, "Are you just going to stare like you wanna eat me, or are you going to fuckin' eat me?"

My dick throbs as my lust for her kicks into overdrive, making me groan with need as I lower her to the ground just inside the door. She smirks and moves to hop on the bed, trying to control the moment, dictating when and where. But that doesn't work for me. Grabbing her arm, I spin her back toward me and slam her back onto the wall. I press my body against hers and claim her mouth with mine. Her protest dies the minute my tongue licks inside her mouth.

My body cages her against the wall as I take control of the kiss. I want to consume her, leaving no doubt that this is where she belongs. She is mine, and I will fight every last man on Earth before anyone takes her from me again.

I drown myself in her taste and savor every flick of her tongue against mine. She tastes like home, just as I imagined for years, but better. I pull my lips from hers and slide them along the column of her neck, my teeth sinking into the soft skin where her shoulder meets her throat, and she shudders against me.

Gripping the hem of her tank, I lift the material up and over her head. Her dark eyes swim with desire as her chest heaves. Gathering her long hair in my fist, I bury my face into her neck, teasing and nipping at her skin with my teeth. Her answering moan spurs me on as my hips thrust against her. Goosebumps break out on her skin as my lips trail a path to her perfect tits.

I flick my tongue over her hard nipple, and she jerks at the contact before I wrap my lips around the flesh. She moans and slumps against the wall, submitting to my worship of her body. I twist her other nipple between my fingers, pinching the bud while my tongue flicks over the other.

I switch sides, and her fingers thread through my hair, scraping at my scalp and holding my head to her breasts. I drop to my knees and press kisses on her stomach, over her scar, and along the band of her panties. Clenching the elastic between my teeth, I tug and release it so it snaps back against her skin.

Her eyes open, and she stares down at me.

I hold her gaze and slide my hands up the outside of her silky legs, over her thighs until I grip the golden globes of her taut ass that make my dick weep. "Tell me to stop." I press my lips to the top of one thigh. "Stop me, Ana." I lick along the pantyline on her other thigh, and her head drops back against the wall.

She is a fucking sight, her silky smooth skin bare for me. Her breasts heave with her arousal, and she stares at me with so much want, my balls threaten to embarrass me.

"Don't stop," she groans. "Fuck me. Please."

Burying my head in her panties, I slide my nose up her pussy and inhale her intoxicating scent. I'm torturing myself. My dick is so hard, it fucking hurts. Squeezing her ass, I grab the elastic band with my teeth and slide her panties down her legs.

Her core glistens with her desire, and my dick twitches in approval. Discarding her panties, I kiss my way up her legs until I get to the place she needs me most. She stares back down at me, her eyes hooded in ecstasy as my tongue licks through her folds. So. Fucking. Good.

I find her clit and swirl my tongue around it as her knees buckle. "Fuck, Mike," she moans out as her fingers pull frantically at my hair. She tugs and pushes at my head like she can't decide whether she wants me to stop or keep going.

I lick and suck at her, my tongue continually flicking over her tight bundle of nerves. She gets louder and more demanding the closer she gets. Her nails dig into my scalp, and her pussy quivers under my lips, hotter and wetter with each pass of my tongue.

My briefs are soaked with precum, and my cock is so painfully hard, but I need her to come first. Once I'm inside her, I won't last.

I slide my hand between her thighs, and her legs part, inviting my touch. I press a finger inside her and squeeze my eyes closed as anticipation zings up my spine. She is warm and tight and so fucking wet for me.

"Oh, God. Faster. I'm so close. Please," she begs between panted breaths, and I slide a second finger inside her. I pump them in and out, curling then slightly as her hips roll and thrust, chasing her orgasm.

"Come for me, Ana. I want to taste you. Come on my tongue, baby. Give it to me," I growl before suctioning my lips over her clit.

She cries out her release, her pussy fluttering around my fingers, and I pump my fingers harder, trying to draw out every ounce of pleasure I can from her body.

She pants as her body jerks with aftershocks. I slow my movements before pulling my fingers from her body. She watches me through a haze of lust as I bring my fingers to my lip, sucking her essence from them until there's nothing left.

Shifting to a seated position, I grab her hips and pull her down to straddle. She squeaks at the sudden movement and groans when I position her over my rigid length. She grinds down on me, and I claim her lips and groan into her mouth. Fisting her hair, I pull her head back, exposing her neck, kissing and licking down one side and up the other.

My balls tighten, and I hold her hips still. Panting and trying to get myself under control, I tug her bottom lip with my teeth. "You keep doing that, and I'll blow my load."

"Blow it, then," she retorts hungrily, her tongue flicking out and licking my bottom lip. Squeezing her ass, I grind her down against me.

"I want to feel you."

"Yes," she answers instantly. Shifting, she scoots down my legs and peels my briefs down as she goes.

Throwing them to the side, she crawls back up my body until her lips press against mine. As her tongue licks into my mouth, I grip her hips, my fingertips digging into the muscles of her toned ass. She straddles me again and grabs my cock, sliding her palm along the length.

"Fuck." I rip my mouth from hers and drop my head to her shoulder. "Ana."

"Hmmmmm?" Her tongue snakes out, sliding over the skin of my shoulder. "Kiss me."

With a growl that sounds more animal than human, I fist her

chocolate tresses in one hand and tug, slamming my mouth over hers and squeezing her ass so hard with my other hand, I'm sure it'll leave bruises. I tug her lip with my teeth before licking to soothe the sting.

The head of my cock slides alongs her core as she positions herself above me. Then she drops her body weight, swallowing me whole. She bounces, her body sliding up and down my length. I feel her juices flowing from her pussy to coat me. I grip her hips, and using my own strength, I thrust my hips up, impaling her every time she lowers herself. Her head falls back on a gasp, and I take advantage, sinking my teeth into the flesh of her exposed skin.

Her pussy tightens, and I thrust harder into her, chasing euphoria. "You're heaven. Made for me. I'll never get enough," I grunt.

"Come, Rett. Come with me," she cries, her tits bouncing, head thrown back, and her pussy clenches so hard, I can feel every ridge and sensation inside her.

I groan, pleasure spreading like wildfire. It shoots down my spine straight into my balls, tightening them and swelling my hard dick even further. "Now, baby. Come for me!" I roar as I explode. White-hot cum spurts from my cock as I bury it so deep inside her, the head of my cock punches against her womb.

She screams, following me over the ledge, her pussy rippling around me, milking the cum from my body as my teeth sink into her shoulder. My body shudders with every wave, my cock pulsing with an orgasm that seems to go on for forever.

Our skin is slicked with sweat, and our hearts are racing. Wrapping my arms around her, I hold her to me and bury my face in her neck. Her arms cling to me as we both feel the emotions washing over us with our reunion. The connection that's always been there fuses back together, never to be broken again.

I won't let it.

She is mine.

23

MILA

I WAKE with my leg tangled between Garrett's and the sound of his steady heartbeat beneath my ear. His breath puffs out evenly in his sleep, and I am too scared to move in case I wake him. He normally rises before me.

I tilt my head to study his sleeping form only to find his lips twitching with humor. I slap his chest, and he lets out a deep grunt. "I thought you were sleeping."

"I was. You moved," he chuckles, and I can't help but smile.

Being with him last night was everything I didn't know I needed. Feeling our connection and solidifying our renewed bond meant everything to me. *He* means everything to me, but I still haven't told him about his son.

Shaking off my thoughts, I try to push them to the back of my mind and just enjoy being here with him. "Are you always a light sleeper?"

He purses his lips before responding, "Missions were fucked. Sleep was either non-existent or staggered. My body was forced into a routine that I haven't been able to pull myself out of." He gives me a sheepish smile. "Until last night, apparently."

"Who knew all you needed was an empty ball sack to get a good night's rest," I say playfully.

"Best load release of my life," he chuckles, and I love that sound. It's become one of my favorite things to hear—Garrett's sleepy chuckle.

"Considering you've only had sex twice, we might need to test the theory," I murmur, lifting myself over him so I sit astride his thighs.

His eyes heat and slide down my body. "Should definitely test the theory. I'm all for experimentation." His cock twitches beneath me in agreement.

I lean over, sliding my tongue across his bottom lip. "It's my turn to taste." I roll my hips and slide my slit up his length.

"I think I can handle that," he moans before gripping the back of my neck to kiss me.

His kisses are like a drug. They smother me in a haze until my eyes cross, and I can scarcely breathe. I always want more. His tongue demands entrance, and I open my lips. He licks into my mouth and lights up my taste buds with the most erotic flavor.

A damn hurricane could rip this room apart, and I would have no idea. That's what he does to me, what he's always done.

I rock against his length, and like it has a mind of its own, it lines itself up. Too far gone, I slide down and groan when he fills every part of me. He is thick and long and so fucking hard for me that it becomes to much to resist. Pushing myself up, I use his chest to brace myself as I ride him.

He stares at me like I am his every desire and fantasy, making me feel powerful and bold. Sliding my hands up along my body, I grip my breasts, rolling the nipples through my fingers. His dick twitches inside me, and my pussy clenches in response.

Groaning, he grips my hips and pistons into me. He takes over, controlling the pace and building me up to explode. My skin flushes with the need to come. He groans every time I slide down and hit his balls.

He shifts suddenly, throwing me off. I land on my back with a gasp as he crawls over me. His lips wrap around my nipple, his teeth sinking into the flesh, tugging at my nipple as he thrusts. His cock slides inside me so deep, I almost pass out from the pleasure.

"Oh, God," I groan, my nails clinging to his skin.

"I love this," he grunts. "You are so fucking beautiful."

My vagina flutters around him more urgently. "Fuck me," I order as I pin him with challenging eyes. "Make me come."

Grabbing one leg, he turns me so I'm laying on my side with him still inside me. His body covers mine, and his hands hold my body down so I can do nothing but feel as his thrusts become harder, burrowing into me, hitting my g-spot until spots line my vision, and my screams become a jumbled mess.

He leans over, tugging at my earlobe with his teeth as he thrusts over and over again. "Squeeze me baby. Come, Ana!" he growls, and my pussy fists around him.

I arch back as my release overwhelms me. He roars as I scream. His cock throbs as wave after wave of pleasure rocks his body, every jerk filling me with his seed. He groans out my name as he pulses, and my pussy responds by clenching around him.

He collapses beside me and pulls me into his embrace. I snuggle into his arms as he showers my face in soft kisses before his perfect lips press against mine. The kiss is slow and full of everything we're both too afraid to face.

My phone rings from the bedside table, and I pull away from him, pressing a quick kiss to his lips before I make a grab for my phone.

He holds my waist, trapping me. "Leave it."

I grin and kiss him again. "I can't." My stomach clenches with guilt. It could be Mama. Something might be wrong, and he wouldn't ask me to ignore my phone if he knew. It's my fault he doesn't.

Sighing, he rolls to his back and releases me. I giggle at his disapproval and receive a smile as a reward.

Snatching up the phone, I frown at the number before answering, "Hello?"

"Miss Diez?"

"Who's asking?" I shift, throwing my legs over the side of the bed and sitting up.

"My name is Kathy. I work at the Community Hospital emergency department. I believe we have your mother here."

My heart stops, all the air leaving my lungs. "What happened?"

"I'm not at liberty to say over the phone. The doctors are with her, and they'll be able to give you more information when you arrive."

I jump to my feet and begin yanking clothes from my dresser drawers. Garrett is up doing the same, sensing my urgency. "I'm on my way."

"See you soon. Ask for me when you get here, and I'll be able to bring you to her."

"Thank you." I hang up and toss my phone on to the bed.

With shaking hands and a stomach full of concrete, I begin to get dressed. I can feel Garrett's eyes on me, but I don't know how to explain this to him. I don't know how to tell him he can't come. He can't find out about his son this way. I thought I had more time.

Tired of waiting for me to speak, Rett drops to his knees in front of me as I sit on the bed, trying to shove my boots on my feet. "What's going on?"

My gaze flicks between his eyes before dropping to my lap. "Mama's in the hospital."

"What happened?"

I shrug. "They said they'd give me the details when I get there. I need to go." I stand and force him from my personal space.

"I'm coming with you. I'll drive."

Panicked, I practically yell at him, "No. You can't. They said family only."

He folds his arms across his chest and narrows his eyes at me. "Then I'll wait in the fuckin' car if I have to. I'm not waiting here when you might need me."

"I'll be fine."

"I'm coming. Fight me on it, I don't care. But I'm not staying here."

I bristle at his words. "This is my mother, and I don't give two shits what you want. Just because you were inside me, doesn't give you a fucking right to demand shit."

"No, it doesn't. You're right. The fact that I love you, though, does," he snaps. "Don't you fucking dare push me away now. You can make demands, Mila, and I will listen. But you're being unreasonable right now and slinging hate-filled words because you're defensive." He comes toward me and wraps his arms around me. "You can be defensive. I can take it. But don't push me away."

He's right, and I'm tired of trying to keep him at arm's length because I'm scared. He said he'll love me no matter what, and I have to trust in that. "Okay."

He lifts my chin and raises my eyes. Giving me a thankful smile, he presses a tender kiss to my lips. "Okay."

An hour later, Garrett pulls into the parking garage of the Community Hospital. On shaking limbs, I make my way inside. He places a comforting hand on my lower back, and I can admit to myself that I am thankful he's here. I have no idea what waits for me inside.

We find reception, and I ask for Kathy. Taking a seat, I cling to Garrett's hand as we wait. He is silent the entire time, and just like before, it's comforting in a way I can't describe. Just him being here is helping.

"Miss Diez?"

My head jerks up to find a young nurse smiling in my direction. "Yes?"

"I'm Kathy. If you'd like, I can take you to your mother now."

I nod and squeeze Garrett's hand before standing.

"I'll be right here if you need me," he says, and I mouth my thanks before following the nurse from the waiting area.

She's silent for a bit as she leads me through sterile corridors and past rooms filled with people. Hospitals always have this sick person and astringent smell to them, and it makes my uneasy stomach twist more painfully.

Eventually she speaks, "Your mother was brought in at about three this morning. We have no idea what happened, but she was badly injured. The doctors operated on her while we tried to track down her next of kin. We would've contacted you sooner, but there was nothing on file."

"How did you find me?" I ask.

"Her cell phone. It was locked, so we had to wait for the authorities to use a generic code to unlock it. She only had you and two other contacts. After some Googling, we found out 'hija' means daughter."

I nod. "How is she now?"

"She's heavily sedated. Her injuries were quite severe. Do you have any idea who would have done this to her?"

I do, but I don't want her to know. If this was Levi, I'm going to kill him. It's better that it isn't traced back to me. "No," I say, shaking my head. The nervous butterflies in my stomach turn to angry wasps as I ask, "Was there anyone with her?"

The nurse frowns and replies, "No. She was alone when the paramedics picked her up."

"Who called?" I choke as fear sinks its claws into me. *Where the fuck is my son?*

"We don't know. She was lucky, though. Any later, and she would have died." She stops outside a room. "This is her room. I'll let the doctors know you're here. Take all the time you need."

"Thank you."

Taking a deep breath, I step into the room. The minute I lay eyes on mama, I fall to my knees as pain and guilt buckle me beyond what my body can handle. She is unrecognizable. Bruises cover every inch of her swollen face. A bandage wraps around the crown of her head and one side of her cheek. One arm is in plaster and her leg is suspended in a brace.

Huge choking sobs rip up my throat, making it hard to breathe. I can't see as tears blind me. A chill buries itself deep within my bones. I shiver, clutching my midsection as I rock on the cold sterile hospital room floor.

This is all my fault. I brought this on my family and Mama paid the price.

24

GARRETT

THE MINUTE MILA disappears from my sight, I call Scott, who picks up on the second ring.

"Michaels?"

"I'm at the hospital."

"What's wrong? Is Mila okay?"

"I think so. Her mom's here, but I don't know the details."

Silence greets me, and he takes so long to respond that I pull the phone away from my ear to see if the call is still connected.

"Scott?"

"Is she with you?" His voice sends the hairs on the back of my neck standing up.

"Mila? No. She's in with her mom."

"Find her. Stay with her! We're on our way."

The line clicks as he hangs up. I stare at the phone for a split-second before I'm on my feet. I follow the corridor she went down, and by some luck, I run into the nurse that took her in.

"Excuse me?"

She startles but recovers and gives me a warm smile. "Can I help you?"

"I came in with Miss Diez."

"Yes, I remember. Is something wrong?"

"Maybe. Can you tell me which room she's in?"

"Yes. Room five-oh-four B. Continue down this hall as far as you can go, then take a left. It's the last door on the right, across from the nurse's station," she smiles.

I frown, confused. "Isn't there a strict policy that only allows patient's families in? I mean, I appreciate your help, I'm just a little confused."

"In most cases, yes. But Miss Diez didn't give us instructions to keep anyone out."

She lied to me. "Okay. Thank you."

I take off down the hall, a million questions running through my mind. Why didn't she want me in the room? Does her mother hate me, and she's trying to shield me from that? Is she so stubborn, she wanted to do this alone?

My mind races back to before she got shot, when I hired the private investigator to track down her mother. Does it have something to do with that? What doesn't she want me to know?

I screech to a stop when I set foot in the room. My eyes fall on Mrs. Diez's beaten, abused body, and I suck in a sharp breath. Gut-wrenching sobs draw my gaze over to Mila. She clutches herself, as if in agony, and rocks, mumbling something I don't understand.

"Fuck! Baby!" I squat in front of her and palm her cheek, bringing her tear-soaked gaze to mine. The pain I see is enough to break any man a thousand times over. "Mila?"

"It's my fault," she sobs, tears rolling down her cheeks, her eyes and nose red with her grief.

Tucking my arms under her body, I lift her from the cold ground. Taking the visitors chair, I sit and cradle her in my lap. "Shhh, baby. It's okay. I'm here."

I rub soothing circles into her back and try to comfort her as she cries and clings to me like I tether her to this life.

I feel useless. I have no idea what's wrong or how to fix it. I reassure her as best I can and hold her as tightly, wishing I could absorb some of her pain. If I could take even a fraction of it, I would do so freely and try to shoulder some of her burden.

She speaks, but none of it makes sense. My shirt is soaked with her tears and the run-off from her nose, but every time I move to get up, she clings and begs me to stay.

Eventually, her tears slow, and the shuddering of her body eases until she falls asleep. Resting my head on the top of hers, I try to slow my heart rate to an even rhythm. I've never seen her break down like this, seem so shattered. But I vow that, somehow, I'll fix it. I won't let anything hurt her like this again.

I don't know how long we've sat here, but eventually, Scott comes in, followed by Blair, Greg, Roxy, Ayda, Ryder, Logan, and Charlie. Almost the entire team is here, and I can't help thinking it's lucky no other patients occupied the other two beds in the room.

Taking in Mila's sleeping form, they silently nod hello before scattering around the room to wait in silence. Greg moves toward the bed and picks up the chart. He scans the paperwork, his face pinched in concentration as he flicks through the pages. Chart still in hand, he moves to check the machines hooked up around the bed. Finally, he puts the chart back and takes a seat beside me.

His face is grim as he shares a loaded look with Scott. Roxy and Logan don't miss it either, their frowns matching mine.

About an hour later, Noah walks in, followed by two other doctors. Greg gets up and greets his brother, who proceeds to introduce him to the two other doctors in the room.

"This is Dr. Kimberly Harper and Dr. Peter Nash. They operated on Mrs. Diez earlier," Noah explains.

"Is she going to be okay?" Mila asks, lifting her head from my shoulder.

"Mila, your mom suffered a lot of traumatic damage to the frontal lobe of her brain. There was a lot of swelling, and we had to operate to relieve some of the pressure. They have her in a chemically-induced coma at the moment to ensure she rests appropriately, and we can monitor her for any signs that what we did wasn't enough."

"And the rest?" Her voice cracks as she looks at her mama, and I tighten my hold on her to reassure her she isn't alone.

Greg settles back in the seat beside me and looks to his brother, silently advising him to let him take the lead. Noah nods. "Her arm was broken in four places and required resetting. Her knee was dislocated as well as her ankle. There was some damage to the tendons in both areas, so they were repaired surgically. We've got her leg immobilized and elevated to aid in the healing process, and those should recover completely. There was a wound and severe bruising to her face, chest and abdomen. But the primary concern at this point is her brain injury."

"Will that be long term?" I ask.

He looks towards me and answers, "Possibly. It's hard to tell this early-on. The best we can do is monitor her and hope that what they've done so far works."

I nod, and the room falls silent as the doctors move around Mrs. Diez, checking the charts and machines, much like Greg did.

Satisfied, they address Mila. "We're both here every day, so if you have questions or concerns, please don't hesitate to contact us."

"Thank you," she murmurs, and I'm relieved to hear her starting to sound more like herself.

"Has anyone else been here to visit?" Scott asks as the doctors turn to leave.

"Not that we're aware of. Is there someone you don't want in here?" Dr. Harper inquires. Mila tenses slightly but tries to hide it by subtly shifting in my lap.

I glance around the room, and everyone else feels thrown off or confused by Scott's question as I am. That's when I realize that I'm not the only one that doesn't know Mila's secrets. Although the girls have an open policy and aren't supposed to keep secrets from each other, it seems Mila still kept this from them.

Except Scott knows. Greg, too.

"We can have a chat outside. I'll fill in the paperwork for the expenses also," Scott replies.

"Sure," Dr. Harper concedes and nods in our direction before leading Scott out of the room.

"What was that?" Roxy moves toward us, hackles raised. "What don't we know?"

"Nothing," Mila answers, her back stiffly upright.

"That wasn't nothing. What the fuck was that?" Roxy's practically almost on top of us now.

Mila, having none of it, jumps to her feet. "It's nothing. That's what I said."

"I'm not stupid, Mila. Something's going on, and I have a bad feeling about this."

She isn't the only one. This whole situation has warning bells blaring inside my brain and my stomach twisting with anxiety.

"Leave it alone. If I want your help, I'll fucking ask for it, you stupid bitch," Mila sneers.

Logan steps in angrily. "Hey! I get that you're upset right now, but if you ever speak to her like that again, I'll fuckin'—"

"What? Huh, Logan?" Mila spits, cutting him off. "What are you going to do? Kill me?"

"Hey!" I stand, suddenly defensive. Wrapping my arms around my girl, I stare at the commander.

"That's enough!" Blair inserts herself between us. "Emotions are running hot, and this isn't helping. Cool it, or I'll kill you both."

"Don't worry about it," Mila snaps. "I need some fucking air." She storms from the room without another word.

I go to follow her, but Blair stops me. "I'll go. She needs someone neutral to extinguish the flames at the moment. I'll bring her back. Promise."

I nod and say, "Fine, but if you're not back in twenty minutes, I'm coming to find you."

"You got it."

I watch as she runs from the room to catch up with Mila.

"What the fuck was that?" Ayda asks, confusion plastered all over her face.

Sighing, I drop down into my seat and glance at the bed. *I bet the only person that knows what's going on is the one person unable to communicate.*

25

MILA

I WALK DOWN THE HALL, chastising myself. I had the opportunity to come clean, and I didn't take it. Partly because Garrett deserves to hear it in private, but mainly because I chickened-out. This is why I don't do happy. Every time I do, something bad happens.

I was fucking Garrett, literally, while my mother was being beaten half to death. My son is missing, and in a split second my whole world's gone. I have no idea where to even start.

Well, that's a lie.

I start by telling those people in that room. I have to tell the truth because if there's any chance of finding Slade, they're the only people that can help me. I can't do this alone.

"You know, for a chick that likes to eat half her body weight in food every meal, you sure move fast," Blair puffs catching up to me.

I grunt in response and push out the hospital doors. Fresh air slaps me in the face, and I greedily suck it into my body, walking around the building before stepping into the underground parking garage. I lean against the brick wall and try to breathe. I need to clear my mind and figure out how I'm going to do this.

Blair stands close, searching the area, no doubt for my husband or his crew. I don't think they're here. They'd have made themselves known by now. He likes to torture me and would want me to know he did this.

"We should probably have her moved," Blair begins, and I nod. "I'll speak to Greg and see if there's someplace more secure where we can move her."

"He's gone," I whisper, and she slams her mouth closed. "Slade wasn't there when the paramedics picked her up." I swallow, take a deep breath, and admit, "I don't know where my son is."

She wraps her arm around me, and I rest my head on her shoulder. "We'll find him. If Levi has him, he needs him to leverage you."

I know that, but it doesn't make it okay. I need to find my son. He'll be scared out of his mind, and if he watched Mama being beaten...I shake my head. I can't even process that right now.

Levi won't kill him. I know that. But that doesn't mean he won't hurt him in some way to punish me. Guilt crushes me; I created this mess, and now my son will pay the price of my mistakes. I straighten up, pulling away from her comfort. I don't deserve to have comfort when my son is missing, and my mother is lying in a hospital bed from injuries she may never recover from. I made this mess, not them, yet they suffer for it.

"How do we know he even has him?" I ask, wringing my hands, trying to stop them from shaking.

"It makes sense, doesn't it? Who else would do this?"

I shrug then answer, "I don't know. But if Levi knows where I am, he'd have made himself known by now. The fact he hasn't makes me think that it wasn't him."

"Would Slade have run? Like when this happened, would he have run somewhere?"

I shake my head. "He's smart. If he did, it wouldn't have been far, and when the paramedics arrived, he would have approached them. He knows to go to them or the police if he needs help."

"Who called the ambulance?" she questions.

"I don't know that either," I sigh, frustrated. "The nurse said it was an anonymous call. So, I have no fucking clue."

"Could Garrett's father have found him?" Blair asks. "Maybe it wasn't Levi after all."

I swallow, straightening up. "I don't think so. I mean, he wanted nothing to do with him before, and as far as I know, Garrett never told him we were working together."

"But do you know that for sure? I mean, he could know, and you'd have no idea he does."

"He doesn't," I argue. "He has no use for him. If anything, he'd do it for Levi. But again, Levi would've made it known by now."

"Does Garrett know yet?" she pushes.

"No," I admit, shaking my head. "And before you say it, I know, I should've told him. Now, I have no choice. I need to tell everyone. But I need you to keep this to yourself until I do. I need to talk to Garrett first."

"The sooner you do, the sooner the whole team is on this."

"I know. I need you to—" my words die in my throat as my eyes zero in on a figure moving swiftly across the parking garage.

Brown hair, the same chocolate hue as mine, glints the moment the sun hits it. I dash in her direction without a single backward glance, moving between cars with single-minded focus and determination. As soon as I'm within reach, I grab the back of her hair and pull, forcing her to flail before crashing to the ground.

"You fucking bitch!" she shrieks, and I'm momentarily stunned. The entire right side of her face is distorted and deformed by scars that spread down her neck and disappear beneath her clothes. Half her hair is missing, having not grown back.

"What?" she sneers. "No snarky remark about my fucking face, sister?"

"Eva," I whisper, knowing how she got those. I did that. "You were in the house." I say with more strength as a few pieces start clicking into place.

She shoves me, catching me off-guard. I stumble before righting myself, and she hisses, "You were always such a fucking whore. You were never satisfied I was happy, and now you stole this from me." She aggressively points toward her face. "I hate myself every time I look in the mirror. Levi can't stand the sight of me."

Her words dissolve the pity I fleetingly felt for her.

"Yeah? I don't need a mirror to hate the sight of you. Where is he?" I snarl.

"Who? Slade?" she cackles like the damn witch-bitch she is.

Like this is some sick game, she's trying to bait me. She wants to play, but I'm not playing this time. Gripping the back of her head, I slam her face into the hood of the car in front of us.

As I pull her head back, it brings me deep satisfaction to see the line of blood leaking from her nose. She claws at me, trying to free herself from my hold.

"I'm not fucking playing, Eva. Where the fuck is my son?"

She glares at me sideways, sneering, "Go to hell!"

I growl and slam her face down harder. Then with a roar, I throw her back to the dirty pavement.

"Did you do this?" I thrust a hand toward the hospital. "Did you beat her?"

"Fuck you."

"She could die! Is that what you want?"

Her face drops, and her eyes flick to where I know Blair stands. When her eyes finally reach mine, I see the guilt swarming just beneath the surface.

"You called the ambulance," I stutter. "Why?"

"He wasn't supposed to hurt her," she whispers.

"Levi," I establish. "How did he even know where to find them?"

"Some PI was digging around, and Levi figured it out. Knew you'd come for Slade. Mama shouldn't have been there. It's your fault she was!"

"Where's Slade?"

"Fuck you, you bitch. This is your fault. You did this. You ruin everything you fucking touch." She tries to get up, but winces and falls back to the ground. "I was raped because of you. I lost my home because of you. The man I love hates me and can barely look at me. Your son deserves to rot in hell!"

She cries out as I slam my foot into her ribs. Then boot her a second time for good measure. Footsteps pound against the pavement, but my rage has me too far gone to care.

I drop down on top of her, clench my fist, and smash it into her face. Blood spurts and bones crunch. She cries out, but I'm done caring about this bitch. Each time my fist connects with her flesh, a sliver of pain lifts from my chest.

Warm arms wrap around my stomach and pull me back. I flail, kicking out and hitting at the arms that hold me hostage.

"You stupid fucking slut!" I scream. "Let me go!"

"Mila, stop!" Garrett demands, grunting when he receives an elbow to the stomach.

"I'll kill you, you fucking piece of shit!" I yell venomously as Eva tries to climb to her feet.

"Eva?" Garrett freezes his backward motion, his arms staying like steel cages around me.

She shoots me a surprised look as a smile spreads across her face. "Isn't this a fortunate turn of events."

"You ruined my life!" I yell. "You'll pay for it. I'll destroy you."

"Not before I destroy everything you love," she spits back spitefully.

"Take her!" Garrett orders, handing me off to Logan.

Panic punches me in the gut, and I struggle harder. "No. No!"

Grabbing me from Garrett, Logan grunts as I try to pry myself from his hold. "Stop fighting. Let him deal with this. He knows what he's doing."

But he doesn't. He can't find out like this. Not from her. She'll twist it and make it so he won't let me explain. The smile she sends my way is enough to make me want to vomit as Garrett helps her to her feet.

Red rings of rage line my vision, and I drop my body weight, instantly freeing myself from Logan's hold, and I race toward my sister. My nails bite into my palm as I clench my fist and slam it into her face, knocking her back to the ground where she belongs.

"Stay away from him," I roar, spit flying from my mouth. She shuffles back on her ass in an attempt to escape. She knows exactly who I'm talking about. "He is *mine*. You touch him, and I'll fucking slit your throat with my fucking nails."

Arms band around me again. "Stop. Ana! Stop, baby." Garrett presses his face into my neck, and surrounds me in his warmth.

"Don't let her in. She can only hurt you if you let her. Baby, stop. Calm down, bring yourself back to me."

"Let me go," I grind out, but I can already feel myself calming.

"No," he whispers. "Do you trust me?" I nod, keeping my eyes locked on my sister. I trust him. It's her I don't trust. "Go with Logan. I'll deal with her."

Without waiting for an answer, he hands me back to Logan. "Get her out of here," he orders him.

"Rett, no!" I plead as Logan begins dragging me backward. "Please!"

Out of desperation and fear, I turn to Rox. "Kill her."

Roxy rears back at my demand. "I can't just kill her. What's going on?"

"Please! Do something!" I beg.

"I'll stay with Garrett," she tells Logan.

I watch with burning tears blurring my vision as Garrett helps Eva to her feet again. Roxy moves to stand with him, but it doesn't make me feel any better. It makes me feel worse.

Everyone I love is about to find out I've lied to them. My body sags against Logan, resigned to the reality of this situation. It's over.

Eva wins again.

26

GARRETT

Eva brushes herself off, and I hand her a wad of tissues from my pocket. When Mila walked out of the hospital room earlier, I grabbed them in case she needed them. I wanted to be prepared.

She dabs her nose, wincing when she presses too hard, while I study her scars. Burns, long healed, disfigure her face. She was once a beautiful girl, and if you look close enough, you can still see the beauty under the scars. But she was never as beautiful as Mila.

I can't help but think that it's kind of symbolic. She used to be beautiful in a superficial way. But underneath the exterior she was as ugly as they come. The scars that distort her face now simply reflect the monster she truly is. A warning of sorts.

"She's a fucking psycho," Eva snarls, trying to staunch the blood flowing from her nose.

I nod, shoving my hands into my pockets. "She's my psycho."

"Want to tell us why you're here, and why my friend wants me to kill you?" Roxy asks coolly.

Eva opens her mouth to respond, but I interrupt, "No, she doesn't. She was about to leave." My voice is stern, as if admonishing a spoiled toddler.

That's what Eva is.

"No, it's fine, I have time," she slyly smiles and looks at Roxy.

"Except we don't want to hear it. I don't want to hear it. Nothing that comes out of your mouth was ever good, and you've had a vendetta against your sister since forever. I don't want to hear shit from you."

"Sister?" Roxy frowns. "Mila is your sister? You must be Evangelina."

"Yes. Though, Eva is fine."

"Or whore? Slut?" Roxy provides wryly.

"You don't know me, bitch, so go fuck yourself!" Eva spits and turns to me. "If you want to live with your head up your ass while Mila lies and hides secrets, that's your problem."

I snort, "I know she has those, just as I know she's the one I need to hear them from. Not you."

She narrows her eyes, and injects a sultry tone in her voice. "You know, I always loved your loyalty. We worked once upon a time. Don't you remember? We were good together, Rett."

"It's Garrett, and you need to find new tactics," I growl. "Your predictability is boring. Get out of here."

"You liked it at one time." She flutters her lashes before dropping her gaze pointedly at my dick.

"Bye Eva." I turn, grabbing a glaring Roxy as I pass.

"She didn't want you then, and she doesn't want you now! She left you!" she yells after me, and I shake my head.

Half-turning back, I stare at her. "Why would you think that'd make a difference?"

"If you knew, you wouldn't walk away from me. I want you. We were good together."

"You never got it, did you?" I state coldly. "It wouldn't matter if she didn't want me. It wouldn't change a damn thing for me. She'd still be the only one that I want. She's all I have *ever* wanted. That doesn't change just because she decides she doesn't want me."

"It'll change when you find out the truth," she snarls, hinting, trying to draw me back in.

"It won't." I retort confidently. "There isn't much I wouldn't forgive when it comes to her. I tried to live without her, Eva. Nothing can be worse than that. I won't ever let her go again."

Turning my back on her, I find Roxy staring at me with profound gratitude and approval. Smiling, I head toward the garage exit with Roxy on my heels.

We find the rest of our group near our parked cars and join them at the same time Scott appears.

"Medical expenses are sorted out. Greg's going to stay with your mother while we figure the rest out," he assures Mila, though she isn't paying attention to him.

She's staring at me with worried eyes and a wobbling lip. She's frozen to the ground, frightened. Stepping forward, I wrap my arms around her shaking body and press my lips to her hair.

She tenses slightly at the contact before relaxing into me. I hold her tighter, trying to soothe her. "Are you okay?"

She shakes her head against my chest as our friends look on silently. Pulling back a little, I palm her cheeks, forcing her to look at me. "Talk to me, Ana."

She sniffles, "Why don't you hate me?"

"She didn't tell me anything," I whisper, and her eyes widen and flick to the area where I left her sister.

"He wouldn't let her," Roxy adds.

"Why?" Mila whispers.

"I know her just like you do. She spills lies like she spreads her legs."

"Where's she now?" Scott inquires with a heavy brow.

"Gone, I imagine," I supply.

"You shouldn't have let her go," Mila whispers and draws my eyes back to her.

I blow out a breath. "I need to know what's going on. I know you wanted to tell me yourself, and I know that's why you were worried about leaving me alone with her. But whatever it is, I need to know."

She squeezes her eyes closed and a single tear slides down her cheek. "I know." I brush the tear away from her skin, and she steps back and turns to the group. "You all need to know, and I *will* tell you. But I need to talk to Garrett first."

Scott steps forward, placing a hand on her shoulder and squeezes. "We're going to head back to HQ. Take your time."

She turns to him and confirms my assumptions from earlier. "I need to be the one to tell them. Please don't say anything until I get back."

"We promise," he responds.

"Thank you."

She grabs my hand with a tentative smile, and I hate that she already thinks I'm going to push her away. I tighten my hand around hers, and she leads me to the Mustang.

She holds out her hand, silently asking for the keys. Digging my hand into my pocket, I pull them out and hand them over without argument. I want to make this as easy for her as possible. She's already a nervous wreck. Making things more difficult will only delay everything.

I slide into the car as she starts the ignition. She pulls out of the parking spot, passes the exit, and away from the hospital. We drive in silence. Whatever she's about to tell me hangs heavy and thick in the air. I can't say I'm not getting nervous.

Her knuckles are white with the grip she has on the steering wheel, and her eyes consistently flick to the rearview mirror. We drive for ages before I start to recognize the neighborhood.

I grew up here. Mom still lives here. I find it strange she brought me here to tell her story. Not that this place didn't hold good memories for me, but she ran from this place. Why would she want to come back here?

I'm completely thrown off when she pulls into the driveway of my mother's house. Switching off the ignition, she simply stares at the house in front of us, and I watch her eyes slide through emotions as she gets lost inside her own mind.

Eventually, the silence becomes too much. Reaching over, I put my hand over hers that's resting against her leg. "Why are we here?"

She snaps to full awareness and clears her throat. "Does your mom still live here? That's what you told me, right?"

"Yes, but what does that have to do with anything?"

"She knows the truth. That's why when you first arrived, I attacked you. I was scared you knew. I thought she told you, and you were back to take it all from me. We don't have time for you to second-guess or question what I'm about to tell you."

"What does she know?" My jaw ticks with tension facing this unknown.

She purses her lips, blowing out a nervous breath. "We should go inside."

"You want her there when you tell me?"

She nods. "Some of it might be hard to believe. She'll be able to back it up."

"She could lie," I grind out.

That earns me a small smile. "You're Garrett Michaels. You can sniff out most lies before people even tell them."

"Apparently not, considering she never told me where you were or what happened. She knew, and she lied about knowing."

"Come on. I need to do this before I lose my nerve." Not waiting for a reply, she pushes open her door and steps out.

My heart pounds as I follow her up the porch steps. I don't bother knocking, I just walk in. "Mom?" I yell out, and it echoes around the room.

"Garrett?" I can hear the smile in her voice before she steps into the entrance. It takes her three seconds to realize I'm not alone, two more to realize who it is, and one more for the smile to fall clean off her face. "Mila?"

Mila inclines her head, staring impassively at my mother. The openness I felt in her the last few weeks is shielded by barriers again. She's protecting herself from my mother, instantly putting me on alert.

My mom's eyes and sheet-white face turn to mine. "You found her?"

I nod. "No thanks to you, apparently."

"Does your father know?"

My brows drop as my eyes narrow, but before I can answer, Mila barks out, "Give me your phone!" She holds out her hand to my mother, who stares at it like she lost her damn mind.

"Excuse me? How dare you?" Mom gasps, clutching at her pearls.

Reaching around, Mila pulls a Glock from the waistband of her jeans, and my heart jumps into my throat. She unlocks the safety in warning, and I step forward. "What the fuck are you doing?"

Not taking her eyes off my mother, who looks completely petrified, she responds, "I trusted you earlier. I need you to trust me now. I won't hurt her, but we need her phone."

Nodding because I do trust her, I turn back to Mom. "Where is it?"

She swallows hard and responds, "Kitchen."

Moving past her, I go into the kitchen, grab the phone off the counter, and head back to where I left them. Handing the phone to Mila, I raise a brow. "Can you put the Glock away now?"

Smiling sweetly, she lowers her weapon and shoves it back in her pants. "Thanks. What's the code?" she asks Mom.

"Six-five-seven-four," mom answers.

Unlocking the phone, Mila checks the call log and messages. Pleased, she locks the phone and moves toward the living room. "Let's talk."

Mom looks at me, regret evident all over her face. Mila was right. Mom has known all along and didn't say a single fucking word. Pursing my lips in a scowl, I follow Mila.

The three of us stand in my childhood living room in silence, like everyone's afraid to start the conversation that needs to happen. I like silence, but in this case, it scares the living shit out of me. I always thought whatever Mila was hiding might hurt me. Now, I'm starting to believe it might destroy me.

Whatever it is, someone needs to tell me, fast. I can't handle this not-knowing anymore. I've been patient. I've waited. I proved that she could trust me. I've shown her I love her. I don't know what else I can do to explain to her I'm not going anywhere. I'm in this for life.

"Someone needs to start," I growl, my impatience getting the better of me.

Mila turns to mom and raises a brow. "Do you want to tell him, or should I?" When Mom thins her lips in response, Mila nods and turns to me. "I want you to know, I didn't mean to keep any of this from you. I love you, and I really hope that, when this is all over, you still want me. If you do, I promise this is it. No more lies or secrets."

I nod, my blood roaring in my ears. This is it.

She takes a deep breath and begins. "When you were away at boot camp, I got sick. Mama was worried, so she asked Mrs. Michaels to take me to the doctor."

My stomach drops. "Sick? Like, dying?"

Mila shakes her head, and Mom falls into the sofa, burying her face in her hands.

"Not dying," Mila continues. "I was pregnant."

The blood that was rushing hotly through my veins ice over. My body is robbed of oxygen as I stare at the woman I love and see raw honesty flowing off her in waves.

"It was yours, Rett. I was pregnant with your baby. Our baby."

The words rattle around my brain but don't settle. I hear what she's saying but it doesn't make sense. She doesn't have a baby. I've lived with her for months and never saw a damn kid.

"What happened to the baby?" I whisper, not able to pull my eyes from her.

She smiles, and it's the most radiant smile I've ever seen. She glows while I float around in darkness. "He was born in a hotel room on March thirtieth. Healthy and so fucking beautiful."

"You had the baby?" my mother gasps.

"You knew she was pregnant?" I snarl at her incredulously.

"Garrett, you don't understand!" she pleads.

"I don't need to understand. You knew I had a son, and you didn't fucking tell me? You kept Mila from me, and maybe I could have forgiven that! But my son?"

"Garrett, please. I had no choice." She stands, her eyes glistening with tears, but I don't feel an ounce of pity for her.

"Rett—"

"Don't!" I snarl. "Just fucking don't."

Scrubbing my hand through my hair, I try to process the onslaught of emotions threatening to choke me.

I have a son.

A son that was kept from me.

Spinning fast, I slam my fist into the drywall. My chest heaves with the need for more air. I need air. Without a backward glance, I storm from the room and out of the house.

27

MILA

I WATCH the only man I love break so hard, he lashes out. The giant hole in the wall could be framed as a historical moment. *The Day Mila Broke Garrett Michaels.*

"Look what you've done!" Mrs. Michaels scolds stridently.

I bristle immediately. "What *I've* done?" I turn my gaze to her and put as much venom as I can into my voice. "You let your husband send me away, too busy drowning yourself in the closest bottle of booze! He sold me while I was pregnant with your grandchild, and you're trying to blame me?"

"You should've stayed away. Garrett was happy!"

"Was he?" I snap. "Or did he spend his whole time looking for me? Or drowning his fucking pain with battlefields?"

"I told you to stay away from him." She stands, scolding me like I'm a child.

I step forward and smile when her eyes turn wary. She should be worried. I'm not the same girl who left here nine years ago. "I pity you. You're a sorry excuse for a woman. You sat by, drinking your whiskey and being fuckin' oblivious while your husband abused you and sold me," I spit at her.

"You've no idea what it's like!"

"I do, no thanks to you. I know exactly what it's like because I was forced to marry a monster. I survived my nightmare and came out fighting, but you'd rather roll onto your back and submit like a mutt."

"How dare you!" she exclaims, blanching.

"Truth fucking hurts. All those years, you made out that Garrett was too good for me. That I was the poor girl no one could love. It was never me that lacked love, it was you. That's why I pity you. I pity your lack of backbone and your need to beg for the slivers Anthony tossed at you. Word of advice—you were better than that, but now, after what you did, you're just as bad as they are."

I don't bother wasting more time on her. She loses at the end of the day because she missed out on the love of her grandchild. If she thinks she's coming anywhere near my son, she's mistaken.

The bitch can rot in hell.

I slam the back door closed and make my way across the yard. A wave of nostalgia rolls over me when I stride past our old home. I know where Rett went. He might hate me, but he'll still go to the willow, if it's even still there. It was as much a comfort for him as it was for me. Separate from the world and the problems life brings, it was always our slice of peace...mine from Eva and his from his parents.

I can't help but smile when I see the willow tree. It's bigger now, but it calls to me in the same way it did when I was a teenager. I left here a quiet, scared kid. I return now, grown and confident. The only thing that scares me is losing my family.

It's a good reminder of what I'm fighting for and how much I've grown. I hate that Rett and I were torn apart, but we've been given a second chance. We can come out stronger and be the parents we always should've been for Slade.

I just hope he lets me explain.

I find him standing a few feet from the willow, his back is to me and he stares at the ground. He knows I'm here, just like he always did. I take a seat, my back against the tree trunk. He needs time to process, and I need to let him. There's still so much left to explain, and I don't want to overload him right away. He needs to process this huge chunk before I can tell him the rest.

I look back toward the house and find Mrs. Michaels on the back porch. She looks in our direction, but I'm sure she can't actually see us. I've said everything that needs to be said to her, and it feels freeing. I didn't realize how angry I was at her for doing nothing until the words poured from my mouth.

Frowning, I turn back to Rett when something catches my eye. I stare at the rough wooden trunk of the willow, my finger tracing the words carved neatly into the wood as my heart stalls inside my chest. I read each one, knowing they're meant for me.

"Esta vida es mía. Pero esta corazón es tuyo." *This life is mine. But this heart is yours.*

"I wrote that the day Alpha Team recruited me," Garrett says in a rough whisper.

I turn to him, blinking away my tears. His face is saturated in misery, and I hate that I'm the reason for his heartache.

"Why didn't you tell me, Mila?"

"I couldn't," I whisper. "Not in the beginning. Then when I could, I had to protect Slade. I couldn't risk your family knowing where he was."

"His name is Slade?" His eyes fill with tears, and my heart breaks a little more.

Pushing off the ground, I stand to face him. "Yes. His name is Slade Michaels. He's almost nine. He looks just like you, except he has brown hair like mine. He's smart and so fucking kind."

He swallows and drops his head. "I need you to explain this all to me. I'm trying so hard to not be angry with you."

"You should be angry," I whisper, shoving my hands into my pockets. I really want to touch him and comfort him the same way he did for me in the hospital, but I know how unwanted that may be right now. Instead, I force myself to take a step back before unloading the past.

"I found out I was pregnant a few days before you were due back from boot camp. Eva figured it out and threatened to tell everyone. I was so afraid of your parents finding out that I attacked her." His eyes go round with shock and disbelief, because the old Mila wasn't aggressive. Nodding, I continue, "In my head, I needed to protect our son. I thought if I could keep it secret until you got home, we'd be able to figure it out. I attacked her to get her to shut up, but it backfired."

"It pissed her off."

I nod, "And she told your parents."

"Then you left."

I shake my head and swallow the lump in my throat before admitting, "No, then I was sold."

His head snaps up and he chokes, "Please tell me you're fucking joking right now."

"I'm not," I state. I have to force myself to continue the story calmly as the emotions I had buried slowly roil to the surface. "Your dad gave me an ultimatum. I could either abort the baby, sign a contract to never have contact with you again, and be deported along with the rest of my family—"

He makes a pained noise in the back of his throat. "What was the second choice? The choice you made?"

"I got to keep the baby on the condition I marry Romeo."

"What?" he yells, losing the tenuous control he had on his emotions, just like I knew he would. "No!"

I nod, "Yes. I stupidly thought he was the best choice I could make at the time that would keep our baby and my mother safe. He wasn't."

"There was no commune?" he asks, needing confirmation.

"No. There was a motorcycle club called the Chaplains. It was run by men and sustained by pussy, drugs, and gun-running. Levi Romero, Romeo as I knew him, was vice president under his dad, Mika. His MC was full of criminals, and you only had rights if you had a cock."

Rett tugs painfully at his hair and drops on his haunches. "I saw him. I asked him where you were, and he said he had no idea."

"I married him less than twenty-four hours after I left here. I became Mila Romero, and they rushed it on purpose."

"So, I couldn't find you because I was looking for Mila Diez."

I nod, sadness making it difficult to get the words out. Garrett's in so much pain, and I still haven't got to the end of it. "I became his property. His father vetted me at dinner the night your family had dinner with them. The one you stormed out of. I was deemed good breeding stock to create heirs with." I roll my eyes. "Me being pregnant was unexpected."

"You said you gave birth, though?" he asks, confused.

"I did. Greg delivered our baby," I smile.

"That's what he meant," Garrett muses. "What happened after that? I'm assuming the team doesn't know about the baby, which means he isn't with you."

"Levi forced me to give him up. I wasn't allowed to keep him with me, so I had no other choice but to send him with Greg. Greg kept him safe until I got out."

"Who has him now?"

"When I left, Scott arranged for Mama and Slade to live hidden away in a safe-house not far from HQ. Everything is in Scott's name, so there'd be no way for Levi to find them. Just like you'd been looking for me, Levi's been looking for me too. For different reasons, though. Levi doesn't have an issue with using Slade to get me to fall in line."

"Your Mom—"

"Yes. Your PI found them. The investigation must've alerted Levi and helped him find them."

"Where is Slade?" My heart flutters each time he says our son's name.

"Levi has him."

"How do you know that?" he argues.

"Eva. She came to live with Levi and me as his live-in pussy, which actually helped me keep him at bay. She basically told me Levi has him."

"What happened to her face?" he inquires pointedly, likely knowing it had something to do with me.

"When I escaped, I needed a distraction. I blew up the house we lived in with her inside it, evidently," I state without an inch of regret.

He blows out a heavy breath and falls silent. Now that he knows everything, I'm anxious to get back to the team. I need to find Slade. That's the most important thing right now. I needed to get the truth out there, then find him. As the silence stretches out, I become jittery and impatient.

"Say something."

"I don't know what you want me to say. This is a lot to take in." He gives me a defeated look, and my heart cracks inside my chest.

"I know, and you don't know how sorry I am. I should've told you sooner, but I was scared. I didn't know you, the older version of you. I needed to make sure Slade was safe. That was my only priority."

"We don't have time for this right now. We need to find him. The rest will have to wait," he says decisively as he stands, trying and failing to keep his anger completely out of his voice.

"Garrett—" I reach for him, but he steps away from me. I avert my eyes to hide my hurt at that, knowing I deserve it. "I love you."

He squeezes his eyes closed as if in pain. "I need time. I know I'm not the only victim here and that you were hurt too and had to live through all that. I'm trying hard not to be angry with or blame you, but I need some time to wrap my head around it all. Please, give me that."

I nod, "I'll give you anything you need. Just please, don't give up on me."

28

GARRETT

THE PAIN inside my chest is so intense, I feel like I'm having a heart attack. Maybe I am. My mind is spinning, and I'm struggling to grasp on to some control.

I have a son.

The whole time I've been with her, living in her fucking apartment, she never told me. I feel robbed. I don't find anything more amazing than knowing something was born from the connection we share.

The weight those words held as they left her mouth almost debilitated me. She crushed me and gave me new life at the same time.

Out of all the possible secrets she might have been hiding, I never would've anticipated this.

I remember our night together before I left for MEPS. I'll never forget it. It's burnt into my brain as the best night of my life...last night's events being the second.

Which is how I know, I never wore a condom that first time. In fact, the need for one didn't even cross my mind, not until a few hours ago when she dropped that bomb on me.

I clear my throat and broach the subject. "We...ah. Are you on birth control now?"

She snorts, glancing away from the road to look at me. "Yeah. I have been since I gave birth. Greg gave me the implant that day. I was glad, too. Levi wanted an heir, and at least he can't hold that over me."

"An heir? Did you—" I swallow the bile climbing up my throat. "Did you sleep with him?"

Her eyes lose their light, and she turns her attention back to the road. She doesn't need to answer, but she does. "Yes. Didn't have much choice. Once Eva moved in and I put a stop to him sneaking in my room, he didn't try as much. He mostly used Eva when he wanted to fuck."

"He raped you?" I stare at her and silently beg her not to say yes. I don't think I'll be able to stop myself from killing him if he did.

She doesn't answer, and somehow, that's even worse. She knows my triggers, saw them the night he drunkenly groped her at a party. I know why she's silent, trying to protect me from myself. But the silence speaks so much louder than any words ever could.

I chew on my anger the rest of the way back to HQ. She parks the car, and we get out, silently making our way inside. We ride the elevator without saying a single word. I know she's sorry. I feel it.

I can't bring myself to even look at her for fear I'll lose the slim hold I have on my control. I know I'm hurting her by ignoring her and pushing her away, but I'm only going to make it worse if I lash out.

I finally understand why she's the way she is now. She had to shield herself and do what was necessary, no matter the cost, to get out of there and keep our son safe. She became his protector, and I'm proud of her for keeping him safe.

Before she steps into the meeting room, and before I lose my nerve, I grab her around the hips and spin her back to me. My lips press against hers before she can speak a word. The kiss is brief, but meaningful, as I remind us both about what we fought so hard for.

When I pull back, tucking her hair behind her ear, I stare into her tear-filled eyes and feel the sting of my own. "I still need to work through this, but I love you too, and I wanted to thank you."

"For what?" Her voice cracks as she tries to hold it together.

"For being a good mother to Slade. For loving him enough to sacrifice yourself. For protecting him."

She chokes and a sob bursts free. I wrap my arms around her and bury my head into her neck, inhaling her intoxicating scent. We cling to one another, and I realize having her in my arms is what I needed. What I *always* needed.

"Let's go find our son." I pull back and swipe the tears from her cheeks. "This time, baby, you don't have to do it alone."

Nodding, she straightens her back and takes a moment to regain her composure. Once she deems herself ready, she steps into the room.

Everyone looks up as we walk in, and Mila glances at me for direction. I pause, trying to find the right words, when she announces, "I have a son. Well, we do." She points between the two of us.

Mouths drop open. Half the men are frozen in place, and the women are gaping like fish out of water. Everyone is registering shock except Blair and Scott. I knew Scott was in the know, but I had no idea Blair knew.

"What the—" Roxy starts.

"Fuck?" Ayds finishes.

Mila nods. "He's almost nine. He was living with my mom in secret so my husband couldn't find him."

"Husband?" Logan blanches, his eyes flicking to me in question.

"Levi Romero. Garrett is Slade's father. Levi was the man I was sold to by Garrett's father when he found out I was pregnant."

"I...I need to sit," Austin whines and plops down onto his chair. "This is a lot."

"You need to back up and explain," Lucas speaks for the first time. "How is the baby nine? Did you and Garrett know each other before last year?"

"Yes. Her family worked for mine," I answer. "Mila and I grew up together."

"We knew that part," Ayda states.

"We didn't." Austin says, nearly pouting.

"Shut up!" A chorus of females yell.

"I was forced to marry an asshole, and I had the baby in secret. Garrett didn't know any of this until today."

"Where was the baby while you were stuck in that hell-hole?" Roxy asks softly.

"With me." Greg materializes into the room behind me. Looking sheepishly in my direction, he adds, "I had Slade with me until Mila was out."

"Then Scott and Blair helped me move him in with my mother."

"Wait. Where is Slade now?" Roxy moves forward, already fitting the pieces together.

"With Mila's ex-husband," I announce as a heavy weight presses into me, knowing my son is with a monster.

"Well, legally, he's still my husband." Mila winces, and my body locks up. "I got as far as getting divorce papers written up, but it's pretty hard to divorce a man when you're running from him and don't technically exist on paper."

Shaking off this new revelation, I focus on the more urgent issue. "We need to get Slade back."

Everyone nods in agreement and support, which I knew they would.

"How do we do this?" Logan asks.

"We could give him what he wants," Mila suggests, bringing my anger rushing to the surface again.

"No. Fucking. Way." I snarl. "You're not going back there. There has to be another way."

She nods, "There might be, but if it doesn't work, we may not have any other option. If I can get in there, I can figure out where he's keeping Slade. Roxy already knows where the location of the complex is." Roxy nods an acknowledgement. "We can come up with some plan to get me out."

Anxiety coils around my stomach like a snake. "What's the first option?"

She lifts her head. "You ask your dad. He sold me to Levi and the MC and should still be in contact with them."

"What if he isn't?"

"Then we already know our next step, but I think you'll find he still is. I used to do ammunition runs for the MC, and I could be wrong, but I think your dad was the seller. There were two contracts on his desk on the day I was sold. One was for my marriage. I didn't get a good look at the second, but I think it had something to do with the buying and selling of firearms."

"Are you sure?"

"Not one-hundred percent, but the guys I collected guns from were familiar."

"I remember them," Roxy adds. "Like Beavis and Butthead."

Mila snorts, "I'd seen them before. I used to walk to school early on Tuesdays. I almost always walked with you, but there were a few times I didn't. I saw them in a car, parked out in front of your property. I didn't think anything of it until I saw them years later."

I think back to those mornings, and I don't remember any strange men. I can remember Mila's smile, or the way her laughter made my chest tighten, but I don't remember the houses we passed or any cars out of the ordinary.

I just remember her.

"I'll call him," I offer.

"If that doesn't work, we need a Plan B," Mila determines.

"What did you have in mind?" Ayda takes a seat on Ryder's lap.

"I think the quickest way is for me to give myself up." She turns to me, just as I'm about to protest. "I know you don't like it, but I know what I'm doing. I don't want to go back any more than you want me to, but I know that world. I survived it once. I *can* do this."

"And if you can't?"

"Then you'll know where I am anyway. Let Levi believe we've no idea where he is."

"How do you know they haven't moved?" Logan questions.

She sighs, "I don't, but we don't have many options here. The longer we wait, the worse it could be for Slade."

"You could wear a tracker," Lucas suggests.

Mila shakes her head, "They'll strip me as soon as I get there."

I fucking hate this plan.

"I meant in your vagina," Lucas adds, and I gape at him. "What? They make waterproof ones."

"Fucking hell!" Austin sputters, staring at Lucas like he grew a third eyeball.

"That could work," Mila shrugs, and I have an urge to hightail her ass out of this room and spank her.

"Okay. Let's say that works. How do we know when to come get you?" Roxy asks.

Mila's eyes come to mine, and I frown at the apology I see there before she looks away. "I have a friend that will help me. He has access to certain things. I should be able to get a burner or something and get a message to one of you."

My teeth grind. It's obvious that she's referring to the friend that she has history with; otherwise, she wouldn't be avoiding my eyes.

I really fucking hate this plan.

"Right. Then what?" I growl.

"I get Slade out, send him out the back way where there are less people. If that changes, I'll let you know. Then I'll find Levi."

"No," I shake my head aggressively. "Absolutely not. I'm going to take care of Levi."

"No," she denies, pinning me with a firm glare. "You'll be waiting for our son. You need to get him out of there."

"You're not going after Levi alone," I snap.

"She won't *be* alone," Roxy says firmly. "We'll have her back. Mila's right. If she sends Slade out the back, and she goes out the front, we will have her covered."

"How do you know they'll even follow you?" I push. "This isn't some high school game you're playing. There's no guarantee."

"There is—"

"There isn't!" I growl, tired of her arguing with me. I won't let her sacrifice herself. She's done enough of that already.

"You can't move on that complex until you have your hands on Slade," she argues. "I can get him out the back and draw the fight away from you."

"You can come that way too." As soon as the words leave my mouth, I already know her answer.

"Levi wants *me*. At the end of the day, even if he saw Slade escape, he wouldn't care. All he'll be concerned about is making sure I stay." Her tone simmers down, and she moves toward me. "I made this mess. I'm the only one that can fix it."

"It wasn't just you that created this. I did too. Let me help you."

"You will be. I need you there to get our son. I know you'll keep him safe, and once he is, I can focus on getting myself out of there and finishing this."

"This is option B. We still have to try option A first," Ayda interrupts. "Call your father, Garrett. Set up the meeting."

Mila's phone chirps, and she pulls it from her pocket. Checking it, she frowns before dismissing it and placing it back in her pocket. She looks at me and raises a brow. "Are you going to call him or what?"

"I'm going to call Mom. If I call him directly, he'll know something's up. If she's the one to call him, it will be less suspicious."

"Is that wise? Considering she knew about this the whole time?" Roxy asks, voicing what half the room is thinking.

The other half know Mom, know how far she's come, how disconnected she is from him. She hates my father almost as much as I do. She might have kept this from me, but she didn't do it as a favor to him. Her reasons were purely selfish.

Mila watches me and nods. "It's fine. If Garrett trusts her, then so do I. He wouldn't do anything to hurt Slade."

29

MILA

GARRETT DECIDED to stay in his apartment tonight. He may not hate me, but he still needs time to come to terms with everything. He spoke to his mother, and she's organizing a brunch for the morning.

I don't hold out much hope for this meeting. His father's never been the reasonable type. He is arrogant and a narcissist. The only way is his way.

I believe that's why he got rid of me. He knew he couldn't control me and, by default, Garrett. I may not have been as outspoken as I am now, but I still held firm to my morals and values and stood by my choices. I wasn't going to be told how to live my life, even then.

The only person that has a say in it is Garrett, and he's the *only* one, other than the other members of Ghost Team, that would never abuse it.

I've prepared myself as much as I can for Plan B. I've chewed my nails down to nothing while pacing my apartment floor so many times, I've worn track marks into the carpet. I watched the minutes tick over on the clock.

The sun sets and plunges the room into darkness before I make my way out of the uncomfortably quiet apartment. I got so used to having Garrett here that his absence makes it feel lifeless.

That isn't my home.

He is.

Though, I don't blame him for needing time away from me. It's the way he is. He needs solitude, much like Roxy used to. I take the stairs to the communal living level and crack open the door to make sure the coast is clear.

Almost everyone should be in the meeting room or in their apartments, but I still hold my breath, listening for any sign of life. When I hear nothing, I slip through the door and into the room.

As silently as I can, I make my way across the room and out the front door, making a beeline to the cars. Finding the car I need, I slide into the backseat of the black SUV.

"Hey."

"Hey, wanna tell us why we're sneaking around?" Roxy asks from the front passenger seat as Logan starts the car.

"I didn't want everyone to come," I answer simply, honestly.

"And where would we be going?" Ayda nudges my shoulder. I smile and glance down at her fingers intertwined with Ryder's. A pang of envy stabs me in the chest.

"We're going to visit my mother-in-law."

"What?" Roxy snaps, spinning in her seat to look at me.

I nod, "I got a text earlier asking me to meet her. I agreed, but I'm not stupid enough to go alone."

"Does Michaels know this?" Ryder asks, likely knowing the answer already.

"No. Clara, Levi's mother, helped me a lot while I was there. She was another woman selected for her ability to breed. She only stays for her son, and I really don't believe she'd do me any harm, but I want to be careful. Showing up with the man I love isn't exactly going to earn me brownie points if she's trying to help."

"Why wouldn't she help if she's in the same position and hates that place?" Logan asks, hitting the turn signal.

I punch in the coordinates I was sent into my phone and pass my phone to Roxy. "Because she's still a mother. She stays for Levi and won't abandon him. But it doesn't mean she agrees with his methods. I want to hear what she has to say."

"That's why we are taking the SUV," Ryder surmises.

"So Garrett doesn't think you left. He only saw one car leave, and it's Logan's," Ayda concludes.

"Smart cookie." I smack a kiss on her cheek.

"Why didn't you ever tell us?" Roxy asks, staring straight ahead and not looking at me. Logan reaches over and slides his fingers over the back of her neck, massaging the muscle to soothe her.

"I'm sorry." The car falls silent. "My life was so messy when I first got here that I spent a lot of the first year trying to work it out. I kept Slade so locked up, talking about him became taboo for me. Then more time passed, and I'd buried myself so deep in this secret that I couldn't find a way out."

"The kid's Tylenol." Ayda narrows her eyes at me. "I thought you stole it."

"No, that was a gift from Slade. He wanted the girls to feel better, so he gave me some teddy bears and the Tylenol to give to them."

"So you've been in contact with him this entire time?"

"Yeah," I nod, relieved to finally be able to share my son with this other part of my life.

I didn't realize how much this secret weighed on me until I lifted it. Not sharing him with my extended family caused me misery I didn't realize I was suffering. I should've told them from the beginning. Garrett too, but I can't rewrite the past.

"The booty-calls weren't booty-calls, were they?" Roxy smirks.

"No. I haven't been with anyone since I left my husband," I take a breath and wince, "except Garrett."

Logan snorts, "Yeah, we got that memo. To be honest, I don't think he's ever been with anyone the entire time we've been working with him."

"The only girl I ever heard about was the one he was looking for." Ryder leans forward to see me past Ayda and grins. "I guess we can assume that was you."

"What can I say?" I throw my hands up. "I've got a twenty-four karat pussy."

"Jesus Christ," Roxy mutters, and Ayda slaps my arm.

We continue talking as the GPS leads us through the streets. They ask me what Garrett was like growing up. How Slade is. What Slade likes. Whether he goes to school or not.

The chatter dies down as Logan pulls into the underground parking garage, the tires squealing on the concrete as he moves down through the levels. The atmosphere in the car is thick with tension as we scan the vacant levels for any sign of an ambush. Clara might have helped me while I lived in that horrible place, but at the end of the day, I disgraced her son. I don't know what kind of effect that may have had on our tenuous friendship.

"Ten-o'clock," Logan informs everyone, and we turn to look.

Clara, still as beautiful as the day I met her, leans against the hood of a car. She, like me, didn't come alone.

"They're club whores," I inform my friends as my eyes scan over the women surrounding Clara. "I'm not sure why she brought them. Generally, they aren't allowed to leave. They're not a threat. They have no training. The only purpose they have in the club is to ride dicks and flash flaps."

Roxy snorts, "You have a way with words. I hope you don't kiss your son with that mouth."

Logan parks the car and switches off the ignition. "How do you wanna play this?"

I unclip my seatbelt and lean forward. "She came to talk to me, according to her text. I only agreed to this because she probably knows something about Slade. So, we'll talk. Any funny business, we defend ourselves. Trust me when I say that we've got the upper hand. Clara isn't dumb. If this was to be an ambush, she'd have brought a carload of cock, not the pussy-parade."

Logan chuckles, "Stay alert anyway."

We climb out of the car and make our way over to the group. Clara slides her butt off the hood to meet us, and her entourage of four skanks move in closer to her.

"Mila, is this really necessary?" Clara gestures toward my friends. "I was hoping for a civil discussion."

"It will be. They're here for the same reason you brought club pussy—because you're not stupid."

She sighs but concedes. The girl on the end shifts, drawing my gaze toward her. Her blue eyes darken lustfully as she ogles Logan. "I'm more than just pussy. I can give you the ride of your life."

"You can try," Roxy sneers, glaring at her dangerously. "But if you lay one fuckin' finger on any part of him, I'll ride you all the way to Hell."

Taking a step back, blue-eyed slut pouts. Rolling my eyes, I turn back to Clara. "Does Levi have Slade?"

She smiles, "I always liked your straightforward approach. When you first arrived, you told me you wanted out. And look," she thrusts a hand toward me, "you're free."

"I'm not entirely free, but you already know that. I didn't come here for a trip down memory lane. I came as a courtesy because you helped me while I was trapped with your son and because I thought you might have information about Slade. If you want to waste my time, we can leave."

She winces apologetically. "Sorry. I don't get out much. Mika tightened my chains when you left. Fear does strange things to a man." Her eyes turn mournful. "They do strange things to my son."

"He took Slade?" I question again.

She nods, clasping her hands together. "He did. He has him at the complex. He wants to draw you out of hiding and knows you'd come for your son. I came to ask you to spare my son's life."

I narrow my eyes at her plea. "Levi won't stop. You understand that, right? He'll keep coming. It's been over four years since I left, and he still won't give up."

"I know, but he's my son. Do what you want to Mika. God knows that man deserves to rot in Hell, but I don't want to lose my son."

I shake my head, "You're asking me to only be able to provide a half-life to my son. He doesn't leave the house; he's being home-schooled and doesn't have friends. I've been hiding him this entire time, and it was for nothing."

"Not necessarily."

I pause before asking, "Then what are you asking me to do?"

"I asked you to spare his life. I don't care how you do that. You can rip him from his throne for all I care. That club is poison."

"It's not just the club, Clara. It's the people that control it. There are few good people in that group." *Kage is one of them.*

"I know what I'm asking of you is unfair. I know my son put you through hell. Still is. But he's my child, and I can't watch him die."

"How will I get Slade back?"

She gives me a pointed look. "You probably already have a plan in place. I might've been stuck with brain-dead men for over twenty years, but I know you, and you don't sit pretty and wait."

"Is he okay?"

"Slade?"

"Well I don't give two fucks about Levi, so who else would I be talking about?"

"Kage," she states and I tense up. "Like I said, I'm not stupid. Yes, Slade is fine. Scared but unharmed. Levi knows you won't come peacefully if he hurts him."

I blow out a relieved breath as Ayda growls off to my side, "I swear to God, you fucking touch him again, I'll shove my pretty little knife up your damn snatch!" She steps in front of an older club whore who's been edging closer to Ryder. Her fake boobs threaten to fall out of her too-small shirt, and her stomach hangs over the top of her skirt.

"He looks like he needs a momma," Pudgy winks at Ry.

He blanches and scowls at her. "Hard pass." He wraps an arm around a pissed-off Ayda's waist and brings her back into his chest. Ryder's face is a little green as he uses his fianceé as a human shield. When Pudgy licks her red lips, I swear he's going to hurl.

"My ass is tight, baby. You can have a taste." Pudgy licks her lips again, and my own stomach rolls uncomfortably.

Lightning fast, Ayda shoves out of Ryder's arms and draws her dagger from her thigh sheath. Pudgy blinks, and the blade is pressed against her throat. "Say it again. Give me a fucking reason to slit you from throat to twat, right now."

"Get off me!" Pudgy shrieks.

"Keep your slimy fucking thoughts to yourself. You so much as *look* at him again, you won't even know I've cut you until you breathe your last breath." Ayda shoves her over so hard, I swear her ass bounces a few times on the concrete. Then she spins toward the blue-eyed-slut, who also had been sidling a little toward Logan on my other side, and points the dagger in her direction. "You think I'm scary, you keep moving toward him, and she," she nods toward Roxy, "won't even fucking warn you."

Blue-eyes freezes, her eyes flicking to Roxy, who spears her with a death-glare. It's enough to send the skank stumbling back, fearfully eyeing the weapon Roxy has clutched in her grasp.

"I'm asking one mother to another," Clara pleads, bringing my attention back to her. "Spare his life. How you do that is up to you, but I can't watch my son die."

She and I are a lot alike. Both of us have made sacrifices for our children. She stayed in a loveless marriage, being treated like shit, for her son. She's never asked me for a single thing, yet she helped me for years in the small ways she could.

Maybe she knew I'd get out, and it was an investment on her part in case this happened. I don't know, but Clara isn't the problem here, and I'm finding it difficult to hate her for asking me this. If the situation was reversed, I'd do the same thing.

"I can't make promises," I state honestly, and her whole body deflates as sadness weighs her down. "But if I can, I will. I know you're only trying to protect your son, but I have to protect mine as well. Slade is innocent in all of this, unlike Levi. If it comes down to a choice between saving one or the other, I will always choose my son."

Her teary gaze stares at me with understanding. "I had to try."

My heart skips at the fear and grief this woman feels. Reaching out, I take her hand. "I will try, I promise. But only for your sake, not his."

"Thank you."

30

GARRETT

I'VE BEEN STARING at the phone for hours. I called Mom and listened as she apologized a million times, but I'm just not ready to forgive her. I wouldn't have called her at all, except for the fact that Slade's missing.

My son is missing.

The words don't feel real. After the shock wore off, and reality trickled in, I realized how right they sounded, but I still have to wrap my head around it. None of it feels real yet.

Not Mila being sold. Not Romeo being her husband. Not the fucking hell she lived in. None of it.

But it is. Instead of taking time to process it all, I'm thrown into the worst situation imaginable. My son's been taken by a damn psycho who happens to be my girlfriend's husband.

I click the power button on my phone, and the screen lights up, showing me no notifications. I called Mom; she was supposed to confirm Dad agreed to tomorrow. I'm on edge because if he refuses to meet with me, we have to go to Plan B. I may need space from Mila, but there's no way I want her handing herself in to her damn husband.

Plan B has so many holes and uncertainties in it that it makes my skin crawl. There's no guarantee that she'll be able to contact us once he has her. There's absolutely no guarantee he will even let her near Slade. There are no guarantees at all.

She'll be a sitting fuckin' duck, and I will be out of reach.

Tobias lifts his head, his ears pricked up, and a low growl vibrates in his chest. Frowning, I follow his line of sight just as there's a knock at my front door. Standing, I give him a quick pat and head to the door.

I peek through the peephole, and my confusion heightens. Swinging the door wide, I step aside to let Scott in.

"You got time to talk?" he asks, scanning the room. "You're definitely a military brat, huh?" he chuckles. "It's so clean in here, you make me wanna throw something on the floor, just to see what you'd do."

"Make you pick it the fuck up. Just like a normal person would if someone purposely threw something on the ground," I growl. "Is there a reason for your visit, or did you just want to nitpick my habits?"

Smiling, he moves toward the couch, drops down onto the cushions, and props up his dirty-ass feet on the coffee table. Tobias takes it as an invitation and props his head on Scott's lap for a scratch. "I want to have a chat," he grins, his fingers getting Tobias' sweet spot behind his ear. I glare at the traitor, but he just adverts his eyes and ignores me.

I turn my attention back to Scott. "Like the pep-talks you gave to Logan and Ryder when they started their relationships with the girls? No offense, but I don't need advice," I state wryly.

"Nope. Not like that. I'm pretty sure there isn't much I could say that you don't already know. Mila does a good job at expressing herself, and you have a keen eye. Not a lot gets past you, but I did want to make sure you're prepared."

"Prepared for what?"

"Plan B." His initial teasing vanishes, replaced with leveled seriousness.

I swallow thickly. "We don't know that Plan A won't work."

"But we *can* assume your father is the same person he's always been."

"What are you saying? That we should just aim for Plan B anyway? Without even trying?"

"No. I'm saying that the likelihood that Plan A will work is slim. You're strategically-minded, trained to look at this from every angle, so you know what I am saying is true."

I don't want to think about it, but he's right. The chances of getting my dad to talk and help Mila are poor. He sent her away, paid some asshole to marry her and never looked back. He won't care that his grandson is in danger.

"I have to try," I croak. "Sending her back there feels like giving up. I lost her once. I can't lose her again."

"You didn't lose her. You were separated, yes. But losing her implies she died or something, and she's very much alive."

"What if sending her back is as good as killing her? What if he blackmails her with something? Or does something so horrible that it breaks her? I can't help her if I'm not there."

"Do you know why I chose these women for this team?" He leans forward, resting his elbows on his knees.

"Because they're skilled?" I choose the obvious answer, not voicing my opinion that these women are crazy too. Beautifully crazy, though.

"That too," he grins. "Women are supposed to be emotional creatures, drama queens or whatever other label we men like to tape to them, when all it is, is being better at communication. They feel it, and make sure everyone knows about it. Men typically hide what they're feeling because society says that's what a man should do."

"So you work with them because they express their emotions?" My face pinches in confusion.

He snickers, "Shark week is a bitch. But yes, sort of. They latch onto feelings and are much harder to sway. In particular, these girls have a strong sense of will. Material things don't matter to them; loyalty and family do. They don't care about money or diamonds. They can't be wooed or flattered into compromising their beliefs."

"So, you're saying I need to trust Mila and her strong will?"

"You shouldn't be worried about her being caught in some blackmail game or being persuaded. That girl is fucking loud as shit and will not sit and take a hit without reprisal. The damn ground could collapse from under her, and she'd still stand strong." He sighs, "I know you don't want to hear this, but she did this before you came back into her life. She fought and won. She isn't a victim."

"I'm not the kind of guy that would stand aside and watch while she fights."

"And she isn't the girl that cries to Daddy when she finds a bug in her hair," he retorts. "Support her. Trust her."

"I do."

"Then you need to let her do this. She needs to go in there with a clear mind, not worried about you and what you'll do."

That's the crux of my dilemma. I don't doubt Mila's abilities. I'm just scared. I'm scared for my son and the girl I've loved for half my life. Mila can see that; she knows me. I'd never send a man into enemy territory with a clouded mind, yet I'm probably doing that to her.

"She spoke to you?" I ask.

"Nope, but she doesn't really need to. Two people owned her heart when she arrived. Those two people are pulling it in separate directions now. Erase that choice. Help her."

I nod in agreement.

"Good man." He stands and Tobias huffs his disapproval. Scott claps me on the back. "You're good for her. And I approve."

"Thanks," I scowl.

"Sorry 'bout the dirt," he snarks, laughing as he goes to let himself out of the apartment.

Clumps of dirt stick to the white tile at my feet, not to mention the bits of grass and shit on the coffee table. "You're an asshole."

"Just preparing you for kids. Spawns are messy," he grins before closing the door behind him.

I walk to the kitchen and grab the dustpan and broom. Sweeping up the mess, I smile. I don't know why, but his statement made me happy. Imagining life here with Slade. I've been so caught up in everything that's been going on, I didn't stop to think what it would be like to be a family.

I didn't realize that Mila gave me the most priceless gift of all.

I dump the dirt into the trash, toss the broom and pan into the corner, grab my keys and phone, and shove them into my pocket. I call Tobias and he runs in my direction and out the door. Then I lock the apartment door behind me.

31

MILA

I've barely walked into my apartment and taken my shoes off, when my door reopens, and Garrett walks in, Tobias hot on his heels. Tobias heads straight for his bed by the sofa, while I do nothing but stare at the man in front of me.

"I was wrong. I shouldn't—" He pauses and takes in my state of dress. "Did you go out?"

I nod nervously.

"Where?" he frowns.

"Don't be mad."

He snorts, "Well, starting the conversation like that is a sure way to make me think I'm about to get mad."

I smile like a love-sick puppy. "I went to see Clara."

"Romero?"

"Yes, and before you get mad, I didn't go alone. I took Roxy and Ayda and their guys."

His lips thin with disapproval. "You forget to add me to your list?"

"No. I thought if you came, she wouldn't be as straightforward with me."

He sighs, "Okay. And what happened?"

"She confirmed Levi has Slade."

"We already figured that."

"I know." I bite my lip, knowing he'll hate this part. "She also wanted to ask me to spare Levi's life."

"You told her to go to hell, right?" he asks incredulously. I glance away, and he continues, "For the love of Christ, are you serious? You told her you would?"

"Clara helped me, Rett. She's a mother, same as me, and if I was in her position, I'd make the same request."

"Our son will never be like Levi," he growls.

Walking forward I press my palm to his chest and feel his racing heart beneath my palm. "I know. But it isn't her fault he's like that. She's trapped in that place and sacrificed a lot. She stays for *her* son. Monster or not, he's still her child."

He stares at me, his eyes reaching into my soul and latching onto it. The bone-deep connection between us flares and zaps like electricity. He isn't touching me, yet I feel him surrounding me, affecting every inch of me.

I thought my secrets would leave us floundering, that they'd create a rift between us that we wouldn't be able to cross. But he's stayed true to his word. His love is unshakeable, a solid foundation I crave in my life, and I am so thankful for him.

I will never deserve him, but I'm done fighting this.

"I love you, Mike," I whisper, overwhelmed by how much I feel for him.

His hands frame my face as he steps in closer, his eyes drilling into mine with so much power and intensity. "Don't ever keep anything from me again."

I shake my head in his hold, "Never. I promise."

"I live for you baby. I always have. Ésta vida es mía. Pero ésta corazón es tuyo," he whispers. *This life is mine. But this heart is yours.*

"Mi corazón siempre fue tuyo. Cada segundo de cada día," I promise. *My heart was always yours. Every second of every day.*

His lips brush against mine softly, barely a whisper against my skin, but they send a rushing current over my skin.

"Te amo, Ana."

I groan as he presses his lips harder against mine, taking the kiss from gentle to positively indecent in a single swipe of his tongue. His fingers thread through my hair and grip, tugging my head back, and I love this aspect of him.

He gives me the freedom I need, but when we're intimate, he takes control. He forces my body and mind to stop and surrender to him, to his body, the way I need to. I've been touched by other men, but I never gave them this.

I've never surrendered like I do with Rett. I didn't want to because it's always been just for him. He's the only one because he is mine just as much as I am his.

I pout when he pulls away, but it morphs into a smile when he grabs my ass to lift me up and wrap my legs around his waist.

He carries me to the bedroom and gently lays me on the bed, hovering over me. He brushes my hair away from my eyes tenderly before claiming me with another searing kiss. My hands slide over his muscles, and my core clenches with need. His tongue slides against mine before he changes it up and bites my lip.

Ooh. Rett's a biter.

I tilt my head back as his lips kiss down the column of my neck, and my insides pulse and ache to be filled by him. Pinching the front zipper on my top, he drags it down slowly, and I feel every ridged tooth as he undoes it. By the time my top falls open, I'm panting and ready to beg.

I grab the bottom of his shirt and pull it over his head as he watches me with potent desire, his military tags dangling from his neck. Grabbing the chain, I pull his mouth down to mine to kiss, lick, and bite at one another. His hand slides over my breast, skating along the soft skin of my abdomen, and finding the button of my jeans.

His hands shake with his need as he flicks it open and slides the zipper down. Sitting up, he grabs the sides of my jeans and panties, pulls them off, and tosses them to the floor.

I watch him with hooded eyes as he gets up and does the same with his own, releasing his magnificent cock. I lick my lips, salivating over how fucking amazing his body is. Rippled abs, eight if you're counting, framed by the perfect V pointing to what I want most.

His thigh muscles flex as he moves back toward the bed. He keeps his eyes on me as he crawls over the top of me to press his cock against my core. It pulses against me with promise while his eyes devour my every emotion.

"This is it, baby. This is forever." His lips brush over mine as he speaks.

"You have me. You always did. We are forever until every last star in the galaxy dies."

He thrusts, sliding inside me with ease, sealing our promise to each other. He kisses me, swallowing my pleasured moans. Every stroke of his cock is tender, loving almost, but potent just the same. Electricity skitters everywhere under my skin until my whole body ignites.

He grinds against my clit until I see stars, his lips showering me in kisses and promises of our future. He grunts in his own pleasure, his momentum picking up speed.

"This is us, baby," he whispers as his lips trail down my neck. His teeth sink into my skin, branding it and my pussy constricts around him in pulses.

Gripping his hair, I pull and bring his eyes back to mine. "Come with me," I pant. I need to feel this with him.

Reaching down, he grips my knee and pulls it up to my chest. I almost arch off the bed as the new angle brings him deeper, ramping up my pleasure to delicious heights.

"Come, baby." He kisses me, swallowing pleas.

Each thrust becomes harder as his cock swells and grows inside me, hitting me right where I need him.

"Rett!" I scream, ripping my lips from his. "Fuck!"

His teeth sink into my neck again, and I explode. Warmth rushes out of my pussy as it pulses with tidal waves of pleasure. He grunts, his teeth still pressed into my skin, sending another rolling wave of euphoria over me.

His cock throbs inside me, pulsing jets of warmth over and over. His chest heaves, and his heart races in time with mine. He presses gentle lips against my bitten skin, soothing the sting, then kisses me, silently telling me how much he loves and treasures me.

This is how it should've been. The first time we made love when we reunited should've been without secrets. There shouldn't have been anything between us. I understand my mistakes now.

I snuggle into his side, content to just lie next to him in silence.

But, for once, he isn't. "We need to talk about Plan B."

Turning, I press a kiss against his chest. "I know you don't like it, but it might be our only option."

His chest rises and falls as he takes a deep breath before speaking. "I know, which is why I want you to know that I believe in you." A little stunned, I lift myself up on my elbow and stare at him, and he continues. "I'm not saying that it doesn't scare the shit out of me that you're going in there alone, but I have faith that you know what you're doing. If Plan B happens, I trust you."

I press a kiss to his lips. "Thank you. You can trust me. For a long time, I didn't know if fighting for you was worth it." He winces, and I smile. "I was wrong. I won't just fight, Rett. I'm ready to go to war. Nothing will stop me from getting our son out of there, and nothing will stop me from coming back to you."

"If you don't come out of there, I'm going in. I walked away once, baby, but I won't do that again. I'll burn down the entire fuckin' city if that's what I need to do."

"I know. I've never doubted you."

"About Slade..." he starts.

"Hmm?"

"How will he know who to run to? You said you'll send him out to me, but how will he know I'm the one he needs to run to and not from?"

I grimace a little. "He knows who you are."

The color drains from his face. "What?"

Sitting up, I wrap the sheet around my naked body. "I never hid you from him. He knows who you are and what you look like. He even knows you've been working with me. In fact, the picture he has is one I took while you were in the gym downstairs."

I smile, but Garrett doesn't return it, his face full of pain and guilt. "Does he think I abandoned him?"

"What?" I frown before clarifying the situation for him. "No. No way. He knows I'm the one that never told you, I swear. We spoke about when I was going to let you know. He knows this is on me, Rett, not you. I promise he knows the whole truth. He's always known, even when he was a baby and stayed with Greg. He knows who his daddy is, and he doesn't think you abandoned him."

"Jesus." He shifts against the headboard and squeezes his eyes closed. I watch silently as he processes this new information. After a while, a smile spreads across his lips. "Daddy. That sounds weird, right?"

"Well, he calls you Papa."

"Still weird."

I giggle, "It's totally weird, but adorable."

"He speaks Spanish?"

I nod, feeling a proud smile tug at my cheeks. "He does. He's been learning from Mama. His teacher helps, too."

"His teacher? He goes to school?"

I chew on my lip. "Not exactly. We couldn't risk it. But Scott and I found a tutor, and Blair did a full background check. She's really good with him, and it helps that he's naturally smart. Her name is Miss Livi. I can introduce you, if you like."

His eyes, filled with worry, come to mine. "Can we do one thing at a time? I want to meet my son first, and then we can move onto the other stuff."

Nodding, I smile and lay back down on his chest, and his arms automatically wrap around me. "Don't worry. He loves you already. Just like I love you."

His lips press against the top of my head. "I love you too."

32

GARRETT

MOM IS DRESSED like she's going to Sunday brunch at the country club. It annoys me, but some things never change. The world could be imploding, and she'll still want to find her pearls. She moves around the room, straightening furniture and fluffing pillows.

Years of being married to an OCD drunk have left their scars. She used to say it was the military that created that side of him. She might be partly correct. I hate mess, but I'm not arrogant about it. If I want cleanliness, that's on me. I'll clean it.

"Mom, sit down," I snap and instantly regret it when she jumps ten feet in the air. I lower my voice as I continue, "It's fine. The house is fine. He doesn't live here anymore. You can have a pillow facing the wrong way if you want."

"Habits," she mutters before taking a seat.

I glance towards the kitchen at Mila who sits perched on top of a stool at the breakfast bar. She winks and smiles in my direction, spiking my heart rate with joy.

I'm so lovesick, it's not even funny.

Now that our relationship is solid again, we need to get our son back. If we hadn't fixed us first, I honestly don't think we'd have been able to work together to get our son back.

We agreed that she'd stay hidden until after my father was in the house. Her presence might spook him enough that he'd leave. We have less chance of that after he's settled in a little. That's mom's and my job: play the part, make him comfortable, and get him inside the living room.

Mom startles when the doorbell rings, and she turns to me with worried eyes.

"It'll be fine. Give him coffee and cake. I'll do the talking," I reassure her as the new housekeeper answers the door.

Dressed in a dark navy suit, he saunters in the room like he still owns the place. He runs his gaze over the furniture and photos, his face twisting in disgust. "Don't you clean for your guests?"

"Only the important ones," I state defensively.

"I see your manners haven't improved since leaving the military."

I shrug, brushing off his insult. "I see your new trophy wife has done nothing for your personality."

"Coffee?" Mom asks, trying to dispel the tension.

"Thought you'd have had it ready by now," he snarls, taking a seat in the single brown leather chair.

"Oh, she did. She was just waiting for me," Mila chirps, coming in the same way he did.

Her position in the room blocks him from leaving, and in my position, I block the only other way out of the room.

He stares at my girl in utter shock, his mouth opening and closing, but no words come out.

She tilts her head to the side. "What's wrong? Nothing to say now?"

"What is this?" he stutters out, blanching.

"These are the consequences," she spits at him.

He turns to me and rushes out, "You can't believe a word she says. She left you! Claimed she loved you and fucking left!"

"With my son," I growl.

"She *says* he's your son," he argues, and my blood heats with anger.

"He *is* Garrett's son. You're confusing me with my slutty sister, Anthony," Mila challenges.

"If you're smart, you'd stop playing games. I know what you are doing, and it isn't going to work. I didn't believe you then, and I don't believe you now," I snarl.

"Fine, he's your son, but she still left. Son, a woman in love doesn't just leave you."

"Stop!" Mom yells, startling all of us. "Just stop. You sold that poor girl to a monster. You blackmailed her mother into signing the consent forms. Stop lying, for Christ's sake!"

"How dare you!" he roars, jumping to his feet, face reddened with anger.

I move, flying out of my seat, but a distinctive *click* tells me I don't need to.

"Hit her. I dare you. Give me one tiny reason to blow your brains out," Mila challenges, Glock pointed straight at him.

She stares at him, unmoving, hands steady and waiting. He turns slowly in her direction, hands up and panicked eyes on the barrel of the gun.

"Not a little girl anymore, huh?" She shifts the gun, indicating the chair he just vacated. "Sit."

He moves slowly toward the chair before lowering himself into it. "What do you want?"

"We need you to speak to your friend Mika," I supply.

"He has our son. We want him back, unharmed," Mila adds, keeping the gun trained on my father.

"We aren't friends anymore," Dad says calmly.

"So those aren't your guns he's purchasing?" Mila snarks.

"They are," Dad nods, a smile spreading across his face.

Mila's wide eyes come to mine, and that's when I hear the thunderous roar of motorcycle engines getting closer, telling me that our plan was fucked from the beginning.

"You knew, didn't you?" I snap at my father.

"He contacted me yesterday about an hour before you did and informed me that they had Sam."

"Slade," I growl dangerously.

"'Bastard' is better, don't you think?"

Mila slams the butt of her gun on his head, knocking him the fuck out. She tosses the Glock in my direction, and I catch it by reflex.

She hurriedly pulls her shirt from her jeans as I move to the window. Four bikes turn onto the street, followed by a sedan. The sound of ripping material has my head turning back to Mila.

"What are you doing?" I shout.

She has her shirt, now ripped clean up the middle, twisted into a knot below her breasts. The black lace of her bra peeks out and screams for attention.

My dick, ignoring the fact that we're in danger, springs to life in my pants.

"There isn't time," she urges, pulling her hair from her ponytail and letting it fall in soft waves around her face.

"What do you mean? What the fuck are you doing?" I say, alarmed.

"We have to go to Plan B." She walks to the window as the riders pull up in front of the house and kill the engines.

That's when I realize what she's doing. She is getting herself ready for him. "No."

"Rett, we talked about this." She steps away from the window and turns to me. "We always knew this was a possibility."

"Not like this. You have no tracker on you. Nothing. This isn't what we planned."

"It's how we have to do it." Rushing over to me, she grips my face. "Trust me, okay? Please?"

My brain scrambles, searching for a different way, but I can't see one. As I stare into her exotic brown eyes, I see a confidence there that never existed the last time she was in this house. I don't have a choice. I have to trust her.

Seeing my resignation, she presses up onto her toes and brushes her lips against mine. "Whatever happens, you can't help me. Stand down, soldier. Trust in me. Te amo."

"I love you, too." I press a hard kiss to her mouth, and she pushes away from me just as the front door bursts open.

Cocking her hip, she smiles as Romeo walks into the room. "Hi, husband. Did you miss me?"

Her eyes flick quickly to the man beside Levi before going back to her husband. The man watches her, but not with the same disdain as the other men. His eyes reflect sorrow and longing. This must be her *friend.*

Fuck!

Levi charges in her direction and smacks a hand across her face. "Fucking bitch! Do you have any idea what you did?"

My entire body shakes with rage. The only thing that's holding me back is the smile she has on her beautiful face.

"I'm sure you found another pussy to shove your dick into," she croons cruelly.

Gripping her throat, he leverages her off the floor. Her eyes flick to mine, pleading with me to stay where I am.

"Ah, Michaels. So nice of you to join us," Levi says as he notices me for the first time. "Did you keep her cunt warm for me?" He buries his face in her tits and bites until she cries out.

Movement in the corner of my eyes catches my attention as the guy with light-brown hair clenches his fist and takes a single step toward them.

My eyes flick between him and Mila. She gives him the same look she gave me, silently warning him to stay out of it. He drops his head and squeezes his eyes closed. That's when I know he's in love with her.

"Where's Slade?" Mila's jaw ticks with hatred as she stares at her husband.

"Safe, provided you do as you're told," he smiles, like half-choking my girl is a fucking walk in the park.

He releases her, and she drops to the ground. Turning to the men behind him, he orders them to take her. As they advance on her, a vise clamps down on my heart. Then I see her eyes, shielded by the thick curtain of her hair. She silently mouths that she loves me.

"She's mine," Levi growls from the doorway, his eyes flinty and trained on me. "She was never yours, rich boy. She's Chaplain property."

He disappears through the front door, though I can see him waiting from where I'm standing. I watch as three men lift my girl as she claws at them and screams for them to let her go. They carry her through the living room, past the man that loves my girl, and out the front door.

Her *friend* follows them, touching the vase with my mother's prized roses, before slipping out the door, and I watch my girl disappear from my life for a second time.

I rush to the window just in time to see them close the back door to the black sedan. The bikes roar to life, and in a matter of seconds, they're gone.

My heart squeezes painfully in my chest, and I pray to God that someone keeps her safe for me. She isn't alone this time. This time, she has an army coming for her.

My eyes flick to the vase and frown. Walking over, I grab a black device that was tucked out of sight behind it and roll it over in my palm.

A burner phone.

I cling to the phone like a lifeline. I have no idea who that guy is, and I'm not particularly excited about the fact that he's in love with *my girl,* but he seems to want to help her. I can only hope that he can.

Pulling my own phone from my pocket, I press dial and bring the phone to my ear. I grit my teeth when Mom's sobbing becomes louder. She's been in the corner, crying this entire time. She has no right to be upset, and I have no desire to comfort her. She could've stopped this years ago. She can swim in her guilt; it's the least she deserves.

The 9-1-1 line connects, and I quickly give them the address and request the police. After I hang up, I dial Scott.

"Michaels?"

"Plan B has been executed," I mutter, my heart pounding with each syllable I say.

"What happened?" His voice becomes urgent, and I can hear him moving around.

"Levi showed up at the meeting. He knew we'd be here. It was a trap. We had no other choice. She's gone." My voice cracks on the last sentence, reflecting the pain inside my chest.

"Get back here. I'll call everyone. We'll get her back, I promise."

"Slade too," I add.

"Slade too. Both she and your son are strong. Have faith. I'll see you soon."

I glance at my father slumped in the chair. "I have something to take care of first, but I'll leave here as soon as it's done."

"Anything I can do?" he asks.

"No, I got it."

I hang up and walk over to my father. Digging through his pockets, I locate his phone. I press his finger against the sensor to unlock it. Scrolling through his settings, I turn the locking option off before shoving the phone in my pocket along with the burner phone.

"What are you going to do?" Mom whispers, her voice thick with tears.

"I called the police. He's selling and distributing guns illegally. I'm sending the asshole to jail."

"Is that wise?"

I turn the full force of my rage towards my mother. "Wise? He sold the only girl I ever loved. He took away my child before I even knew he existed. Then, when I needed his help getting Slade back, he fucking ripped my girl away from me all over again!" My teeth are clenched so hard, I swear I hear a tooth crack.

"She's no good for you, and that bastard doesn't deserve my name!" my father mutters as he's regaining consciousness.

My hands clench at my sides as my blood boils. I turn around to find him staring at me, clutching at his head. "It's my name, too," I growl, barely holding my anger at bay.

"If you wanted a pussy to fuck, I would've supplied you one. One that didn't come with a fuckin' child!" he shouts, and I snap, losing the precarious hold I had on my anger.

Grabbing his shirt, I lift him off his feet. "You're going to rot in fucking jail. You'll be a cheap hole other men fuck on lonely nights. I hope they rape you. That's what you deserve for giving Mila to a monster. He raped her, made her life hell. I had to stand here and watch him manhandle her and take her from me. I told you, I fucking warned you, if I found out, I'd destroy you. I'm going to make sure you spend the rest of your pathetic life behind bars like the animal you are."

I shove him away from me, disgusted that this pig shares genes with me, and he lands back in the chair, rocking it back dangerously.

"You aren't a cop. You can't arrest me," he challenges. "You have no proof!"

"I might not be with the police, but I am a military man. I'm a fucking Ranger. My word has weight. I'd be willing to bet your phone has some interesting information on it and that all your paperwork in your organized office will have even more," I smirk.

He fumbles in his pockets, and when he comes up empty, his narrowed gaze comes to mine. "You!"

He launches his body out of the chair and in my direction. Clenching my fist I viciously slam it into his face. "Sit the fuck down," I growl.

He groans, trying to shake off my hit. "You can't do this!"

I brace my hands on the arms of the chair and shove my face in his. "I can, and I will. Happily. Are you proud now? Your military son is finally accepting his duty," I spit out at him.

Fists pound against the door, and his eyes turn fearful. Standing, I move toward the entrance. "Do you want money? I'll give you whatever you want!" he pleads, and it grinds down my spine.

"Everything I ever wanted, you took from me. You have nothing left I want." I swing open the front door and let the cops in. "He's over there. Possession and distribution of firearms," I state.

"And you are?" The first officer asks, clearly hesitant.

"I'm his son," I supply. Turning to my father, I smile and add, "Staff Sergeant Garrett Michaels of the Army Rangers and recently retired from Alpha Team."

"My apologies, sir," he says. Then, turning to the rest of his team, he nods. "Arrest him."

33

MILA

THE ROAR of motorcycles sends shards of ice through my blood as we travel back to the complex. Memories I had long pushed into the recess of my mind hit me with renewed vigor. I ride, and Roxy's always on Widow, her motorcycle. But they aren't Harleys, and the riders aren't Chaplains. Levi says nothing as he sits beside me, silently stewing in anger, no doubt.

"Where's my son?" I snarl.

His hand whips out and cracks across my face. My skin burns as dots float across my vision. "Don't you EVER disgrace me again, you fuckin' bitch! How dare you do that to me?"

I bark out a forced laugh, "Do that to you? What about everything you've done to me? And you want respect? Fuck off, Levi!"

He raises his hand again, but I'm ready for it this time. Grabbing his wrist, I block his strike and pound my fist into his face. With a roar, he unbuckles his seat belt and lunges for me. He pins me against the car door and wraps my own seat belt around my throat. The material pinches my skin and restricts my airway.

His seething face fills my vision. "You're a damn whore. That's it, that's all you'll ever be good for. A nice pussy to fuck. Did you fuck him?" He tightens the belt, and waves roar in my ears as my eyes start to lose focus. "Did Garrett touch what belongs to me?"

I sputter, unable to breathe. I try to swallow, but I can't force the spit down my throat.

His hand slaps against my vagina and squeezes, sending stinging pain through my pussy. "I can't wait to fuck him out of your mind. I'm going to destroy this cunt, like your bastard son destroyed it for me."

My eyes shutter and my limbs grow heavy from the lack of oxygen. When he slaps me again, I barely register the pain as my head flops to the side.

Then the solid support at my back vanishes, and I'm free-falling.

"Fuck!" I hear a man's voice distantly as arms catch me before I hit the ground. I know his voice. I remember it.

Kage.

"Get your fucking hands off her!" Levi roars as my blood rushes to my head and makes me dizzy.

"She can't fucking stand, Romero," Kage growls. "You almost killed her. Give her a second."

"I'm okay." I pat his chest lethargically. "Put me down."

His lips thin, but he does as I ask. My feet touch the gravel, and I wobble slightly before getting my bearings. Pain slices through my cheek again, and I hit the ground, crying out as gravel bites into my skin.

"Don't you dare help her, Daniels." Levi commands.

Slowly, I struggle to my feet, almost collapsing a few times before I eventually stand. Levi is glaring at Kage as they have a silent stand-off.

"Where's Slade?" I whisper. "Please, just let me see him."

Levi shoves Kage away before turning his attention back to me. "Strip," he snarls.

I narrow my gaze, but do as he asks. I knew I'd have to. The men crowd around as I begin pulling my clothes off. I watch Kage's jaw tick and hands clench in anger out of the corner of my eye. He doesn't watch though, his eyes focusing on the ground in front of him, offering me a tiny sliver of privacy.

The other men don't. They lick their lips and make lewd gestures with their hips. Their eyes swallow me up and refuse to spit me out again. Levi laughs, clearly enjoying his games.

That's all this is, a game, just like Clara said from the beginning. Levi thinks I'm embarrassed, and this is his sick way of trying to dominate me. But I have no shame in my nakedness. I don't care what these men think.

It doesn't matter to me if they find me sexy or hideous. Either way, not a single one of them will touch me. The only person that gets to decide if I am sexy or whatever, is me.

When I stand in front of them in nothing but panties and a bra, I fold my arms and raise a brow in question. Levi's smirk drops from his face as his eyes focus on someone behind me.

"I see your wife has returned, son," Mika's voice skates down my spine, like nails on a chalkboard. "Perhaps you can hold on to her this time."

A warm palm slides over my butt cheek before Mika moves to stand in front of me. "I believe we have something of yours," he states, staring at my boobs. "Daniels, take her to her room in my house."

"Your house?" I question suspiciously.

He leans forward pressing his nose against my ear. "Mmmm. Seems you need to learn a lesson from a real man, seeing as my son failed. You and your brat will spend some time with me and Clara. Perhaps my wife can show you how a real old lady behaves, and I can show you what happens when they don't." He slaps my ass and nods to Kage.

I narrow my eyes at Mika as Kage grabs my arm and starts dragging me away. "Cool it, Mila. Now isn't the time," Kage whispers through clenched teeth.

Levi steps up beside his father, his face red with barely contained fury. I bite back my grin. Kage dragging me away pisses him off because he doesn't want me anywhere near him, but he can't challenge his father.

We enter the house, and I see not a lot's changed since I left. It's still pretentious and sterile. I hate it. Like his son, Mika has pornographic "art" on the walls. The floors glisten and sparkle enough to make your eyes hurt from the glare.

Leading me to the kitchen, Kage drops my arm. He opens and

closes cupboards until he finds a first-aid kit. Silently, he pulls out antiseptic wipes and tubes of creams.

Guilt claws its way through my body as his silence continues. He's angry, refusing to make eye contact as he cleans my lip and cheek. He checks the cuts to ensure they are thoroughly clean before tossing the used wipes in the trash.

When he starts rubbing aloe cream on the friction burns on my neck and still hasn't said anything, I do. "Say something."

"What's left to say?" he says, his tone short and laced with wounded barbs.

Placing my hand on his wrist, I halt his ministrations. "I had to leave. You knew that I was going to," I whisper.

"I didn't know the night you broke things off was goodbye. You just left. Blew the place up and rode off on the back of a bike. Did I mean that little to you?" He finally looks at me, and parts of me wishes he didn't. His hurt and pain slice at my heart.

I didn't want this. I never wanted to hurt him. "I didn't say goodbye because I couldn't. I do care about you, and saying goodbye would've killed me."

"So you ripped my heart out instead?" There isn't any anger in his words, just sadness.

"I shouldn't have—" I choke on the tightness in my throat. I swallow hard and straighten my spine. "Being with you was selfish. I was never available, and I shouldn't have brought you into this mess. It was selfish. I let you go because you deserve better."

"But not you?" He takes a step back, and my stomach drops. I thought I would have a friend here, but it's clear now it was only wishful thinking. I can't ask this of him.

I look into his tormented eyes and hope he can see how truly sorry I am. "I care about you, I really do. Please don't doubt that. But I'm not your forever girl, Kage. I belonged to someone else before we even met."

"Your ex?" he guesses, and I nod. "He was the one at the house, right? You said you weren't going back to him."

I exhale an exhausted breath, "I wasn't. I didn't. He found me."

"So that's it then? He's it?"

"He was always it. We could just never be together. We're both different now. He knows the truth. All of it."

Kage nods, his throat bobbing as he swallows whatever it is he wants to say. I want to go to him, try and heal some of the hurt I've caused, but it'll only make it worse for him. So I do nothing but stare at the guy that helped me survive, hoping that I'm saving him in the long run.

"Mila?" I spin toward Clara's voice.

"Where's Slade?" I insist, stepping around the counter toward her.

"He's in his room." Her eyes slide to Kage. "I'll take you."

I nod as she begins to leave the room. I turn back to Kage to thank him, but he's already halfway out of the door. My stomach drops, and I realize something. I thought my mistakes were mine to bear alone, but they aren't. They continue to hurt everyone around me, and I hate it.

I follow Clara up the stairs and into another hallway. She seems fidgety, on edge.

I frown, "Are you okay?"

"No. There's been a lot going on since you left that you don't know about. The underground is sectioning off, and Mika believes a war is brewing. That's why they needed you back. They need to project a solid front to the rest of the club and to our enemies, and having a missing wife doesn't do that."

"I've heard something might be happening," I muse.

She stops at the last white door on the left. "This is Slade's room. Yours will be across the hall."

"Thank you."

She nods and leaves. I practically barge my way into the room, startling my son, who screams from his seat on the bed.

His scream dies off as he realizes who it is. "Mama?"

"Baby!"

I rush to his side, and he dissolves into tears. I pick him up and cradle him in my lap. I breathe him in, my heart finally settling after hours of unease. Deep down, I knew that Levi wouldn't hurt him, but I was never one-hundred percent sure. I hold him as tightly as I can and plan my next move.

34

GARRETT

EVERYONE'S HEADS immediately turn in my direction as soon as I enter the meeting room, their worry evident on their anxious faces. I try to block out their concern, though. I have to focus on what I'm able to do right now, and that's to come up with a solid plan.

I need to keep my mind clear so I can get my family out of there.

Ignoring their sympathetic looks and the anger we're all feeling, I move to the front of the room to fill everyone in on the current status. "The meeting with my father was a trap. As of now, my father has been arrested and will be charged." I look at Roxy. "You said you knew the location of the complex?" She nods. "Can we pull it up?"

"Already done." Blair taps away at her tablet, and the screen behind me lights up showing a map.

I stare at it, waiting for someone to say something. When no one does, I growl impatiently, "Does someone want to explain what I'm looking at?"

"Are you okay?" Ayda asks. "I mean, we can see you're not harmed, but you just watched Mila being taken."

I purse my lips at the reminder and search the team's worried gazes. Sighing, I drag a hand through my hair. "Not really. My son and my girl are missing. But I need to do something, not talk about it."

"They aren't missing," Roxy reminds me as she steps forward. "We know where they are."

"The road into the compound is a housing estate for the Chaplain riders and their families. There is one road in and one out. We have to go through the Chaplains's army to get to the main gate," Blair explains, highlighting the direction on the map.

"From there, we have to figure out a way in the main compound," Roxy adds.

"How did you get in last time?" I ask, confused.

"We didn't. Mila opened it from the inside," Charlie supplies. "She had a burner phone and arranged a time with Scott. We were waiting on the outskirts."

I nod, "I have a burner. One of the guys that picked her up earlier hid it in my mother's vase on his way out."

"Why would he do that?" Logan questions suspiciously.

"He must be the guy that helped her last time," Blair supplies.

"Her friend," Roxy nods in acknowledgement.

I snort, "He's in love with her. I'm pretty sure he wants to be more than friends."

"Too bad for him then, huh?" Ayds giggles and I feel my lips twitch.

"Once we're through the gates, you have the main clubhouse," Roxy continues as Blair highlights the building on the screen.

"There are three other buildings on site. Levi's house, Mika's house, and a storage shed," Blair says as she highlights each of the buildings for us.

"Okay, so where would Mila be? Levi's?" Logan asks.

Roxy shakes her head. "Maybe not. There was a lot of uproar surrounding Mila's departure. Levi was disgraced and shamed for not having control over his wife."

"So, what? They'll teach her a lesson?" Austin gasps, and my molars grind.

"Maybe. But I have a feeling that his father might be the one issuing the punishment."

That has my attention. "Why?"

"Because these men are a lot like Lex. They're probably a big part of the syndicate he controlled. When I first met Mila, she recognized me. That was about a month after Ayda and I escaped. Lex would only trust those in his control with that information."

"So Lex went to the Chaplains for help in searching for you?" I ask.

"That's what Mila assumed by the meeting she attended, yes."

Plan B fucking sucks.

"Okay, so if we assume Mila is here," Blair's inserts, highlighting Mika's house, "then she's in the center of the main complex."

"Making it super difficult to get to her," Lucas concludes.

"But not impossible," Scott adds.

"This seems like a suicide mission. It's one way in, one way out. How do we maintain enough of a hold over them to get out without dying?" Austin winces when he looks up and sees four girls and me glaring at him.

"We're going in, no matter what. We're a team, and if you can find your balls, you're welcome to stay home. We will get Mila and Slade out," Roxy snarls. "There is no other option."

Throwing his hands up in surrender, his face paints the picture of innocence. "I was just saying. Sheesh. I got my balls. Don't worry, Mortemous. They might be blue, but they work just fine."

Charlie snorts, "Is your hand broken or somethin'? Jack off like the rest of us. We don't need to hear that shit."

Austin blanches, "Are you filling in for Mila while she's away? If so, my lap's free darlin'. Wanna ride?" He winks, and I slam my hand down on the table, startling them both.

"Are you two done?" When they remain silent, I continue, "What's our next move?"

"My guess is that phone will ring in the next twenty-four hours," Ayda nods towards the burner.

Roxy nods in agreement, "I agree. I think we should wait until we hear from whomever is going to call. If it was her *friend,* then he may offer us a way through we don't know about."

"We might need some help," Logan sighs. "While Austin is being a dick, he has a point." He stares at Roxy, and I know he is worried about losing her.

"I'll be fine," she murmurs her reassurances.

"I don't doubt you, baby, but I think seeking help might be smart here. I know you don't like outside help, but we need to be pragmatic here."

"I might know someone," I announce. "Leave it to me."

"Do you trust them?" Blair questions.

I nod, "With my life."

"Call them," Roxy relents. "In the meantime, we need to figure out how to get in on our own."

"Explosives are out," Austin muses, and I really want to knock him the fuck out.

Then I remember something. "Not necessarily. Mila has a room in her apartment. I'm pretty sure there are some explosive devices already made and stored there. We could use those."

"Nobody knows explosives like she does," Roxy says, frustrated. "We may have them, but we have no one to set them up."

"I do. I know how to rig an explosive. I just need the diagram and design to figure it out. Both are in that room," I answer. My heart pounds with excitement as a plan forms. "We can deploy the same strategy she did last time, right? She used an explosive as a distraction. What if we rigged a series of timed bombs to draw them to one area, away from the front gate?"

"Wouldn't they be expecting that?" Ryder inserts, and I shake my head.

"Not from out there. Mila said it took years for Levi to allow her outside the gates. There's no way he'd allow that this time. So if we set them up outside the main gate in the community of houses, he won't think she set that up."

"He'll think there was an attack," Roxy says as her brain ticks over.

"Exactly. He'll draw the majority of his men to that area."

"Limiting the number of guards on the front gate," Scott finishes.

"What about an exit strategy? He won't fall for the same thing twice," Charlie frowns in thought.

"We won't have any vehicles close by," Logan adds.

"If we're quick enough, he won't have time to draw his men back, and if he does, they will come in waves rather than one massive group," I answer. "If he's smart, he won't dismiss the bombs as random. He'll split the group, sending one part back to the main area while the others stay behind."

"We can handle that many," Austin winks.

Scott looks at me. "We need those explosives. Go and check out her room. Take the phone." Then he turns to the rest of the room. "Everyone keeps their phones on them."

We all nod in agreement.

"This is the plan for now. We'll see what happens when we get that call. Ayda, Roxy? I've ordered a shipment of weapons from Owen. Can you guys pick them up?"

"Fuckin' seriously?" Ryder groans. "Fuckface?"

Ayda jams an elbow into his stomach, and he folds over. "Yeah, we'll go."

"Alone," Roxy adds, staring pointedly at Logan.

"Is there something I should know?" Scott inquires, his gaze bouncing between the four of them.

"No."

"We're going," Logan insists.

Chuckling, Ryder throws an arm over Ayda's shoulder. "Come on. It'll be like old times. I bet Fuckface missed us."

My lips twitch as Ayda and Roxy both groan in unison.

35

MILA

I'M startled awake early the next morning by the stench of whiskey and cigarette-scented breath. I open my eyes to find Mika's face barely an inch from mine. I reflexively strike out and slap him across the face.

His head whips to the side, and a smile spreads across his face. "I always like my women with a little fight in them."

Clutching my chest, I work hard to slow my heart rate. "You like women who beat you? Find me some handcuffs, and I'll give you a real show," I sneer.

"My son thought you were the be all and end all, and I must admit, when I first met you, I didn't think much of you. But at that dinner, you showed a certain finesse that made my dick hard."

"Just what every girl wants to hear. How hard she makes her father-in-law's dick," I retort sarcastically.

"Then you don't wanna hear what that little fight with your sister did to me," he whispers in my ear, and I feel like puking. "I thought you would be easy to tame. Perhaps we chose someone with too much strength. Clara was sassy like you, but once the bitch slipped out a kid, I had the lock and key to her life."

"Good for you. Would you like some perverted award for arrogance? Or would a sandwich suffice?"

He chuckles, "It's going to be fun breaking you. I look forward to it." He stands and does nothing to hide the bulge in his pants. "Stay in here. You do not leave this house."

"Goodie. Can't fucking wait," I roll my eyes and wait for the door to close.

There's no lock on it. I figured that out real quick. I guess they're getting a little smarter. Flipping off the covers, I pad barefoot across the room. Once I check to make sure the coast is clear, I skip through the door and into Slade's room.

Smiling at my sleeping boy, I lift the covers and slide in beside him. He nuzzles into my body and smacks his lips. He reminds me so much of his dad that my heart aches for Rett. I know how worried he is right now. If I could only tell him that our baby's safe, that I'm with him and won't let anything happen to him.

"Mama?" His sleepy voice makes my heart swell inside my chest.

I press a kiss to his hair. "Morning baby. How're you feeling?"

"I want to go home," he whispers sadly.

"I know. Listen to me." I lift his chin and look into his green eyes so he knows I'm serious. "I'm going to get you out, okay? My friends and your dad will help."

"Papa?" His voice is a mix of shock and excitement.

I nod, smiling. "Yeah, Papa knows about you. I told him, and he's very excited to meet you. But we need your help to get out of here."

He sits up a little straighter, instantly fully awake. "Okay. What do I do?"

This beautiful boy has such unshakeable trust. His faith in me keeps me strong, and I love him so much for it. "When the time comes, I need you to run. Your Papa will be waiting for you. Do you remember what he looks like?" He bobs his head up and down, fast. "Good. If I tell you to run, you go out the back of the house and keep running until you find him. Don't stop running until you do. Don't come to the front. Just keep going, and Garrett will find you. Okay?"

"What about you?"

"I'll be right behind you. I just have to help my other friends first."

We both jump, gasping in surprise as a fist pounds against his bedroom door. Swallowing, I press a kiss to his forehead and whisper,

"Stay here, okay? Always in here. I'll come get you when it's time. I love you."

"I love you, Mama."

"Good boy."

Standing, I walk to the door and crack it open. Frowning, I open it fully when I only see Clara standing on the threshold.

"Here." She thrusts out a dress. "Put this on. You're required at a meeting."

Confused, I stare at the black dress. "With whom?"

"His highness," she supplies before walking away.

"Well, that was helpful," I say, muttering to myself as I close the door.

"That's pretty!" Slade exclaims.

"Pretty things come with a price, baby. Turn around."

He does as I ask, and I pull off the night dress that Clara gave me. I slide into the black silk dress. As it slides against my skin, I'm strangely reminded of Garrett's hands. Once the dress is secured, I move to the bed.

"Give me a hug, baby. I gotta go."

Slade turns, his green eyes swimming with worry and fear. "I don't want you to go."

I grip his cheeks and press my forehead to his before speaking to him in Spanish. "I'll be in the house the whole time. If anything happens, scream, baby. I'll hear you, and I'll come running."

"Okay, Mama."

"Be ready, baby. Be ready to run." I press a kiss to his cheek as another knock sounds at the door.

Standing, I smile and try my best to give him strength and reassurance. By the time I get to the door, he's smiling back. I wink at him, open the door, and step out before closing it behind me.

"Should've made her wear yellow. She looks fucking ugly in yellow," Eva sneers as she hangs off Levi's arm.

"Aww, what's wrong, sister? Can't find the right concealer to cover your shit side? Maybe you should try putty," I snark.

"It's your fault I look like this."

"Keep going, and I'll make the other side match," I threaten.

"Enough!" Levi shouts, looking in my direction. "You're wanted downstairs."

Smirking, I move past them and make my way down to the main level and wait for Romeo and Juliet to catch up before I follow them into the living room.

My heart stops. I'm completely rooted to the spot as I stare at the man standing beside Mika.

"Leave!" he orders everyone but doesn't take his eyes off me.

Mika bristles but doesn't say anything as he nods to his son and leaves the room. My heart rate goes from stalled to coronary-inducing palpitations as he waits for them to leave the house.

The front door *snicks* shut before he starts, "Mila Diez. Ghost Team member and my sister's friend, right?" Jake smiles, but it doesn't reach his eyes. The darkness that lingered in his eyes the first time I met him seems to almost drown out the blue of them now.

"What are you doing here? What do you want?"

"I should ask you the same thing," he retorts.

He stares at me with suspicion, but I school my features, not giving anything away. I won't let him ruin this by trying to stop me.

"I wouldn't tell you." I lift my chin defiantly.

"Neither will I. Though, I do have a question." He moves closer, and his partner, Jaxon if I remember correctly, moves with him. "What do you know of Katarina?"

"Why? What's she done now?"

"That's my concern," he snaps. "What do you know?"

"That's my concern," I retort. "I'm not your fuckin' minion or some floozy messenger. You don't get to flick to bear mode and have me bow at your feet. You want information, you tell me why."

He smirks, "I can see why my sister likes you. Fine. I believe she's in talks with people that threaten my territory."

I frown, "I thought she was underground. In the city somewhere."

"She is. Though, we can't get a fix on her location. Turns out, my mother's an elusive woman." My eyes narrow at the faintest layer of pride his words reveal.

"We found camera footage of her and a girl," I admit.

"What girl?"

"Her name's Melanie. She was kidnapped and is being held captive by Katarina. We got the case about a week ago."

"That's all you have?"

I throw my hands up. "Er, yeah. In case you didn't notice, I haven't exactly had much free time."

"What are your plans here?"

"What are yours?" I raise a brow, knowing he won't tell me. He purses his lips, and I nod. "Exactly what I thought."

He nods towards Jaxon, who watches me like he has a million questions. Jake settles his gaze on him for a moment before slowly turning back in my direction. "How are my nieces?"

I rock back in shock. "Why?"

"Curious."

"They're safe, and it needs to stay that way. Don't you dare try and take them, Jake. You won't win. They're happy and trying to move on from their mother's death." I catch Jaxon's wince, and I kind of regret the heartlessness in which I delivered the news. "Their parents are gone. Leave them be."

He stares at me for a long moment, like he has more to say, but then decides better of it. Giving Jaxon a nod, he makes his way out of the house.

Just before Jaxon walks out the door, I step forward and address him quietly. "I'm sorry about Mia. I know she wasn't the best person, but she was a good mom. She saved them. But I am sorry for your loss."

He drops his head for a moment, absorbing my words before he finally looks at me. "I haven't lost everything. Not yet."

With that, he leaves, shutting the door behind him. I stare at it for a long moment and wonder what his story is. He seems more tormented now than he was years ago. But at the same time, there's more clarity in his eyes that wasn't there the last time.

"Hey."

Clutching my chest, a scream lodged in my throat, I spin on my heel. Kage motions for me to come closer. Looking toward the door, I hurry in his direction.

"We don't have much time. They can't find me here," he whispers urgently.

"What's going on?" I react, his urgency putting me on high-alert.

"You need to get out of here. Tonight."

I frown at him. "What? Why? Not that I don't want to get the fuck out of here, but why so urgent?"

"They're going to kill you, Mila." His voice is full of concern and anger. "Your escape enraged them, and Levi wants to make an example of you, so they're going to do it publicly. I assume that's why Jake's here."

Fear slides down my spine and turns my blood to ice. "And Slade?"

He averts his eyes and nods. "People are refusing to support Mika. This is his way of righting the wrongs done to his running of the club. He wants to show them he has control, and to do that—"

"He needs to kill the person that shook it up."

36

GARRETT

I'VE FIGURED out half of the explosives in Mila's arsenal. If I wasn't so impressed, I might actually be worried about the woman that sleeps beside me. They're so intricate and detailed that after ten hours of being in here, I'm only half-way through.

She wasn't joking when she said she likes this shit.

Tobias growls from his position beside the table, and I lift my head from the plans in front of me. I'm sliding out of the chair to stand up just as there's a knock at the front door.

I open it and head back to work as Logan closes the door behind him. Dropping into my chair, I pick up the plans and begin studying them again.

Whistling in amazement, Logan walks in with wide eyes. "Is your girl part terrorist? This is nuts!"

I smirk, "It's kinda scary."

"Remind me not to piss her off."

"Noted."

He grabs a spare chair and takes a seat next to me, looking over my shoulder at the plans. "No call?"

My lips thin, and I shake my head. "Not yet." My eyes fall to the frustratingly silent burner phone on the table.

"Roxy thinks it'll be soon." He leans back, giving up on trying to figure out the schematics and crosses his arms.

"What if she's wrong?" I muse.

He raises a brow. "She might be, but don't say that to her."

I chuckle, remembering the last time Logan tried to tell Roxy she was wrong. It didn't turn out so well for him.

"Look, Roxy isn't always right. But when it comes to this stuff, she is. That's what she does, what Lex trained her to do. Trust her."

"I don't like waiting," I huff out an inpatient breath.

"I get it, I do. When Roxy was kidnapped, I was out of my mind with worry. It doesn't matter that we know they can take care of themselves. It's the unknown, the factors we don't see, that we can't shake. Did you call your friend?"

I nod and put the plans down. "Yeah, they're free. I just need to give them a time and location. I just need that fucking phone to ring."

Tobias whimpers before resting his head on my lap, sensing my distress. I hate feeling in limbo. Memories of Levi hitting her are burned into my brain and play repeatedly. Each time, it sickens me more.

I get it now. I understand where her strength was born, why she isn't the girl I remember. That girl wouldn't have survived. There was no way. But instead of suffering and submitting, she grew her wings and became wild.

Understanding all of that, seeing it with my own two eyes, has allowed me to connect the two completely. I was missing the middle part. I had the beginning and end, but they didn't make sense without the middle.

"Did you get the weapons from Owen?" I ask, deciding to change the subject.

"His name is Fuckface. Just get on board. Ry and I need wingman support on that one. Roxy and Ayda already have enough of a say around here." Logan chuckles.

My lips twitch into a small smile. "What did he do?"

"He's a complete asshole. Ayda and he went on a date before she and Ry happened. Then, this guy wouldn't accept she didn't want him. He started saying she was a cock-tease and shit."

"So Ry punched him?" I guess.

Logan grimaces, "No. Ayda took care of it, but that's not the point. He was rude, and he shouldn't have spoken to Ayds like that."

I nod, "The girls seem to be over it."

"Good for them," he snarks back.

I bark out a laugh, and it feels good. I've been wound tight for hours, so it's nice to have someone else's problems distract me for a moment.

The shrill sound of the burner ringing breaks the good mood, and heaviness comes roaring back in. Fumbling it slightly, I grab the phone and hit the green answer button.

"Hello?" I say, my eyes flicking to Logan sitting silently beside me, watching attentively.

"Michaels?" A deep voice responds, and my heart deflates. I was truly hoping it'd be Mila on the other end of the call.

"Speaking," I answer, doing nothing to hide my disappointment.

"I need you to get Mila out of here tonight."

I sit up straighter, responding to the urgency in his voice. "We're ready, but what's going on?"

The responding silence tells me everything I need to know. I don't know this guy, but I do know a man in love, and he loves her. His urgency and his silence could only imply one thing. They're going to kill her.

I swallow and ask for confirmation, "They're planning to execute her, aren't they?"

"Yes."

"When?"

"Tomorrow night. Slade too."

My body heats with anxiousness and rage. "What do you need me to do?"

"Mila said you know where to go? I'll get her out of the house."

"We need the gates open. I have a team, but the gate will be the biggest challenge," I respond as Logan nods his approval. His gaze is focused, and I know he can hear the entire conversation.

"I can get the gates open, but I can't give you an exact time. These guys don't operate on a schedule."

"That's fine. We'll get into position and wait."

"It has to be tonight. I won't be able to get her out in the light of day."

"We'll be there." I growl, annoyed that he's second-guessing me. This is *my* girl and *my* son.

"I'm counting on it."

The line clicks, and he is gone. My heart pounds inside my chest as I stare at the phone and pray he gets her out safely.

Logan already has his phone to his ear as he begins rounding up the troops. When he hangs up and notices that I still haven't moved, he claps a friendly hand on my shoulder.

I turn to him and voice my single biggest fear, "What if this doesn't work? What if we fail?"

"We start thinking like that, and we *will* fail." Scrubbing a hand through his hair, he sighs, "Look, I'm the last person that's okay with Roxy going into battle, but she's good at what she does. So is every other person on this team. I'm not saying we're invincible because we aren't. But the skill set we have is like no other team I've heard of. You need to have faith in your friends and your girl."

"I do, but this is my family we're talking about," I worry.

"It's their family too. Mila and Slade are as much a part of us as Rhian and Layla are now. We're not leaving without them. Like Roxy said, we get them out. There is no Option B."

"We could die. I'm okay with that, but I—"

"Don't do that. Every single one of us has risked their life at some point. If we can do it for the good of strangers, then we'll have no issue doing it for family. We know the risks, and we choose to do it anyway. So that guilt you're carrying can fuck right off."

I snort, "Roger that, Commander."

He claps me on the back. "Let's go get your girl. I wanna meet the famous Garrett Michaels two-point-oh."

Feeling some of my fear edge away, I stand and follow him from the room. He stops abruptly, and I almost run head-first into his back.

"Eavesdropping is impolite," he chuckles as I stop beside him.

Roxy shrugs, "Sounds like you have a little girl-crush on me, Commander."

Laughing, he hauls her into his chest. "Not little, baby. Big crush. The forever kind." He presses his lips to hers and I turn away to give them privacy.

Austin stands back with his nose scrunched up. "Where's my girl at? I feel left out," he whines jovially as I join him. "You get a girl. Logan has one. Ryder, too. But I don't? Where's she at, huh?"

I shrug, "Maybe you don't get one."

"Yeah, 'cause Greg is hogging them all!"

I bark out a laugh and clap him on the back. "You need to get over that, dude. He likes both genders, but that doesn't mean he has all of them stored in his bedroom at one time."

He snorts, "It's not like we'd know! We didn't even know he liked both. What other secrets is he hiding?"

"Leave it alone!" I order, laughing at his ridiculousness, and turn to Roxy and Logan, who are talking quietly amongst themselves. "Let's go. We don't have much time."

Roxy pulls out of Logan's arms. "Why? What's happened?"

Grimacing and swallowing my panic, I answer, "Mila's execution's been set for tomorrow night."

37

MILA

KAGE RETURNS LATER in the day and informs me of the plan for tonight. When he tells me he talked to Garrett, I almost pass out.

"How? Why?" I ask, confused.

"I left a burner phone at the house before I left yesterday," he answers nonchalantly.

"You planned this?" I rear back, suddenly cautious.

"Shit's different around here. Mika and Levi have lost their damn minds over the last four years," he scolds.

"I know you hate me for leaving, but I'm not sorry. It sucks that you're miserable—"

"I am, but that isn't your fault. I don't blame you, baby," he sighs. "It's my fault for loving someone unavailable. You were right, and you never lied to me."

"It doesn't make it okay," I whisper. "I'm so sorry."

He reaches out and pulls me into his chest. I wrap my arms around his waist and breathe him in. "Don't be sorry. Loving you saved me. I wanted to be the right man for you, and that required me to fight this system. Loving you brought me clarity." He lifts my chin with his finger. "I won't ever regret you. I'm not sorry. But I can't lose you like this. I can't watch you die. Whether you're mine or his in the end, it doesn't matter."

"What are you going to do?"

He presses his lips to my forehead. "I'm going to finish what my father started."

I shift back. "Your father? What does he have to do with this?"

Kage's father died when he was young, around the same time my father passed away. Kage was old enough to remember him, but he never really spoke about him much. I could tell it hurt him, so I never brought it up. That's why his revelation surprises me.

"He was murdered by Mika," he snarls. "He got out. Mika granted him temporary leave because he wanted to be a doctor. In Mika's eyes, he'd serve a purpose for the club if he did. He was the one that delivered Levi when Clara gave birth."

"What?"

"Mika killed him when he tried to cut ties completely. My father didn't want me to become like the rest of them. But Mika killed him before he got the chance and forced my mother to live here and raise me as one of them."

"How long have you known that?" I gasp, my heart breaking for him.

"Right after Mika killed my mother because she threatened to tell me. Except she already had, and he was too late."

"Oh my God, Kage. Are you okay?" I press a hand to his chest, trying to comfort him with my touch.

"I wasn't. I lost you and my mother in the space of a few weeks. I was a mess. But then Clara came to me and helped me understand the need to break the club's foundations."

The pieces start falling into place. My meeting with Clara, Kage's history, it all makes sense. "You're going to overthrow them."

He nods, "Shit needs to change, and I can do that. When Mika told me that they'd found you, I knew this was my chance."

"You know about my team?"

"I found you a year after you left. I needed you. I was in a dark place, but you had this brand new life, and I didn't want to bring you down. I need you now to help me finish this."

He'd never before asked anything of me. He continued to help me over and over again. He still does, and I owe him this much. "I will, but I need to get Slade out of here first."

"We will. I promise."

He left, promising to return after dark when the time was right. This is the most unorganized mission I've ever had, and it's the one with the most risk. Rett would be breaking out in hives right now.

As the sun starts to set, I change into the black jeans and black, long-sleeve shirt Kage gave me. No doubt he got them from Clara; they reek of her perfume. I secure my hair in a ponytail, and shove the Glock Kage gave me into the back of my jeans.

Then, listening through the door, I make sure the coast is clear before I slip into the hallway and into Slade's room.

"Mama?"

"Shhh, baby," I whisper, moving to his side. "Remember what we spoke about earlier?"

"Running?"

"Yeah. We need to do that tonight. Your dad will be here soon, and he'll be waiting." Tossing the backpack on to the bed, I pull out the other set of clothes Kage gave me. "Put these on."

Slade slips out of bed and strips out of his dirty pajamas. He puts on the dark-colored pants and shirt, then ties on the sneakers. They're slightly too big, but they'll do. I hold the jacket out for him, and he slides his arms in before I zip it up and pull the hood over his head.

"Baby, when I say run, you run, okay? Don't look back, even if I'm not following you, okay?" I push as much urgency as I can into those words. I don't want to scare him, but I also don't want him trying to come back for me.

"Will you be hurt?" he whispers.

I sigh and think of the best way to explain without either lying or making him even more scared. "Remember all those times Mama showed up and had bruises or cuts?" He nods, smiling. He was always impressed with my battle-wounds, and loved to hear stories of how I got them. "This is the same. I might get hurt, but I'll be okay. Just like all those other times."

"Will your friends help you?"

"Yes," I say with confidence. I know, without a shadow of a doubt, that my friends are coming. That's who they are, and I love them as much as they love me.

We move onto the bed to wait. The sun sets, and night replaces day. The room is dark except for ambient light coming from the clubhouse. We sit and talk. I tell him stories to pass the time and to keep his mind from wandering. The more time that passes, the greater my anxiety.

I trust Kage, and I trust my team, but relying on someone else doesn't sit well with me. I need to be in control, to do something. I keep reminding myself that I'm doing my job and guarding my son.

But the longer I sit here, the easier doubt begins to creep its way into my mind. The 'what ifs' start to form and spread like poison.

I tense when footsteps pound against the stairs. *That's not Kage.* Panic slices through me, and I push away from Slade and whisper, "Do not move off this bed. Stay here."

I don't give him a chance to respond as I shift, putting myself between the door and my son. My hands shake, and I jump when the door flies open and slams against the wall behind it.

"How did I know you'd be in here?" Mika snarls.

"Whatever this is, my son doesn't need to see it," I state, trying my best to remain calm.

The back of his hand rockets across my face, and Slade screams as I fall to the floor. He flips me over, and I kick out, my foot bouncing off his thigh. He grabs my legs and holds them open.

He's going to rape me. In front of my son.

My gun bites into the skin of my back as I try to reach for it. Realizing I can't, I roll and try to wiggle my way free. He grabs my hair and pulls so hard, I cry out.

"It's my turn to have a little fun with the whore who ruined everything," he sneers.

"Fuck you!" I shout.

"That's the plan, and your bastard gets to watch."

The reminder that my son's watching sends a surge of fury through me. I bring my free leg up and snap my foot into his balls. He chokes on a groan before he shoves an arm into my back, pinning me to the floor.

"What do we have here?" he grunts, and I feel his hand brush against the Glock in my pants. "You planning to escape, little slut?"

He pulls the gun from my jeans, and I freeze, feeling the cold metal press against the back of my head.

"The only way for you to leave is by death. You brought disgrace to my name and destroyed my reputation." He jams the barrel against my head with each breath he takes.

"You're a coward. I hate you, and I hated this life. I could never stay here. I'd rather die than live another fucking day as your son's wife."

I struggle against his hold, but I'm pinned down as he holds me against the ground with his entire weight. He's just too heavy for me to shift. The click of the safety is drowned out by my son's cries. I hate that it's going to end like this.

"Slade, baby, close your eyes for me." I stare at my baby boy, huddled on top of the bed.

"Mama, no," he sobs and shatters me.

"It's okay." I choke back my grief and pray that whoever's listening that this doesn't ruin his life. "Close your eyes. I promise it'll be okay. I love you, baby."

He sobs harder, clutching the pillow to his chest. I smile, doing my best to show him I'm not afraid, that everything's okay. I lie to my son for the first time in his entire life and hope he will forgive me one day. I watch his face press against the pillow as Mika presses the barrel of the gun harder against my scalp.

"Don't worry. You'll see him again. He's next."

A gunshot explodes in the room, and Slade screams. His cries pierce the night, birthed straight from his soul. The gun Mika holds drops to the ground beside my head, and his weight crushes me. I barely register the warmth of his blood against my cheek before his body is shoved off of me.

Kage falls to his knees beside me. "Are you hurt?" I grab his arm and pull myself up, shaking my head. "Fuck," he says on a outward rush of relieved breath.

I scramble to my feet as Slade screams turn to sobs. Grabbing my son, I pull the pillow away from his face and grip his cheeks. "I'm okay, baby. I'm okay."

"Mama!" He launches off the bed and into my arms and clutches me tighter than ever before as he cries against my neck.

I turn to Kage. "Thank you."

"You can thank her, too." He nods toward the door as Clara steps into the room. "She told me he was here. I'm sorry, Mila. I had eyes on him all night."

"It's fine." I breathe. The *whooshing* in my ears gradually silences as my heart slows.

"We have to go," Kage urges, already moving toward the door.

That's when I hear it: explosions. "The gate?" I remember.

"It's open. That's what I was doing. That's why I lost sight of Mika."

"You have to go!" Clara insists.

I press a kiss to Slade's cheek as his cries begin to taper off to whimpers. "Baby, I need you to get ready to run."

His arms tighten around my throat, almost constricting my airway. "No, Mama. I wanna stay with you!"

"No, baby. We need to stick to the plan. You promised me, remember? I'll be okay. I promise."

38

GARRETT

I HOLD my breath as the first explosions go off. I'm in position, just where Mila told me to be. Kage opened the gates more than ten minutes ago, and we've been in position for seven of those. I stay low, camouflaged at the fringes of the long grass just in front of the tree line. My M-16 is positioned in front of me, locked and loaded.

"You got eyes?" I whisper into my comms unit.

"Affirmative," Anderson responds.

"Anything?"

"Negative."

My old team's helping us as a personal favor to me. We knew there would've been no way this mission would've been officially sanctioned by their commander, even though the Chaplains are being actively investigated by the DEA and the ATF. There just wasn't any time to get through all the red tape bullshit.

Whether on the books or off, I'm glad they're here. We needed the manpower, and I trust these men with my life.

"We have movement. Eleven o'clock," Anderson's voice comes through clear.

My eyes swing around to the reference point, and my heart jumps inside my chest.

Slade.

His tiny legs race across the grass, his eyes wildly searching the area before swinging back to look behind him.

"We got company. Sector Three-B." Hexon warns.

"Contact," Anderson confirms as I see three men racing around the side of the house.

My heart jumps into my throat as I push to my feet. "Send it!" I order, already rushing toward my son.

Raising my M-16, I hear the *crack* of the rifle fire from our sniper. One man drops as the others continue in the direction of my boy. I raise my rifle and aim, squeeze the trigger, and another man drops.

"Papa!" Slade yells, and my heart explodes. He rushes toward me as another M-16 fires, and the final guy is neutralized.

Dropping to my knee, I catch Slade as he jumps onto my body. Wrapping my arms around him, I push off the ground and rush toward the cover of the trees. As soon as we're clear, I drop down into a squat, put my weapon down beside me, and wrap both arms around my boy as he clings to me.

His face is buried into my neck, and his heart pounds against my chest. I breathe him in for the first time ever and take a moment to reassure us both that this is real. I'm here, he's safe, and I'm never going to let anything else happen to him.

He pulls back, and I brush the hair away from his wet cheeks. His eyes are puffy and red from crying, but he smiles, and I feel my heart swell inside my chest.

"Are you hurt?" I whisper, feeling overwhelmed with emotions I can barely name.

"No, but they hurt Mama! That man was hurting her." A single tear rolls down his face as I share a panicked look with Hexon.

He nods before his voice trickles through the comms, "Begin perimeter search for Miss Diez."

"Copy that," Anderson responds.

"Where was she?" I ask gently.

He turns and points at the house he just left. "In there. She told me to run because I promised her I would. I'm sorry." His tiny voice cracks.

"You did the right thing, Slade." I tilt his face to regain eye contact.

"Hey. You did the right thing, okay?" He sniffles and nods. "See those men over there?" I nod toward Hexon and Anderson.

"Yes."

"Can you stay here with them? So I can go find Mama?" I ask softly as I continue to brush his tears from his cheeks, maintaining eye contact.

I don't care what anyone says. If you stare into the eyes of your child and see your own eyes staring back at you, it creates a love so soul-deep that it both hurts and heals. That's what I feel right at this moment. I love his mother with everything I am, and up until this moment, she was the most important thing in my world. Now, she's been knocked to second-place because I would kill *anyone* that hurt this boy.

My son.

He nods, "Will you come find me?"

Smiling through the sting of tears, I lean forward and press my lips on his forehead. "I will always come for you. I'm sorry I haven't been around, but I'm here now, and I'm not going anywhere. I promise."

"We don't break promises," he recites, and they're the words Mila and I said to each other a million times. "We don't lie."

"Te amo," I whisper.

"Te amo, Papa." He throws his arms around my neck and holds on tight.

Grabbing my weapon, I lift him with one hand and move toward Anderson. Placing Slade gently on the ground, I turn to my old unit.

"Stay here with him," I order. "Parkinson and Forrest, with me. Fergo, stay and cover them. If anyone breaches Section A, retreat. Keep my son out of their reach."

"Roger that."

I nod and drop back to one knee in front of Slade. "Do as they say, okay? They can talk to me at any time, so if you need me, tell them, and I'll come right back."

He nods in agreement, and I stand up. Nodding to Parkinson and Forrest, I move through the trees a hundred meters away before leaving the cover of the trees. If anyone's watching, they won't know exactly where the rest of us are positioned; therefore, hiding my son's true location.

Silently, we move across the grass, M-16's raised and eyes alert. We sweep the area carefully but arrive at the house without interference. Parkinson takes one side of the door while Forrest and I take the other.

"Logan, you copy?" I speak through comms.

"Yeah," he answers instantly.

"Slade's safe. We're entering Mika's house now."

"Copy that. We're moving in now," he replies. They've been waiting beyond the gates so that we didn't alert the remaining Chaplains at the compound that we were here until we had Slade out safely.

On my nod, Parkinson swings the door open, and I step into the doorway. Slowly, I move forward, the guys at my back. We move through the house, clearing the upper floor first before moving back down the stairs to the main level.

I step into the living room and hear the distinct sound of a safety being released.

"Garrett?"

"Jesus," I exhale.

Mila lowers her gun. "Where's Slade?"

I register movement to her right, and immediately point my M-16 at a man wearing a Chaplains cut. He freezes, his eyes staying on me, but he doesn't move to grab the gun on his thigh.

"Rett, no!" Mila shouts, moving toward the man. "This is Kage. You spoke to him on the phone. He's on our side."

He's the same man that left the burner phone at my mom's house, but I don't trust anyone just because they did a couple of good deeds. But since Mila trusts him, and I trust her, I slowly lower my weapon, signaling the others to do the same.

I move toward her, ignoring her friend, and haul her against my chest to breathe her in. "Slade's safe with Anderson." I pull back and cup her beautiful, bruised face. "Are you okay? Slade said you were attacked."

She steps out of my arms and moves toward the window. "I'm okay. It was just a slight deviation from the plan, is all."

Kage's glare tells me that was a lie. She turns back to us, her head moving back and forth between the two of us. "What's the plan?"

"Logan, Roxy, Ryder, and Ayds are moving in now. We wanted to make sure Slade was out first. Less chance of him being caught in the crossfire."

"And the rest?" she asks as Kage moves back to the windows.

"We decided to come in waves. Charlie, Austin, Blair, and Lucas are at the entrance to the housing's road. They're watching the Chaplains investigating the explosions and will move in when the Chaplains do."

"Your team's here. If we're going to do this, we need to do it now," Kage states, replacing the curtain over the window.

Nodding to Parkinson, I murmur, "Send it"

Pulling a grenade from his belt, he walks to the door as we follow behind him. He pulls the pin, rips open the door and hurls it out onto the gravel. Shutting the door, we brace ourselves.

The house vibrates with the force of the explosion. Forrest completes a short countdown before we race out of the house and into the roar of club members.

We take cover behind walls, vehicles, or any other object we can use to shield ourselves. Guns fire, bullets explode, and screams fill the night.

Ayda and Roxy whirl through the men, their weapons slicing through the air with deadly accuracy. Logan and Ryder shield themselves behind the walls on either side of the open gate. They are our eyes for when Levi realizes the explosions were a distraction. They also have a clear view of their women and watch their backs.

Mila drops to her ass and leans against a car to reload her gun. Her eyes widen, and she raises her gun. "On your six."

I spin, gun cocked and finger on the trigger. I aim and shoot. My bullet pierces through the skull of a soldier, and he drops to the ground. Turning back to the battle, I fire off two more rounds as men creep up on Forrest and Parkinson.

"Where the fuck is he?" Mila growls.

Round after round of bullets pop out of my gun. I reload on autopilot and do it all again.

"We have a problem," Austin's voice trickles through comms. "Levi's figured it out. He isn't coming to you guys. He's coming here for us."

My mouth opens to respond, but Mila's already on her feet, racing off toward the gates. I stand, instantly exposing myself, and move to follow her. Dirt sprays at her feet, and she skips nimbly as gunfire rains down on her.

I put down cover-fire as Kage races from his hiding place and tackles her to the ground, covering her with his body. I move in, firing off rounds as Parkinson and Forrest move in from the other side. Together we push the enemy back.

I kick Kage's foot to grab his attention, keeping my eyes on the battle in front of us. "Move! Go!"

39

MILA

I THRASH and scream for Kage to get off me. Levi isn't trying to attack my friends; he's trying to fucking escape. If he does, this will never be over. I need to finish this now!

Kage lifts himself off me, and I race to my feet. Keeping my head down, I fire my weapon at the Chaplains closing in on us.

Kage grabs my arm and tries to pull me off to the side. Ripping my arm from his hold, I screech, "I need to finish this!"

I run toward the gates as bullets ping off the ground around me. I duck and weave, trying to be a harder target to hit. Logan spots me and tries to wave me in his direction, but I ignore him as I race past.

My legs burn, and my heart pounds inside my chest as I push my body harder. A large body slams into me, and I hit the ground hard.

"I got you, bitch," a deep voice whispers before he rolls me over, and I meet angry brown eyes. The stench of alcohol bleeds out his pores, hardly masking the goon's lack of hygiene.

I slam the butt of my gun into his face with a roar. Twisting, I maneuver my body to the side and pound my elbow into his nose with a satisfying *crunch.* He cries out, clutching his face as blood drips through his fingers.

Shoving his weight off me, I jump to my feet. I barely move an inch when the goon's arms band around me and start to drag me back. I kick, slamming my foot into his shin, but he doesn't loosen his hold.

"Let her go!" Garrett growls, moving to position himself in front of me, his M-16 raised. Forrest and Parkinson follow his lead, surrounding us.

"This is club business, and she's a club whore. This doesn't concern you, soldier-boy" the goon snarls, his words slurred with inebriation.

Garrett watches me the same way he's always done. He reads me just as well as I read him. His finger twitches against the trigger, and I know what he needs me to do. He shifts his stance slightly for better balance. He looks like he's watching me, but his eyes are focused just behind me, aiming for the guy holding me. I relax, giving the illusion that I'm giving up.

"Now, baby!" he commands, and I drop my body weight, slithering out of the arms of my captor. The gun goes off shortly after I'm clear, and I crash to the ground.

Garrett races towards me as I'm climbing to my feet and takes a hold of my hand. "Move! Let's go!"

I stumble slightly as he tugs me forward, but I right myself and race toward the gates. Garrett, Parkinson, and Forrest move with me, scanning the area and firing kill-shots at any targets that come in range.

My blood pounds, and my breath heaves with exertion. Gunfire sounds up ahead, and I know we're close. Digging my toes in, I push my body forward.

Austin, Charlie, and Lucas are fighting off at least three dozen men. Searching the crowd, I find my husband, red-faced with rage and firing his gun from behind a gray sedan. I race forward with my gun raised, and shoot. He ducks behind the car as my bullet *pings* off the metal.

Turning, I aim at the men firing on my friends. Bullets explode from my Glock, and, one by one, the Chaplains fall to the ground. Garrett moves to my side, his loaded M-16 firing into the melee. His focus and skill are really fucking sexy.

I reload my gun, cursing the fact that this is my last clip. I aim at the Chaplain stalking Charlie and fire. He drops, his body dead weight. Roxy and Ayda race past us, jumping into the fight. Their swords glint in the moonlight as they fight with determined brutal force.

I turn, and move in the direction of the gray sedan in search of Levi. Gun raised, I whip around the corner of the car, but he's gone. Searching frantically, I scan the area, but I don't find him anywhere. No matter where I look, I come up empty. A scream ricochets through the night, and when I turn, my stomach drops into my stomach.

Charlie clutches her arm, dark red blood staining her snow-white skin.

"Charlie, look out!" I scream as Levi grabs her from behind and presses a knife to her throat.

He smiles maliciously at me and licks her cheek. "I like this one. She has spunk. Don't you think, wife?"

I hold my gun steady, the barrel of my Glock aimed in their direction. "Can you get a shot?" I ask Garrett as I move past him.

"No. It's too risky from this far away," he answers.

"Blair?" I ask, knowing she's hidden away somewhere with her sniper rifle.

"Negative," he answers for her, discouraged.

"Do you trust me?" I ask Rett pointedly.

He side-eyes me for a moment before nodding in acknowledgement. I step out from behind the car with my hands raised and drop my Glock.

"You win!" I yell. "Me for her, Levi. Let her go, and I'll go with you."

I keep moving forward, stepping out onto the road in his direction.

"Let her go, Levi," I plead and ignore Charlie as she tells me to *fuck off* with her eyes.

Too many people have been hurt because of me. They've sacrificed too much for too long, and I won't let him hurt her. I'll trade myself to save her.

His gaze extends beyond me for a moment before coming back to me with a grin. "Nah. Think I'll have fun with this bitch first."

"Mila! Look out!" Roxy roars.

I spin, only to be instantly blinded by headlights as a car speeds toward me. Spots pepper my vision, and as I blink to clear them, Roxy's body bulldozes into me.

We grunt as we hit the ground, and the car flies past us, barely an inch from our feet. It screeches to a stop in front of Levi, and the back door opens.

"No!" I scream, my heart in my throat.

My knees scrape against the gravel as I rush to my feet. I see a flash of red hair before Levi ducks into the car behind Charlie.

I dive for my Glock at the same time everyone begins firing their weapons. Bullets sink into the body of the car, as the tires screech.

My Glock dry-fires, indicating I'm out of bullets just as I see the tail lights disappear from sight. I spin around, searching for a vehicle or something I can use to go after them.

"Blair has a lock on her GPS location," Ayda announces, rushing toward us.

"A GPS location is fucking useless without transport!" I shout, panicked.

Roxy screeches in frustration and flings a knife at a Chaplain. The blade sinks into the fleshy part of his neck, and his body collapses to the ground.

Logan rushes forward and grabs her as she goes for another guy. "This won't help. We need to find—"

We turn at the sound of an engine roaring. The rider wears a helmet and flies toward us. I smile when I recognize the paintwork and the way he moves on the bike. He's edgy and has a streak of recklessness when he rides.

Kage jerks to a stop in front of me and nods to the seat behind him. Rushing forward, I swing my leg over the seat and settle my ass in.

"Ana," Garrett's voice sounds slightly pained, slightly fearful.

I give him a reassuring smile. "Find a vehicle and follow me. Blair will lead you to me. Te amo, Mike."

I grip the leather of Kage's cut, and the bike vibrates underneath us as he takes off. We weave and swerve through the back streets. I have to trust Kage knows where he's going. I never went out on rides, nor do I know what the club did outside the complex. Kage does.

While I'm sure he doesn't know Levi's exact location, he'd know the first places to look.

Kage brakes so suddenly that I have to cling to him to prevent myself from coming off the bike. The back tires slide, but he keeps us upright despite my added weight on the back. I look around his body, and all the blood drains from my face.

I dismount the bike in a rush and scramble toward the wreckage of the car in which Levi had taken Charlie. Kage catches me before I reach it. "Stop! It could fucking blow up!" he growls.

"Charlie's in there!" I yell. "We need to get her out!"

I stare at the car in horror. Plumes of smoke rise from the crumpled engine. Half the front end is missing and lies scattered over the road. The lights flicker, and fear chokes me.

Please, God. Don't let her be dead.

"Charlie!" I scream.

"Stay here!" Kage orders, slowly releasing me. He watches me for a moment, making sure I'm not going to run off, and sprints toward the wreck.

The car's on its roof, so he has to get on the ground to look through the windows. He shuffles forward, checking the front of the car. The back window shatters as gunshots go off, and I scream a warning as Kage rolls to cover and jumps to his feet.

The rear driver's side door opens with a screech as the twisted metal protests. I hold my breath as Kage races back toward me. Beyond him, the person I'd rather see dead crawls from the mangled car.

My jaw clenches, my hands squeezing into fists as Kage reaches my side. "She isn't there."

My head jerks in his direction. "What do you mean she isn't there? He fucking had her in the car. I saw him take her!"

"She isn't in there, Mila. The driver's dead, and he's there," he nods toward Levi as he struggles to his feet, "but Charlie isn't in there!"

I spin around, searching, praying I see red. I need my friend to be okay. When I can't find her beautiful hair anywhere, rage pierces through every part of my body and lodges deep in my soul.

Fury sharpens my vision as I take off toward Levi. He's on his feet, his eyes widening as I approach, and raises his weapon, but he's too slow. I snap my hand out, grab his wrist, and drop my body weight into his elbow, snapping his arm just like Roxy taught me.

He howls and drops the gun as I rain punches on his face. He groans and falls to his knees. Grabbing his hair, like he's done to me a million times, I rip his head back and snarl "Where the fuck is she?"

He tries to swallow, the angle of his head making that difficult. "I don't know," he croaks.

"You took her!" I shriek, my tone full of venom.

"I woke up, and she was gone!" He shoves me, and I stumble before righting myself.

With a roar Garrett would be proud of, I smash my boot into his face. His head whips to the side, and he falls flat to the ground.

"It's time to pay, Levi," I growl. "You're going to *wish* you never married me."

40

GARRETT

"HOLY SHIT" I gasp, stunned. "Stop the car!"

The tires screech as Clara slams on the brakes, jerking us forward violently. Grabbing the door handle, I push the door open and step out of the car as a second vehicle screeches to a stop behind ours.

Kage is standing twenty feet from the overturned car as I join him. Mila roars, her foot swinging out in a round-house kick, smashing her foot into Levi's face as he tries to get up.

“See, Levi!" she spits at him, her body thrumming rage. "You wanted fuckin strong? How does it feel, you fucking asshole?"

She slams her fist into his face until he spits blood. Clara gasps, her hand flying to her mouth as tears gather in her eyes.

She stares in horror for a moment, and her features twist with the fury of an angry mother. Her hand reaches around, gripping the gun at her back, and raises it to aim it at Mila.

I step in front of her gun as Kage raises his own gun, aiming it at Clara.

Holding my hands up, I try to calm her down. "You don't want to hurt her, Clara. That's not who you are."

"I'm a mother first, Garrett. I won't let her kill him!"

I grind my teeth. Her son is a fucking monster, after all, and deserves everything he gets. Clara's gaze bounces between Mila, Kage, and me.

"You either stop her, or I will!" she shouts. "You really think I'm not willing to die? Kage may shoot me, but I promise I'll stop her first."

I take a single step forward, and Clara shoots. The shot barely misses Mila, and my gut clenches. It was a warning. Nodding, I step back, making my intentions clear.

I remember my conversation with my girl before she was taken. She promised to Clara, from one mother to another, that she'd try not to kill him.

Giving Clara a swift nod, I move toward Mila's outraged condemnation. "Ana, baby. Stop!" I put as much authority as I can into my words, but she doesn't hear me.

She's too trapped by her anger for anything other than her need to inflict pain. She kicks, punches, and punishes her husband for everything he's done.

What pushed her this far? To break like this? There has to be something more that fuels her attack.

"Charlie's gone," Kage says, and my head snaps up to find him watching me with an indulgent smile on his face. "That's why she snapped."

I turn toward the others as they move in closer, watching their friend with saddened expressions as she tries to beat her husband to death. "Charlie isn't here. Search the area."

The team races off, dividing up the search, scouring the perimeter. As quietly as I can, I ease around behind Mila.

Her back heaves with labored pants and adrenaline as she lines up another kick. But before she moves, I wrap my arms around her, using all of my strength to hold her against me.

"Get off me!" she screams, bucking and fighting against my embrace.

I bury my head into her neck and bring her back to me the only way I know how. "Te amo, Ana." I press a kiss to her neck and smile when she shudders. Even raw with rage, her body still knows where home is. "You promised Clara, baby. Let me help you finish this the right way,"

Her chest rises and falls, but she doesn't say a word as she watches Levi struggle and fail to get to his feet.

"If this is how you want it, I'll let you go," I whisper, pressing another kiss to the soft skin behind her ear. "I won't blame you. Just do it with a clear mind."

"She's gone," she whispers, her body finally stilling in my arms.

Slowly and tentatively, I release her and turn her around so she faces me. Pressing my forehead against hers, I promise, "We will find her. You and me, together. Everyone's here, and they'll do whatever it is that you want."

She turns around, noticing everyone for the first time. The teams are back, and my stomach drops when I don't see Charlie with them.

Kage's watchful eyes are on us as he stands where I left him. Roxy stands on the other side of the wrecked car, talking into her comms.

"Blair, you got a GPS location on Charlie?" she murmurs.

"Her tracker's still in the same place. Right where you are," Blair responds.

"Like close to me? Or in the vicinity?"

"About thirty feet south of where you are."

Roxy heads off, taking Logan with her, her eyes narrowed as she searches the area. I look on as I hold Mila against my chest and rub soothing circles into her back.

Click.

I freeze. Mila tenses.

I barely register the gun in Levi's hand before the sharp report of a gunshot explodes through the air. Instinctively, I dive to the ground, pulling Mila with me, rolling to absorb the impact and to protect her. I grunt as my head bounces off the concrete, and stars float across my eyes. Gripping her waist, I roll us so I'm protecting her with my body while I work to clear my head.

Wide eyed and panicked, Mila pushes against my chest and starts searching frantically for a wound. "Rett! Are you shot? Fuck!"

I grab her face, equally petrified, and force her to look at me. "Are you?" I know she's moving around, but I've seen men shot in battle and not realize right away. Adrenaline does stupid shit.

"I'm okay," she pants, working to calm herself down.

I look over at Levi as Clara cries out. His body lies on the road, clearly shot, but he's moving slightly. He's not dead. Yet.

"Kage," Mila whispers, drawing my attention to her friend as he lowers his gun. "Oh God. The car's going to blow!"

Her pushing against me becomes more insistent as I see fire spreading quickly from the mangled engine. Jumping to my feet, I grab her and help her to hers. She pulls out of my hold and rushes toward the wreck. "Mila, no!"

Ignoring the throb of pain in my head, I run after her. Mila grabs Clara around the waist, trying to pull her off her son. Clara fights her, clinging to Levi and trying to plead with him to stay with her, to keep his eyes open.

"Clara! The car's about to go up!" Mila demands, trying and failing to budge Clara. "We've got to go."

"I'm not leaving him!" Clara shrieks.

I grit my teeth in annoyance and offer, "Get out of here. I'll get him."

I fucking hate this plan, but the longer Clara stays, the longer my girl does. Clara finally moves out of the way, and I step forward and roughly lift Levi from the ground. He shouts in pain and curses, but I don't give a fuck.

If it was up to me, I'd leave him to die. But...Fucking Clara.

Everybody is moving to clear the blast radius. It's like a ticking time bomb, and we're in the dark about how much time is left on the clock. I hold my breath and pray this asshole won't be the reason we die.

Kage runs toward us, grabs Clara from Mila, and hoists her into his arms as Forrest moves Mila in front of him.

We're barely clear when the deafening explosion rips through the night. The shockwave of the blast propels us forward, and I fall, not even trying to avoid landing on Levi. He grunts as he gets the wind knocked out of him, then cries out when he takes the brunt of my weight.

"You fucking cunt," he snarls.

Smirking, I press his face into the dirt as I push myself to my feet. Parkinson and Forrest move toward us, Parkinson pulling zip ties from his pocket. He secures one of Levi's wrists behind his back, grabs the other and secures them together.

"What the fuck? You can't do this!" Levi shouts at me.

I kneel down near his head and reply smugly, "We certainly can."

"This is bullshit!" He roars.

I grab his face and squeeze it to the point of pain. "You ever come near my family again, getting arrested will be the least of your worries."

"Is that a threat? You can't threaten me!"

I slap his face condescending in a double-tap and stand. "She's mine. Stay the fuck away from *my* girl and *my* son."

"Levi Romero, you have the right to remain silent," Parkinson, who was in the military police before he joined the Rangers, begins, and I turn and make my way back to Mila as he rattles off the rest of the Miranda rights.

She moves away from Clara, meeting me halfway. I open my arms and fold her inside them tightly as she buries her head into my chest. I press my lips into her hair, sighing in relief.

"Thank you," she mumbles.

"I'd do anything for you, Ana. Te amo."

"Te amo, Mike."

My heart skips a beat as she says my childhood nickname, the same way it did when Slade called me “Papa” for the first time. I breathe in my girl and smile. I have my family, and that's all that matters. We eliminated the threat, and they are safe, free.

"What's going to happen to him?" Mila whispers as she pulls back to look up at me. Her eyes glitter, stony with anger, and I know she’s referring to Levi.

"Parkinson will escort him to the hospital and notify the police en route. The cops’ll most likely have to formally arrest him. I'm not sure what other options the guys have on this job other than handing him over, and I don't know which law enforcement entity has jurisdiction. Whoever it is will have a field day gathering evidence back at the compound. Rest assured, he’ll be going to jail, baby, for a long time. By the time he qualifies for parole, Slade will be old enough to have great-grandbabies."

She nods and averts her eyes. "Is it really over?"

Gripping her chin, I tip her face up to mine. "It's over, I promise."

She smiles and relaxes. "It's over."

I nod, my eyes flicking to her lips. "Ana?"

"Yes?" She pants for a whole different reason as I lean in.

"Tell me to stop"

41

MILA

I WATCH the ambulance drive away, Levi cuffed in the back. Garrett went with Parkinson and Forrest in case they ran into any trouble. Anderson's on his way here with my son and will follow behind them once Slade's been handed off to me to relieve Garrett at the hospital.

I join the girls. "Any news on Charlie?"

Roxy frowns, "No, but we found her tracker over there." She nods in the direction of the wreck.

"We also found this." Ayda hands me a small knife.

"A throwing knife?" I ask, confused. "Why would Charlie have this?"

"I don't think this was hers," Roxy replies.

"Was someone else here?" I ask.

"We think so," Logan replies. "We found tire tracks near the area. Blair's looking into it."

"Charlie's alive?" I whisper, hopeful.

"We think so. Until there's a body, that's what we'll assume. Charlie's one of us," Ayda states.

"Mama!"

I spin and barely catch Slade as he leaps at me. Running my hands over his back and hair, I smile. "Baby, are you okay?"

He nods against my neck. "I was scared."

"I know, baby. I'm so sorry." I kiss the side of his head. "It's over now, just like I promised. Nobody's going to hurt you ever again."

He raises his head and looks around. "Where's Papa?"

I smile, "He's okay. He just had to go do something, but he'll be back, I promise."

He gives me a serious-looking pout. "Don't break promises, Mama."

"Never."

I turn toward the rest of my family as I adjust Slade on my hip. "Guys, this is my baby boy. Slade, these are my friends."

He rolls his eyes and exclaims, "I'm not a baby. Anderson said so. He said I was brave!"

"You *were* brave!" Roxy smiles and ruffles his hair. "Maybe even braver than me. My name's Roxy. It's nice to finally meet you."

"I know who you are," he announces proudly, and I laugh. "You're Roxy, and you have cool swords! And you're Ayda. You're Logan and Ryder. And Austin and Lucas. Where's Blair and Charlie?" He frowns.

"Well, Blair's on her way, and Charlie is...uh—" Ayda stutters, glancing at me for assistance.

"Charlie's lost, baby. We have to find her," I explain.

"Lost? Is she hiding?" His forehead wrinkles in confusion.

"We think so, but we'll find her. Are you ready to go home?"

"Yes. I'm hungry."

I roll my eyes as he giggles. "You're always hungry, hijo."

"Where's abuela?" he asks nervously.

"She's in the hospital, baby. We can go visit her tomorrow."

"Actually," Roxy cuts in, "Scott organized a room for her in our infirmary. He's also hired a full-time nurse to stay with her."

"Doesn't she need a doctor?" I ask, my gaze bouncing between all of them.

"Yeah, Noah's helping out," Ayda shrugs. "Apparently, he likes us."

"It's 'cause we're as hot as fudge sauce," I reply.

Logan barks out a laugh. "I was waiting for your usual kind of comment," he says when we look at him strangely, "and hot fudge sauce was not it!"

Ayda giggles, "Fudge sauce, huh?"

I roll my eyes. "Shut up. I have to mature at some point."

Sirens blare in the distance as Blair pulls up in the van. I thank Anderson, Fergo and Hexon for keeping Slade safe, and they shake hands with the rest of Ghost Team. Afterward, my friends and I all pile into the van to get comfortable while Anderson and the rest of his team drive off in a separate vehicle to head to the hospital. I position Slade on my lap, preferring to keep him close for a while.

Our mood is somber as Blair pulls away from the wreckage. Everyone's feeling the loss of our missing team member. I know as soon as we get back, Blair and Lucas will lock themselves in their rooms and search every available database they have at their disposal.

The rest of us will have to wait until we've some sort of direction in which to go. I don't know where to start, and I know the others feel the same. Roxy sits beside Logan, flicking the throwing knife over in her palm. Ayda watches her sister as she snuggles into Ryder.

Lucas is already on his tablet, Austin hanging over his shoulder helping. I just hope that she's okay, that Levi didn't destroy someone else's life.

Charlie's tough, but she's also the youngest of the group, the baby. We've always been protective of her, but she doesn't *need* us to be. She can take care of herself. I just hope she can this time.

By the time we arrive back at HQ, Slade is snoozing peacefully in my lap. We agree to get a few hours rest before reconvening. Blair and Lucas head to the IT room, and I know they won't get much rest. Slade flops bonelessly against me as I try to pull him from the car.

"I got him," Logan offers. Exhausted myself, I nod. He lifts him easily and carries him inside.

I hit the elevator button for my floor, and Roxy steps in after us. When we get to my apartment, Logan carries him inside, and I lead him into the bedroom where he lays Slade down on my bed. Tobias paws his way up on to the bed, sniffing his way around Slade's sleeping form. Once he is satisfied, he hops down and moves out of the room. After pulling the blankets up around him and kissing his sleeping face, I follow Logan out of the room and go to close the door behind me.

Tobias blocks the door, nudges it back open again and walks into the room carrying his bed in his jaws. My lips twitch as I watch him place his bed beside Slade's. He steps inside his bed, spins around in circles a couple of times and then lays down and stares at me. I smile and nod, then leave the door open slightly.

"Slade has himself a protector" Logan muses.

"Mmmm." I nod. When Garrett first arrived here, that dog was the last thing I expected to love. Now, he is apart of the team. A member I love and trust.

"You might need a lock for that door," Logan smirks and nods toward my 'office.'

I shrug, "I mean, he can only blow himself up once, right?" He blanches, and I laugh. "I'm joking."

"Do I need to call child services?"

I tap my chin as if deep in thought, "Depends. Do you want kids one day? 'Cause if you touch my baby, I'll neuter you for free."

Roxy snorts, "We missed you. Are you okay?"

I nod, "Yeah. I just need a hot shower. My family's safe, and the rest is history."

She grins and steps forward to give me a hug. "Slade's lucky to have you, Mila."

My nose twitches with the sting of tears. "Thank you."

She releases me and takes Logan's hand. He leans forward and lands a brotherly peck on my cheek. "If you need us, call. God knows, Layla and Rhian will be banging down your door to meet him."

Roxy smirks in agreement and pulls Logan to the door. I watch them leave, my heart filled to bursting. I'm finally where I belong. It feels amazing when you find your place and your people. The world just feels right again.

I walk to the bathroom and switch on the water. I slip off my clothes, step into the hot water, and close my eyes as I lean against the tile. The water slides over my skin, washing away the last few days and sending the bad shit down the drain.

The nightmare is finally behind me, but I still have two things I need to do. One, I need a divorce. Two, I need to see Kage. He left before I could talk to him, and I owe him a conversation.

He saved my life twice. Three times, if you count the years I spent with Levi. Maybe I'm being selfish again, but I want to make sure he'll be okay.

The shower door opens, and warm arms slide around my waist, making me smile. "What were you thinking about?" Rett murmurs against my neck before his lips kiss softly along my skin.

"Divorce and Kage," I respond. He tenses, and I smile as I turn in his arms. I slide my palms across his pecs and look up into his fathomless green eyes. "I have the divorce papers. I just need Levi to sign them."

"And Kage?"

"I owe him a conversation. I love and choose you. Kage is fully aware of that, but he saved my life, Rett. I need to make sure he'll be okay. I need to offer him closure, if that's what he needs."

"What if he needs you?" he swallows, unsure.

I shake my head. "He may *think* he does, but he doesn't. I think he's starting to realize that. But when you and I were separated, I could never fully move on, and I don't want that for him."

"We're different because it was always us, Ana. We weren't meant for anyone else."

I smile, "Well yeah, that. But also because there wasn't any conversation or anything that closed that door. I need to give him that."

Garrett moves forward and traps my body between his warmth and the cold tile. His hand slides up my arm and across my shoulder until his fingers wrap around my neck. He holds me, his intense eyes staring into mine, reaching into the very recesses of my mind.

He searches, and I let him. I have nothing to hide anymore. Everything that I am, every secret I own, is his, always.

He leans forward and nips at my lips. "I'm coming with you to see Levi. I don't want you going alone. Then you can go and see your friend. Close the damn door because you're mine, and I'm never giving you up."

I groan as his lips claim mine, reminding me exactly who I belong to.

42

GARRETT

I WAKE up the next morning, already smiling. I don't think I've stopped smiling since I went to sleep last night. Slade sleeps peacefully, tucked into the blankets between Mila and me. It was our first night together as a family, and I'll treasure it forever.

Full of contentment, I watch the two most important people in my life sleep. Normally, I'd get up and go to the gym or start breakfast, but I can't bring myself to leave their side. Not for a second.

I reach out and brush Slade's hair back. It's shaggy, and long enough to hang in his eyes. He has the same hair color as his mother, but it's straight instead of wavy. He smacks his pouty lips and smiles in his sleep. My own lips tug upward in response.

"I used to lay awake for hours when I first got him back," Mila whispers, and I look up to find her watching me. "At first, it was because of fear. I was afraid I hadn't hidden him well enough from Levi, that, somehow, the Chaplins would find us. But as time went on, I relaxed a little, and I just liked watching him dream."

"I hate that you did all this alone when I wasn't there. It makes me angry," I say softly.

"I know you're angry with me—"

I reach past our son and stroke her cheek. "I was mad that you lied and kept this from me, but that's all. I'm proud of you, Ana, for everything you've done to keep our son safe and happy. Even with all this happening around him, you still showered him in love. I owe you for that, and I can never repay you."

She turns her head and kisses my palm. "You don't owe me anything, Mike. I just want you, want our family. This right here makes everything else worth it."

I sit up and lean across Slade, pressing my lips against hers briefly. "Te amo. I love you. Even when I say those words, know that I love you more than that."

She slides her nose against mine and smiles with watery eyes. "Te amare por siempre."

I will love you forever.

"Esto es asqueroso," Slade mumbles, and we laugh. *This is yucky.*

Pulling away from my love, I look down at my smiling son. "Morning."

"Morning, Papa," he says confidently. "Do you like kissing Mama?"

I grin, "I do. Is that okay with you?"

He smiles and gives me a big nod. "Does this mean I can stay here with you now?" He looks at Mila with hopeful eyes.

She bops his nose with her finger and makes him giggle. "It does, if that's what you want."

He turns to me, suddenly shy. "Will you stay, too?"

"Yes. If it's okay with you, I'd like to stay."

"We'd be a familia?" he gasps excitedly and sits up.

"Yeah, baby. Just like you wished for," Mila chuckles at his enthusiasm.

He turns to me with joyous eyes and grabs my face, like he can barely contain his amazement. "I wished. I did, Papa. Every year, I blew out candles and wished to be like this. Every day!"

Chuckling, I catch him as he tackles me to the bed. "Well, that's what happens, right?" I look at Mila and stare into her exotic brown eyes. "We make wishes, and we hope. With a little magic and a lot of persistence, it happens."

She leans over and presses her lips to mine as Slade wraps his arm around her. "Rett, you were my wish and my dream. I was *always* yours because you had my soul, and souls are forever."

I grip Ana's hand in mine, our fingers intertwined as we ride the elevator to Levi's floor. He got out of surgery this morning to repair the bullet hole Kage put in his thigh. It was enough to stop him but not kill him. Clara's persistence saved Levi's life, and he'll finally get what he deserves.

We don't know where Eva is, though. I'm sure she'll resurface in the next couple of days. She won't be able to resist her need for revenge, and Mila's planning to wait her out. She's a creature of singular habits, after all.

After this visit, Mila will finally be free from any legalities binding her to either Levi or the remaining Chaplains. We won't leave until Levi signs the divorce papers clutched in Mila's other hand.

Now that all the secrets are out, I see my girl in a new light and finally feel like I understand her completely. Before, I had started to understand, wanted to, but there was always this wall, something that blocked me.

Now, I understand her vulgar mouth is a reminder of her strength. She is who she is. She held onto who she was at her core, fought for it...found her fire and rebuilt herself. She demands respect, and her vulgar, in-your-face attitude, reinforces that.

She is blatantly unrepentant of who she is. She's loud and demands to be heard. She draws attention and won't ever be ignored again. It's different because, for years, I was her protector. When she no longer needed one, I had to struggle to find another purpose in her life.

We're on more equal ground now. For a time, I felt unneeded, but that isn't true at all. I need her the same way she needs me. I breathe a little easier, my problems aren't as heavy, and I'm not alone.

I squeeze her hand comfortingly as we step off the elevator and make our way down the corridor. I give our names to the guard, and Ana's hand tremors a little in mine.

The guard allows us entry, and I press a kiss to her hairline before we go in. Levi sits up in his bed, his face covered in bruises and one eye swollen shut. He's shackled to the bed and watches us suspiciously as we enter the room. When his eyes drop to our joined hands, he sneers with disgust.

I smirk. He's dumber than he looks if he thought for one second I'd ever give her up.

Clara clears her throat, stands from her seat next to his bed, and moves to Mila. Pressing a kiss to her cheek, she squeezes her arm. "Thank you."

Mila smiles and nods before turning back to face Levi. She squeezes my hand and releases it to move toward the bed. Dropping the divorce papers on the table, she narrows her eyes. "It's over, Levi. Sign them."

"No." His voice is hoarse but unwavering.

"There are two ways out of this marriage for you," she says pointedly. "The first is the easy way. You sign the fuckin' papers. The second is harder and a lot less pleasant. For you, that is," she adds with a smile. "I'd enjoy it immensely, though."

He faces me, anger radiating off him. "Must really burn to know I took her from you. Right from underneath your rich-boy nose."

"He's the only one that ever had me," Mila snaps. "Rett is and always has been the only one to own me. I gave him my virginity, freely. He's the father of my first-born and will be the father of my second and third-born children, too. He has me for the rest of my life while you rot in jail." She leans forward and braces herself on the table, ensuring he hears every word clearly. "You lose, Levi. You lost the second you took me from him because I never gave any part of me to you."

"I *had* you," he exclaims. "You're my wife. I was inside you. All you had to do was submit like my mother, and you would've been happy!"

"Is that what you think I did?" Clara says sharply as she steps forward. "That I submitted? That I was happy?"

"You were!"

"No, I wasn't," she says through clenched teeth. "I was never happy. I didn't submit. I chose to stay because of you. I never wanted that life. I didn't want my marriage, and I sure as hell didn't want your father."

"You killed him!" Levi yells at Mila, and I step in her direction protectively.

"No, I did," Clara snarls smugly, "and it's about damn time. He was a bastard and deserves to rot in Hell. You're alive because I asked Mila to keep you that way. Sign the fuckin' papers, Levi."

"You can't be serious," he protests.

"Sign them, or I'll leave, taking your protection with me." She picks the pen up and holds it out to him.

He stares at her and doesn't move an inch. They stare off, the stubbornness of a son against the stubbornness of a mother. I've known Clara since I was a boy. She used to come to our house with Mika, and Levi and I would hang out while they had drinks with our parents.

I always thought she was quiet, timid. But she isn't. She played her part in their game, waiting for her moment.

Levi snatches the pen from his mother's grasp and scribbles his name on the papers. Mila's body sags in relief as Clara gathers the paperwork and hands it back to her.

"Thank you," Mila sighs as she takes the paperwork.

"You know, when I first met you, I was worried. My husband spoke of you as if you were this amazingly strong woman with a vicious streak. But when I met you, you hid beneath your hoodie and barely stood up for yourself. As I watched you grow, I realized my husband and my son made a huge mistake. I knew you'd be the one to bring them down."

"Is that why you helped me?" Mila asks softly.

Clara shakes her head, "No. I helped you because I was feeling powerless and trapped, useless. Helping you helped change that for me and gave me a reason to stand a little straighter."

Mila nods and moves toward me. Her palm slides against mine as she takes my hand, and my body instantly relaxes. We say goodbye to Clara and make our way out of the room.

"She *will* think of me!" Levi hollers, and I freeze halfway out the door. I turn back to see his sneer. "Like poison, I'm inside her. She won't ever forget me."

I snort, "She already is forgetting, and even if she doesn't forget,

I'll be here to remind her everyday what a worthless pig you are. She's mine; she always was mine. You underestimated her, and that's on you."

"I'll always be her first husband," Levi snickers, thinking he scored a direct hit.

"I was her everything in the beginning," I snarl, "I'm her middle, and I will be her end. You might've been her first husband, but I will be her last and, most of all, *her best*. Don't worry, Levi," I smile, "we'll send a picture of what never could've been yours to you in prison, where I'll make sure you rot for the rest of your miserable, insignificant life." I wink and close the door.

Mila leans against the wall, eyeing me playfully. "I would have added something about keeping my pussy warm."

I bark out a laugh as the guard on duty spits his coffee out all over the floor.

43

MILA

I LEAVE the team to troll through security and traffic camera footage in search of Charlie. The guilt over her absence weighs me down like a boulder. It's my fault she's gone, and I won't forgive myself if we can't find her. I pull myself away a while later and leave out of the front gates, the Mustang purring as I hit the accelerator.

I have one last thing I need to do, one last door that I need to close.

Kage.

My heart hurts for him. I love him, I do, but not nearly as much as I love Garrett. Garrett is my forever, and I know that with every inch of my soul. I just hope Kage can finally be free to find his forever.

I pull into the same parking garage where I met Clara and travel through the levels. I came alone because I know Kage won't hurt me. He knows what this is about, just as much as I do. My heart is heavy, but I know I need to do this for both of us.

I park the Mustang beside his Harley. He leans against the machine, his cut proudly displaying his President patch on it. His eyes follow me as I exit my car and move toward him.

"Guess you're the new Prez. Congratulations," I smile. "Who'd you make VP?"

"No one yet. I have to work through the men. There are a lot of people still loyal to the old ways, and I need to change that. Until I find someone I can trust, I'm working alone," he explains.

I nod, and we fall awkwardly silent. I know what I need to say, but now that I'm here, it's a lot harder than I thought. He was my friend for so long. He held me up and brought me light on my darkest days.

Part of me thinks it's wrong to walk away and cut ties, but that's the selfish part of me that wants to hold onto his friendship because I need him. But he wants more than just a friendship, and that's why I need to sever the ties. The longer I hold on, the more hope I'll give him.

"Kage, I'm so sorry," I whisper and work hard to swallow my emotions. I need to hold my shit together for him, one last time. "I'm sorry that I'm hurting you, that I can't give you what you want after everything you've done for me."

He drops his head. "I'd do it all again. Even knowing this is how it turns out, even feeling this pain, I would do it all."

A sob claws up my throat when he raises his head, and I see tears in his eyes. "I hate this."

He pushes off the bike and wraps his arms around me. I grip his waist as a tear rolls down my cheek. His arms hold me tight as his body shakes. He knows this is goodbye. Even though he's hurting, he's still trying to comfort me. He presses a kiss to my hair. "Be happy, Mila. Make it all worth it."

"What about you?" I croak. My body jerks against his, as a sob escapes me uninvited.

He palms my cheeks and lifts my head until I stare into his eyes. His lashes are wet, and his hurt slices through me. "All I care about, all I want, is to know you're happy. I had you for a moment, and I will always remember that."

I nod in his hold, "I want you to be happy, too."

He leans forward and presses his lips lightly on mine. It's short, barely a brush...it's goodbye. He needs this, so I let him. I give him one thing after his years of selflessness. "I need to find a way to let you go, and I need to do it alone," he whispers, his voice thick with tears.

I squeeze my eyes closed from an onslaught of grief. "I love you."

"Just not enough, and I understand," he whispers, and my heart breaks a little more when I hear his voice crack. He presses his lips to my forehead one last time and releases me.

He throws his leg over the seat of his Harley and puts his helmet on. I stand motionless as I watch him start the engine and turn the bike around. It thunders through the garage as he drives away.

Tears roll freely down my cheek. I pray and hope he finds his girl, that his life is as full as mine one day. He deserves it. He deserves it more than I do.

There's always going to be this Kage-shaped void inside me because of his absence. He's my friend, and I will always have a place for him in my life. Maybe, one day, when he finally finds his forever, we'll be able to rekindle our friendship. But for now, this is the way it needs to be, for his sake and for Garrett's.

"Well, isn't this sad," Eva's voice creeps up my spine and ices my blood. "I think I even shed a tear."

I reach around, wrap my fingers around my Glock, and pull it from my pants, disabling the safety before turning to face her.

"It's over, Eva. Your boy-toy is in prison. Kage won't ever let you back into the Chaplains. There isn't anything left here for you."

"No thanks to you," she spits out.

My eyes trace down her arm to the pistol gripped in her hand. I move toward her, slowly but confidently. "You brought this on yourself. I don't pity you. You were stupid, and I am done trying to help you."

"I was raped because of you!" she insists vehemently.

"You were raped because of your own stupidity. I found you and I carried you home. I took care of your injuries. I got us out of Mexico and gave us a better life. I wasn't the one who raped you, Eva. Those dirty cops did. Everything I did was for you and Mama."

"You took everything from me!" she snarls, crazed with her own delusions.

I'm barely three feet from her, using her distracted state to sidle ever closer. "You took my child, my love, and ruined my life."

"You deserved it!"

Grinning, I lunge for her and rip the pistol from her grip. She moves to charge at me, but I raise my Glock and press it to her forehead. "You deserve to rot in hell," I hiss.

"You going to shoot me, sister?" she challenges.

"Why should I be the one to end your suffering? You have nothing left. No family, no man, no club. I bet you don't even have friends left. Karma's a bitch, and she's finally fucked you up the ass."

"I hate you."

"Not as much as I hate you. I despise the fact that you still breathe. Mama should've swallowed you when she had the chance. This is your last warning, Eva. You come after me and mine, I will end your pathetic life. This is done. Over." Shoving my face in hers, I make myself one hundred percent clear. "I will kill you if I so much as see you at the fuckin store. This is all the warning you get."

I press the gun harder against her head, hoping that it leaves a damn bruise. I wait for her response. She doesn't speak, but I see her defeat settle in her eyes. Shoving away from her, I walk away.

I swing open the driver's side door of the Mustang and slide into the seat. Tossing my Glock on to the passenger seat along with her pistol, I start the engine and reverse out of my spot. The tires squeal as I fly out of the garage, relieved to finally see her in the rearview mirror. This time, for good.

Euphoria makes me giggle as I head back to HQ. My family is finally free. Everything I did, everything I lived through, it was all worth it.

Today is the first day of the rest of my life.

EPILOGUE

THREE MONTHS LATER

GARRETT

"PAPA?" I smile and share a knowing look with Mila.

"Yes?" My eyes find Slade's reflected in the rearview mirror.

"What is a ghost's favorite dessert?"

"Mmmm." I tap my chin in thought. "Waffles?"

He shakes his head and chuckles, "Eye scream!" His giggles are contagious. "Okay, how about this one. How do you make a tissue dance?"

"Wave it around?" I frown.

He snorts, "You put a little boogie in it."

I groan, and he laughs as I turn the Mustang onto my mother's street. Mila squeezes my hand reassuringly and gives me a beautiful smile when I look her way.

My dad's trial ended a week ago. Mom testified against him. That, combined with the documentation he had in his office and the information they found on his phone, ensured he wasn't going to beat the charges. He was sentenced to twenty years in prison.

Levi also spent time in court. He was sentenced to life without parole for a stack of felony offenses. Kage came forward and provided a list of locations where Levi had narcotics and firearms stored for distribution. He was also charged with kidnapping and human trafficking.

We haven't seen Kage since the day Levi was sentenced. I know Mila misses him, and there are moments when I know she thinks of him. It doesn't make me jealous like it once did. I understand their relationship more, especially after he saved her life. He was her friend when she had no one else.

He was her brother-in-arms.

Mila finally got the divorce finalized, and we celebrated by going out on our first official date. All of this made me realize that I never really got the chance to do normal things people do in a relationship with her. So I told her to get dressed up, arranged for Slade to have a sleepover with Rhian and Bella, and I took my girl out on a real date. I wooed her.

I pull into Mom's driveway and feel Mila tense in her seat. This will be the first time Slade meets his other grandma, and his mama is worried.

Chuckling, I switch off the car and turn to her. "We can leave."

She expels a heavy breath, "No, it's fine. We agreed, right? That she's different now, and we should give her a chance?"

I nod, holding her gaze. "We did, but if you've changed your mind, I'll understand."

She looks over at Slade, who is suspiciously quiet in the back seat. "We promised normal, and this is normal."

"We don't break promises," I whisper and earn myself a smile.

"Can we go to the willow first?" she asks sheepishly.

I grin, "Cualquier cosa por ti." *Anything for you.*

I send Mom a quick text telling her we're going to the willow first and will be inside in a little bit. I exit the car and wait for Mila and Slade to join me. Sliding my arm around her waist, we walk to the place where we started.

My other hand slides into my jeans pocket, my fingers stroking a circlet of cool metal. Slade races ahead when Mila points out where we're going. We catch up to him at the willow to find his tiny fingers tracing the inscription I carved into the trunk all those years ago.

Mila lifts up onto her toes and kisses me quickly before joining Slade. Taking a deep breath, I drop to one knee and pull the ring from my pocket.

Slade turns, and I give him a nod. Grinning, he says, "Hey, Mama?"

"Mmm yeah, baby?"

"Papa wants to know if you'll marry him!"

"What?" She splutters and turns to me with a frown. Her eyes widen as she takes in my position. "Oh my God."

Slade comes to kneel beside me as I stare into the wide teary eyes of the only person I will ever completely love. "I fell in love with your silence, your perfection, under this very tree. I understood your words without your voice. When I was given a second chance, you were louder and less perfect."

Her nose scrunches up. "I think you're fucking this up."

I snort, "Shush! I love this not-perfect Mila more than I could ever have loved the perfect one. Being open, honest, and free, is love. It's real. You're real and so fucking beautiful. I've lived without you, Ana. I've lost you. I've waited for you. But I never once stopped loving you. Will you marry me, baby? Make this really real?"

I look into her eyes and see everything I'll ever need. I get lost in her as we stare at each other. I swallow when she lets me in and lets me see just how much she loves me. Rising to my feet, I grab her around the waist and kiss her with everything I am.

"Is that a yes?" Slade asks.

Smiling against her lips, I don't need the yes. I already knew her answer. We've waited years to be together. This ring, the ceremony...none of it really matters. We're forever bound to one another whether we have the paper or not.

"Hello?" Slade scolds impatiently. "Did you say yes?"

"Yeah, hijo. I said yes."

The End

But, it not the end of Ghost Team. Next up in the Redemption Series is Rectify. Time to find out what happened to Charlie...

ACKNOWLEDGMENTS

Garrett and Mila were by far my favourite couple to write. Their connection was so pure and explosive, it made me blush.

I hope you enjoyed their love as much as I did.

What's next? I have a certain redhead that has a special kind of man. Can you guess yet?

insert smirk

You can stay up to date via Facebook. I announce all dates/updates there. Including teasers.

Okay…

T, Lita and Amy, I love you SO MUCH. You make me laugh and sing. The three of you fill me with never ending happiness and I know you are for life. (Not that you have a choice. Sorry boo.)

To my editor, Kat. Amazing as always. Thank you for going above and beyond for me (and my readers). You were under the pump for this one, but you pulled through, without sacrificing your perfection.

Amy— my proofreader. You smashed through this book and got it back to me in record time. Thank you.

Yanella- Thank you for your help with making Mila more authentic. Truly, I appreciate it more than you know.

To my friends that surround me with endless love and support.

Thank you. I love you and I appreciate you all more than you could ever imagine.

Finally, to my babies and my fiancé. Life is never boring *laughing* but I love it and I love you all.

Rectify is next. Brace yourselves.

I'm still around. I post a lot of upcoming stuff on my Facebook page, teasers and cover reveals as well. All the fun stuff. If that's something you wanna check out, feel free. I also have a reader group where everyone chats about the books.

Much love to all. Catch ya. X

ALSO BY ELLIE KIRSON

The redemption series *(in reading order)*

Renegade

Reclaim

Mortemous- Early years Novella

Reborn

Revive

Rectify

www.ingramcontent.com/pod-product-compliance
Lightning Source LLC
Chambersburg PA
CBHW031556240626
47153CB00002B/533